STACY M. JONES

Harbor Cove Murders

First published by Stacy M. Jones 2022

First edition

ISBN: 978-0-578-28134-6

This book was professionally typeset on Reedsy.
Find out more at reedsy.com

For Jamie

Acknowledgement

Thanks to my family and friends who are always a source of support and encouragement. Thank you to my early readers whose feedback was invaluable. Special thanks to 17 Studio Book Design for bringing my stories to life with amazing covers. Thank you to Dj Hendrickson for your insightful editing and Liza Wood for proofreading and revisions. Thank you to my readers who are reading this series for the first time and those who have been loyal readers. Your messages are a constant source of encouragement.

CHAPTER 1

The balcony of our hotel in St. Thomas overlooked Harbor Cove in the northern part of the island east of Magens Bay Beach. My husband, Det. Luke Morgan, and I were there to celebrate the wedding of Cooper Deagnan and his fiancée, Adele Baker. Cooper was my business partner and Luke's long-time best friend. We couldn't be happier to celebrate with them. They had opted for a small beachside service with the four of us. Cooper had nearly no family, his father passed away years ago, and Adele's parents were fine with a celebration after the fact.

I was running late to meet Adele, who was with the hotel wedding consultant planning last-minute details before a short rehearsal. My natural wavy auburn hair, challenged by the humidity, proved difficult to tame. Standing on the balcony and watching the waves lap the surf probably wasn't helping. It was such a perfect view and the late afternoon air made it impossible for me to tear myself away.

Our fourth-floor balcony overlooked the cove that had been naturally formed by two larger rock formations. It was a cozy spot that had a soft sandy beach, blue water, and a small dock with boats that mostly offered tourist excursions. Cooper and Adele would marry on the beach and then we'd have dinner in a private section of the restaurant's beach-side patio.

"Aren't you late to meet Adele?" Luke said, wrapping me in his arms and nuzzling my neck in a way he knew drove me mad with desire.

I melted under his touch. "I was thinking about how I'm a terrible maid of honor. Thanks for helping my guilt."

"Always willing to be of service. I'm late to meet Cooper. I'll go downstairs with you."

It was Luke's way of nudging me out of the room. He was never late for anything. I pulled out of his embrace and twirled around, showing him my new strapless blue dress. It had bright pink and white flowers on it and hit below my knee. It was a daring dress and I hoped I was pulling off the look.

Luke dragged his gaze up and down my body and then whistled. "You're making me not want to go downstairs."

It was the confidence boost I needed. I rose on tiptoes to kiss his lips before he led us out of our room and down the hallway to the elevator. His hand never left mine as we flirted. We composed ourselves enough for Luke to hit the elevator button. A moment later, the doors slid open and our jovial mood came to a crashing halt. Inside the elevator, a sobbing woman had her head buried in a man's shoulder.

"I'm sorry," Luke said, stepping back from the doors. "We can wait."

The woman lifted her head and looked directly at us. It was then I saw that she had a stack of papers in her hand. She asked through sobs, "Have you seen her? My daughter is missing."

She handed Luke a flyer. I leaned over him as we studied the young woman's face. Laurie Presley was twenty-two years old. An attractive, dark-haired young woman who resembled her mother. She had gone on a spring break trip with three of her friends and never came home. The flyer had all the pertinent details including the name of the bar where she had been last seen. Sunshine Beach Bar & Grill. It was down the beach from us and we had made a point of saying we'd have to stop in for dinner.

"Was Laurie staying here?" Luke asked, his voice already losing the vacation vibe he'd had moments earlier.

Laurie's parents, Ava and Bill Presley, stepped out of the elevator into the hall with us and introduced themselves. The elevators doors slid closed behind them, making us even later to meet Cooper and Adele.

Bill shook Luke's hand. "Laurie was staying here, and on the last night of the trip, the girls went to the Sunshine Bar, but Laurie disappeared sometime that night. The girls called us the next morning frantic. We came immediately. That was four days ago and the local police refuse to take this seriously. They think she might have run off with a guy she met."

"Did she meet a guy?" I asked.

Ava wiped the tears from her eyes. "No, my daughter has a boyfriend back home. They were dancing and having a good time, but they were drinking. She was on the dance floor with them one minute, went to the bar, and then was gone. They thought she might have been in the bathroom. They looked but couldn't find her. Then they thought she might have gone back to the hotel, but no one was there. The hotel provided surveillance footage and she never came back inside the hotel that night."

Luke squinted down at the page and then back up at Ava and Bill. "No one saw her leave the bar? No witnesses have come forward?"

"We don't know if there were any witnesses because the cops haven't taken the case. They haven't done anything," Bill said, explaining the sad reality of the situation. "We will find our daughter and bring her home on our own if we have to."

I tugged on Luke's arm, letting him know that we needed to get moving. The last thing I wanted to do was embroil us in another investigation, especially during Cooper's wedding. "Don't cause any drama" was his only instruction to me. And I knew exactly what he meant – *don't find any dead bodies, and if you do, step over them like you never saw a thing.*

Of course, he didn't mean that literally. Cooper wasn't a horrible person, but he didn't want anything to ruin Adele's day. My tendency to get swept up in criminal cases needed to be tempered.

Luke understood the tug on his arm. He held the flyer in his hand. "I'll keep my eyes out for anything. We have to get to a friend's rehearsal dinner for their wedding tomorrow, but we will be around all week if you think I can help."

Bill and Ava nodded and walked down the hallway in the opposite direction of our room. Luke hit the elevator button and when the doors opened, we got inside. "I wish you hadn't told them you'd help."

"Did you see the mother, Riley? It broke my heart, especially because she said the local cops are no help." Luke looked down at me and then shifted his eyes up toward the door. "I know I'm usually the one cautioning you about getting involved in things. There was something about them that made me offer. After Cooper's wedding, I'm willing to help any way I can."

"Cooper warned me about not messing up his wedding."

Luke side-eyed me. "You do tend to cause a ruckus." He broke into a wide smile and then he reached for me and pulled me into his side. "We won't mention anything to him about this."

"That's probably for the best."

"I imagine he might hear it from other people since the family is here in the hotel."

"From other people is fine. We can pretend we don't know much."

The elevator doors opened on the lobby floor and we stepped out holding hands. Before we even took two steps, we had to navigate around a man attempting to corral several pieces of luggage and a throng of people milling around – some of them with camera equipment. The long line of people checking in was ten people deep. It took us a moment to spot Cooper standing by the door that led to the outside restaurant. Adele was nowhere in sight.

Luke called his name and Cooper turned in our direction. "Sorry we're late."

"It was my fault," I said, hugging him. "My hair doesn't want to behave in this weather. Where's Adele?"

"The wedding coordinator took her out back to the beach to check out the lay of the land for the wedding tomorrow. I told them we'd meet them out there." Cooper looked toward the front of the hotel and then back at Luke with a concerned expression on his face. "I heard the parents of a missing girl are staying in this hotel. She's been missing for a few days. I saw a CNN truck outside. Most of these people are media."

Even though we had agreed not to say anything to Cooper, Luke gave him the rundown of what we had learned from the parents. "It doesn't sound like the local cops are doing much of anything, so it doesn't surprise me they called the media."

Cooper locked eyes with me and I raised my hands in defense. "I promised you. I'm not getting involved, and I'm sticking to that promise."

"Let's go meet Adele." Cooper led the way to the outside patio. It was two steps down to the beach where sunbathers baked in the late afternoon sun. Others sat in the cabanas the hotel had provided.

I scanned the beach and spotted Adele near the water. There was a lovely quiet area of the beach that was closed off to sunbathers and used only for weddings and other events at the hotel. Seeing it from our balcony did little to showcase the beauty and serenity of the area.

I walked ahead of Luke and Cooper and met with Adele. "This is a wonderful spot you picked."

"I can't believe I'm getting married tomorrow. It's been such a whirlwind." Adele had her hair braided and then wrapped in a bun on top of her head. Her brown skin glowed in the sunshine and her smile beamed.

I reached for her hand. "I'm so happy for you both."

Adele had met Cooper while he was helping Luke investigate the murder of his sister. It turned out Adele's younger sister had been a victim of the same killer. It brought Adele and Cooper together in Atlanta, and shortly after the case was solved, she moved in with him in Little Rock. She set up a criminal defense practice, and right after Luke and I got married, Cooper proposed.

Luke and Cooper joined us and then Mia, the wedding coordinator, got started. She spent the next twenty minutes going over where the flowers would be, how the ceremony arch would be set up, and even when the musicians would arrive. She showed us where we would all stand and how to proceed. We walked through it once, and by the time we were done, we were all starving.

Before Mia let us go back up to the hotel's restaurant, she gave us a warning. "The hotel is expecting a heavy media presence given the missing girls. We've instructed them not to bother our guests, but many are staying with us so they will be around the hotel. Please do not speak to them or give interviews because it will only encourage them."

Adele pulled back in shock. "Interviews about what? Missing girls?" She looked to Cooper and then to Luke and me.

Luke explained that a young American girl was missing from a bar nearby and that her parents were staying at the hotel. When he was done, he turned to Mia. "You said girls. We only know about the one."

Mia's hand went to her throat, obviously uncomfortable. "Yes, well… "

I stepped toward her. "Please tell us. Luke is a detective. Cooper and I are private investigators, and Adele is a criminal defense attorney. There isn't much we haven't heard."

Mia looked around to make sure no one was near and then stepped toward us, gathering us in a small circle. She kept her voice low. "This is the fifth missing girl in a year. The police haven't taken it seriously and no one knows what's going on, but we are all concerned. A part of me is glad the media has been called in, so maybe someone will get to the bottom of it."

We all stared at each other, confusion and fear on our faces, wondering what we had stumbled into – knowing that even if we didn't want to be caught up in it, it was already too late.

CHAPTER 2

Luke finished off his steak and took the last bite of a glazed carrot. "This will not interfere with your wedding, Adele. We promise you that."

Adele hadn't said much since getting the news from Mia. Her face had been drawn and her lips set in a firm line. Luke knew this had to be challenging for her. Both of their sisters had gone missing so it brought them right back to the trauma they had each experienced. Luke's sister, Lily, had been only a freshman when she was abducted from her college campus and murdered by a serial killer. Adele's sister had been the same age and had gone missing from the college she had attended.

Adele sat back in her chair. "I'm not worried about my wedding. I'm concerned about what's happened to those young women. Five in a year." Adele shook her head and her eyes watered.

Cooper put his hand behind her back. "Please don't let this ruin the wedding. There's nothing we can do. I'm sure the media will put pressure on local law enforcement to do something."

Riley leaned into the table. "Adele, this is the last thing you should be worried about. Let's stop thinking about it and focus on something else – like how beautiful you're going to look tomorrow."

Adele nodded. "You're right. It was just so shocking to hear."

"I can't wait to see your dress tomorrow," Cooper said, changing the subject.

Adele reached for his hand. "I hope you'll like it. But either way, I'm going to look fabulous!" She giggled and the mood shifted to something lighter.

Luke smiled over at Riley, both of them knowing the light mood was only going to last so long. He hoped it lasted through the wedding. Already the hotel had grown full of people. Anderson Cooper and Erin Burnett from CNN sat together having dinner with another man, probably strategizing the coverage. Chris Wallace sat at another table with three people. They all had their heads bent low, deep in conversation.

"Luke, I'm headed to Adele's bridal suite for a bit and then I'll be back to our room later," Riley said but Luke only registered half of it. She grazed his arm with her fingertips. "Are you listening?"

"Sorry," he said, turning to her. "You're going with Adele and I'll see you later. Did I get it?"

Riley stood from the table and leaned down to kiss him on the lips. "You got the part that matters." She and Adele walked off toward the lobby and then disappeared.

"Your head is off in the clouds." Cooper moved his chair closer to Luke, and when the server came over, they both ordered another drink.

After Riley walked away, Luke pointed out what he had been staring at. "This has turned serious quickly. Riley told me about what you said about her not getting involved in anything."

Cooper gestured toward the crowd. "Did you see Adele's face? She's already curious about what's going on."

Luke had seen her face and it worried him. Not because she was curious, but it was a familiar look like his own – trying hard to stuff down trauma while desperately wanting to help a family in need. Luke set the feeling aside for a moment and focused on what was important.

They chatted about work and life until the server brought them their drinks. Luke held up his glass and toasted Cooper on his wedding. "You ready for tomorrow?"

"As ready as I'm ever going to get."

"You worried about anything?"

"Everything." Cooper laughed and took another sip of his beer. "I have no good role model for marriage other than you and Riley. My dad had a series of wives and all of those relationships ended badly. I've never seen a good solid relationship that lasts a lifetime. You had your parents as an example. I'm worried about messing this up."

Luke understood the feeling. "We are all worried about messing up. I may have had my parents, but my relationship with Riley is far different than the relationship my parents had. Riley is stronger-willed than my mother, and I love her for it..." Luke didn't finish his thought because he wasn't sure what to say. He realized he didn't have any advice for Cooper. He didn't feel like he knew much more than his friend. "We are all playing this by ear, Coop. There's no rule book to follow other than being friends as much as husband and wife. You and Adele like each other as people and support each other. The respect is there. Make sure the communication is too."

"That sounds like pretty sound advice from a guy who says he doesn't know what he's doing."

Luke kicked his legs out in front of him and leaned back in his chair. "Sometimes I make this up as I go along and it sounds good. It doesn't mean I know what I'm doing." There was a hint of a smile on his face that made Cooper laugh.

"As long as we can always go to each other for advice, I'm good."

Luke raised his glass again to him. "I don't know how I'd navigate Riley without you. She's a handful. It's almost like it takes two of us."

"Never let her hear you say that." Cooper looked back out toward the crowd and then to Luke, shaking his head. "This is going to get wild, isn't it?"

"Seems like it. As much as I hate this for you and Adele, if this has been going on for over a year and there're five missing women, I'm glad someone is finally paying attention."

"Excuse me," a man said from behind Luke. "Are you Det. Luke Morgan and Cooper Deagnan?"

Luke looked over his shoulder and didn't recognize the man who stood about five-foot-eight and had sandy brown hair and round glasses. Luke guessed they were about the same late thirty-ish age. "Can I help you with something?" he asked, not meaning to sound as annoyed as he did.

"I didn't mean to bother you." The man extended his hand to Luke and he shook it. "I'm Grady Campbell with the *San Francisco Chronicle*. The missing girl – Laurie Presley – she's from San Francisco. My editor sent me here to cover the story. I saw you across the restaurant and wondered your involvement in this case."

"No involvement," Luke said and pushed out the chair next to him for Grady to take a seat. "It's by happenstance that I'm here. How do you know me?"

Grady pulled back in surprise. "How does anyone who follows true crime *not* know you? All of you, including your wife, Riley Sullivan. You're all famous. Don't tell me you don't know about the podcast."

Cooper and Luke shared a look, neither having any idea what Grady was talking about. "There's a podcast?" Cooper asked.

"Started several months ago now." Grady pulled his phone out of his messenger bag and pulled up a website to show Luke.

Rock City Killers had a graphic of a knife dripping blood. Scrolling down, there was navigation to recent episodes and a bio page for the podcast host – Cat O'Conner. Luke read her bio but had never met or heard of the woman. He handed the phone back to Grady. "First I'm hearing about it. Does she mention us on the podcast?"

"The whole podcast started with the case where you brought your sister's killer to justice. She covered more of your cases after that."

Luke tried to keep his expression steady and unchanged but inside he grew uncomfortable. "Does she cover other cases besides mine?"

Grady nodded. "There's a handful, but they aren't as interesting. She's even gone to the prison and spoken to a few of the killers."

Cooper seemed as concerned as Luke. "She's never interviewed any of us. I wonder how she's getting her information."

"Freedom of Information Act," Grady said like he couldn't believe they had no idea.

Luke wanted to know more about the podcast, but it wasn't the time or the place. "Have you found out anything about Laurie to indicate where she might have gone?"

"I only arrived this morning but so far nothing. The cops aren't involved and have refused to speak to any reporters. They keep claiming that Laurie ran off with a guy, but the family disputes that."

They had said as much to Luke. "We heard that Laurie is the fifth woman to go missing. Can you confirm that?"

Grady pulled out his iPad and started reading through notes about the past cases. There were five missing women in all – two from the United States, one each from Canada, England, and Scotland. All of the women were in their early twenties and had been in St. Thomas on vacation with their friends. They were all missing from the same bar under the same circumstances. None of the women had been found.

"As you can see, it's a bigger case than any of us knew about. It was never covered here in St. Thomas though. I found articles about the missing women in newspapers in Canada, England, and Scotland, but it never made anything more than local news. Gia Tibbitts, from Colorado, went missing about a year ago on spring break. Her local newspaper covered the story, but it didn't get much press beyond that."

"Why?" Cooper asked with confusion on his face. "I could understand if these young women were missing over years and no one connected it across a few countries. But it's been five young women within a year."

Luke thought Cooper had answered his own question. "It's because they were all from different countries who went missing here. No local women have disappeared."

Grady closed one notebook and pulled out another. "That might not be true." He flipped to a page and unfolded several newspaper clippings. "Amani Hanley was twenty when she disappeared on her way home one night with friends. They had been at the Sunshine Bar. Amani walked the mile home with her friends and then cut off the main road along the dirt path to her house. It wasn't more than two hundred yards she walked by herself, but she never made it. That was two years ago and she's never been seen or heard from since. No one has ever been charged and no suspect has been identified."

"That doesn't mean that it's connected to the others," Cooper argued. He took another sip of his drink and looked poised to say something else but didn't.

Luke was sure this was the last thing Cooper wanted to talk about the night before his wedding. "What's your plan, Grady?" he asked, hoping to wrap up the conversation.

"I'm going to hang out here and do some digging around and hopefully find some information. Will you both be around if I have questions? This case could use your expertise – both of you."

"Cooper is getting married tomorrow so that is our focus. I don't know that we'll have any time or interest in getting involved in this case."

"Understood," Grady said, the disappointment in his voice evident. He congratulated Cooper and then put his belongings back in his bag and stood. "It was nice meeting you and I hope you can enjoy the time here."

When he was gone, Cooper thanked Luke. "I didn't want to sit here talking about the case all night."

"Me either," Luke said. "Let's get out of here and take a walk on the beach. There's another bar right on the beach just down a little from the hotel. Maybe there will be fewer people."

Luke finished off the last of his beer, and as the server walked by, he asked for the check. Cooper pulled out his wallet but Luke told him to put it away.

Cooper insisted. "You can't pay for everything. It's my rehearsal dinner."

Luke brushed his hand away. "The father of the groom usually pays, right? Well, consider me Dad for the night. The least I can do is pick up dinner."

Cooper thanked him. "I don't know what I'd do without you."

"Same," Luke said, not wanting to get emotional over it all. They had each had a few beers and Luke was already feeling a bit off. He shook off the mood and smiled across the table. "Come on, let's go enjoy your last night as a single man."

Later, around one in the morning, Luke stumbled back to the hotel room after making sure Cooper made it back safely to his room and was tucked in for the night. It had been a long time since either of them had gotten drunk, especially together. The night ended up being fun once they got away from the hotel and found a spot at a beach bar.

Luke put the deadbolt on the hotel room door and stripped off his clothes right there in a heap. He took a cool shower and then snuggled up to Riley in bed. He laid his arm across her belly. "You awake?" he whispered.

Riley stirred and rolled into him. "Did you have fun with Cooper?"

"We did, but we both drank too much." He kissed her cheek and snuggled into her. "We met a reporter from San Francisco who told us we're famous. Apparently, someone named Cat started a podcast about us."

Riley patted his arm as if he were talking nonsense, but he was snoring before he could explain fully.

CHAPTER 3

Dressed in a tan suit and bright blue shirt, Cooper stood on the beach under the arch made of bright spring flowers and waited for the music to play and Adele to make her grand appearance. He had tried to sneak a peek at her dress, but she had told him that it was bad luck. Even though neither of them was particularly superstitious, Adele wasn't going to tempt fate.

Cooper turned to Luke who stood beside him and Riley who stood on the other side. He couldn't imagine being at the altar with anyone else. The day had been a blur of waking up late, struggling through a hangover, and then getting ready in the late afternoon. Now it was nearing five with the sun sitting perfectly in the sky and he was about to become Adele's husband. His heart beat a little faster and his palms started to sweat. It was the anticipation that was getting to him the most. It felt like he had been waiting all of his life for a moment he didn't know he wanted until he met Adele.

The music started to play and he turned to look down the makeshift aisle lined with flower petals in the sand. Adele carried a small bouquet of flowers, but their beauty was nothing in comparison to the smile on her face. Everything about her was simple and elegant from the form-fitting strapless white gown that hugged her curves to the pearl earrings on her ears. Cooper had given them to her for her last birthday. There was a naturalness about Adele that attracted Cooper right away. It was reflected today in the way she had planned their wedding.

She came down the aisle flirting with her eyes and then handed the flowers to Riley. She turned to him and held his hands and he told her how beautiful she looked. "You're quite handsome yourself," she said, smiling again.

If he died right there looking at her smile, he'd die a happy man. Cooper couldn't believe he was having such thoughts. Before Adele, he didn't even think he was capable of falling in love. The man officiating was saying words Cooper didn't hear. He was lost in his thoughts about Adele and how amazing she was. She nodded her head to the side and Cooper had to focus.

The officiant said words about love and marriage and the bond that Cooper and Adele shared. Cooper didn't want to be looking at him though. When it came time for the vows, Cooper's voice cracked and he barely got out the words while he tried to hold back the emotion. Adele had the same problem and they were lucky they both didn't end up blubbering messes. They exchanged rings and the officiant said more words Cooper didn't quite process. What he did hear loud and clear was that it was time to kiss his bride – and would he ever.

Cooper took Adele in his arms and kissed her gently on the lips and then pulled her closer. They lost themselves for a moment forgetting about the people around them. Luke cleared his throat after a moment and Cooper blushed, embarrassed that he'd gotten so carried away.

"Sorry," Cooper said sheepishly and then laughed.

"Never apologize for kissing your wife." Adele pulled him closer again for one more kiss before they broke apart and were congratulated by Riley and Luke. Even the officiant seemed overjoyed for them.

They stood for photos of just themselves and then with Riley and Luke. It seemed to go on forever. Relief washed over him when Adele waved off the photographer and put a hand to her stomach.

"I haven't eaten a thing all day and I'm starving!" she cried and pulled Cooper toward the table that had been set up for them.

"That was a beautiful ceremony," Riley said as she sat. "Cooper, you seemed completely lost in your thoughts. Did you hear a word the man said?"

"I heard him. I said all my lines correctly, but I was mesmerized by my beautiful bride. You can't blame a man for that."

Adele leaned over and kissed him again. "I had a hard time paying attention too. All I wanted to do was kiss you."

Luke raised his glass. "Well, that you certainly did!"

They enjoyed the meal that Adele had planned for them. Everything was chosen with Cooper's taste in mind from the appetizers to the salad and entrée and even dessert. She had skipped the traditional wedding cake and had the hotel make a raspberry cheesecake, which was Cooper's favorite. He didn't think he'd ever felt more special in his life and couldn't believe that he'd been so lucky to have met and now married someone like Adele.

As the evening grew late and darkness settled in, all four of them grew tired. Nearing ten, Cooper was ready to call it a night. As they stood from the table, he wrapped Adele in a hug. He started to whisper how much he loved her when a piercing scream cut through the night air.

All eyes turned toward the water. Cooper couldn't see what was happening because the shoreline was too dark. Without even thinking, Cooper released Adele and took off with Luke in a run toward the water.

When they finally reached the source of the screams, they stopped cold. A woman stood ankle-deep in the water staring down at the bloated corpse of a young woman. She screamed over and over again an unintelligible piercing wail that drew many more onlookers than

Luke and Cooper.

"It's okay," Cooper said to the woman, even though everything was far from okay. He put his hand gently on her arm to let her know that she had succeeded in calling for help. "Please stop screaming. It's going to be okay."

"We need to secure the scene," Luke said, looking around at the people who started to gather.

The woman stopped screaming and looked to Cooper for answers, which he didn't have. He gestured to a hotel employee standing next to him. "Luke is a detective and I'm a private investigator. Please take this woman back up to the hotel and call the police."

The hotel employee did as Cooper asked as Luke started backing up the people who had gathered around. Cooper worried that the waves rocking in and out would take away significant evidence, but there was nothing they could do about that.

"What do you think we should do?" Cooper asked Luke, who seemed as shellshocked as he felt.

"There's not much we can do until the police arrive." Luke bent down to look at the body. "I can't figure out if this is the same girl who is missing. Her body is in such a state of decomp it's hard to tell."

Cooper had only seen a photo of the girl briefly when he was standing in the lobby of the hotel the day before. He ran a hand down his face, scratching at his chin. "I don't think it's the missing girl, Luke. She doesn't even have the same color hair – well, what's left of it."

It was never easy for Cooper to come face-to-face with death. He didn't have the strongest stomach, and even though he'd been a detective turned private investigator for all of his career, it never got easier. By the look on Luke's face, Cooper assumed it hadn't become any easier for him either.

"We don't have gloves or anything so I can't go digging around in her pockets for identification. We shouldn't touch the body," Luke said and Cooper agreed.

They stood in the water staring down at the dead young woman as the waves swayed her body. They had agreed that if the waves started to carry her out too much, they'd have no choice but to pull her on shore. Touching her was the last thing they wanted to do though.

It took the police close to forty minutes to arrive on the scene. Cooper stepped back out of their way and scanned the crowd of people for Riley and Adele. He and Luke had left them at the table, which Cooper was glad about. Neither of them needed to see this horror – particularly Adele still in her wedding dress.

"What do we have here?" a cop said, sauntering toward them like he had all the time in the world. His dark thinning head came up to Cooper's shoulder. He turned to Luke. "Heard you were a cop or something."

Luke extended his hand, which the man didn't take. "I'm Det. Luke Morgan, head of the violent crime division with the Little Rock Police Department in Arkansas. This is Cooper Deagnan, a former detective turned private investigator."

The man smirked. "You two cowboys have taken over now?"

Luke's jaw set in a firm line and Cooper knew he wasn't happy. "Hardly. We heard screaming and rushed to the water thinking someone might have been in trouble. We got down here to find a body and a hysterical woman. Cooper asked a hotel employee to take her inside and to call the police. We are standing here protecting your crime scene. A lot of people rushed to see what was going on."

"Heroes come to save the day," the man said, dripping with sarcasm.

"Professional courtesy. We've introduced ourselves, but I didn't catch your name."

"That's because I didn't give it and don't have to." He leaned over the body, waved, then stood slowly. He told the other cops who had come with him to leave. "This ain't nothing but a drowning. The medical examiner will be here any minute and can take it from here. You can go back to getting drunk or whatever you were doing down here from Arkansas."

Cooper pointed to the body. "She has a sneaker on her right foot and remnants of a pair of pants on. I hardly think that's swimming attire. She also has contusions on her face."

Luke added, "She has three fingernails on her right hand ripped off down to the skin. There was some kind of struggle, probably before she went into the water."

"You boys don't know nothing about island living." He jutted his chin toward the body. "We get pretty young girls like this down here all the time getting drunk and partying with their friends. They forget we are surrounded by the ocean. All it takes is a slip and fall near the water and that's it, they're a goner."

Cooper shook his head in disgust. "I understand you know more about what happens on this island than us, but I'm sure we've handled a greater number of homicides. I'm telling you that's what we are looking at here. At least, protect the scene in case it is. My understanding is you have five young women who have gone missing over the last year. This could be any one of them."

The detective straightened his body to his full height, which still left him looking up at Cooper and Luke. He had his hands on his hips and he screwed up his face in a scowl. "You two need to get out of here. I'll be in touch should I need anything." When they both hesitated to go, he threatened them. "I can arrest you for disturbing my scene. How'd you like that?"

Cooper started to say something, but Luke reached for his arm and pulled him by the sleeve to go. They didn't say anything else to the cop who still hadn't identified himself, and he hadn't even bothered to ask Cooper or Luke for their contact information. It was hard walking away knowing someone was going to make a snap judgment, potentially harm a crime scene, and never get justice for the poor woman's family. It ate at Cooper as they pushed their way through the crowd of people and returned to the hotel.

As they entered the lobby, Cooper assumed they were going in search of Riley and Adele so he was taken aback when Luke went to the counter and asked where they had put the woman who had discovered the body.

"She's still hysterical," the man said. He had a pleasant face but seemed shaken by the incident, as anyone would be. "I'll take you to her."

The man brought Luke and Cooper down a hallway to a conference room. The woman sat at the end of a long table with her head in her hands. She raised her red watery eyes and blotchy face to them as they entered. "Are you the detective who I need to speak to?"

Luke shifted his eyes to Cooper. "No, but I am a detective and I need your help."

Cooper held back a sly smile knowing they were going to charge head-on into the investigation whether the local cops liked it or not.

CHAPTER 4

I paced the floor in the living room area of Adele's hotel suite. After Luke and Cooper raced to the water, we heard onlookers talking about a body that had washed ashore. We went back to our rooms to change our clothes. I was half-expecting Adele to fall apart or lament the fact that her wedding had been marred by a tragic event. She seemed to take it all in stride – much better even than I would have if a body washed up on the beach after my wedding.

I had run to my room long enough to change out of my dress into a pair of shorts and a tee-shirt. I slipped on flip-flops and went to Adele's room without even wiping some of the makeup from my face – a decision I now regretted because my eyes were starting to itch from all the mascara and eye shadow.

Adele had finished changing by the time I knocked on her door. She pulled it open looking determined. "Should we go and help them?" she asked, stepping out of the way and letting me in.

"There's nothing we can do. I assume Luke and Cooper are hanging out until the cops arrive and then will be back up here. I texted Luke and told him that we were in your room. I haven't heard back yet."

Adele plopped down in a chair and placed her hands on her knees like she might spring up at any moment. "I don't think I can sit here and wait."

I sat on the couch near her. "Why are you okay with this? I would think you'd be annoyed that this is happening."

Adele looked at me and furrowed her brow. "Riley, young women are missing and a body just washed up on the beach. These girls are barely older than my sister. I feel for the families and want to help. You used to be like that."

Red flamed my cheeks and I wasn't sure what to say at first. "I care, Adele. Cooper warned me not to get involved in anything like this and ruin your wedding day. You know that I tend to fall into cases. I was only thinking about you on your special day."

Adele reached out and took my hand. "I'm sorry. Of course that's your concern. I'm okay though. Cooper probably shouldn't have said that to you. He wanted to make today so perfect for me that he worried any little thing might ruin it. It was the perfect day. I couldn't have asked for anything better, but now, this is more important to me."

I checked my phone again and Luke had texted to let me know they'd be up soon. He didn't share any information with me but said he'd explain all when he saw me. "It doesn't sound like Luke is going to let this go."

"I wouldn't have thought he would." We waited until the lock clicked on the door and Cooper and Luke came in. Cooper went over to Adele and pulled her up from the chair and wrapped her in a hug. "What did you find out?" she asked.

Cooper pulled back. "Are you sure you want to be involved with this? Luke and I talked and he said he and Riley can handle it while we go off to the other side of the island and enjoy our honeymoon."

Adele shook her head. "I couldn't enjoy our honeymoon knowing there were missing young women on the island. Everything happens for a reason, Cooper. You know I believe that. We are here for a reason and we were right there when the body was found for a reason. Don't make me ask again. What did you find out?"

Luke raised his eyes to me in a question, but I wasn't sure what he wanted to know. "We are both okay getting involved, Luke." That seemed to appease him so he sat down on the couch and detailed what happened after they left us at the table.

"The bottom line," Luke said as he was finishing, "is that the cop is an idiot. I tried to give him the benefit of the doubt, but he looked at the body and said she drowned. I've seen bodies in that condition and there's no way that was a drowning. That girl was dead when she went into the water. He didn't even introduce himself. I had to search the police department's website and he's the most senior detective they have. Richard Hanley, which is suspicious because the reporter I met said that two years ago Amani Hanley went missing, too."

"Any relation?" I asked, moving over to the middle of the couch so Cooper could sit on my other side.

"I don't know. I'm not sure if Hanley is a common name here. It might be a coincidence and I didn't find anything online to indicate they were related. Then again, I didn't find much about Amani Hanley other than a short piece buried in a local paper that she was missing. The article provided few details."

"We don't know that it's connected to the others then."

"Right," Luke said, reaching for my hand. "We don't know what we don't know."

"This isn't Little Rock, Luke. How are we going to proceed without access to information?" Adele asked, realizing probably for the first time that being an investigator was far different than an attorney who would file motions in court for information.

Luke looked to me and then to Cooper. "What private investigators do all the time. Ninety percent of the cases Riley and Cooper take have nothing to do with my homicide unit and they have no access to information. I say we connect with the parents we met first and offer our help. That should grease the wheels a little. The cops don't want to take the case so we will take it. Then we can seek out that reporter I spoke to last night and see what other information he wants to share with us. He seemed eager to work with us."

"What reporter?" Adele asked, looking to Cooper.

"Luke and I met a reporter from the *San Francisco Chronicle*. Laurie Presley is from San Francisco and his editor asked him to cover the case. He has quite a bit of background information."

I turned to Luke with my eyebrows raised. "What did you find out?"

"Not much because I was trying not to get involved." Luke ran a hand over his face. "If we commit to getting involved, we have to commit. This could be our whole vacation."

Cooper shrugged. "We can all go on vacation another time."

"You mean that?" Adele asked, her eyes welling up. "You're willing to sacrifice our honeymoon?"

"I'll take you on vacation anytime you want. If it's fine by you, then we're helping," he assured her. Then he turned to me. "What do you want to do first?"

I couldn't admit that I was feeling a twinge of guilt because I didn't want to get involved. I didn't know if it was a gut feeling, or because we were on an unfamiliar island with no local resources and no equipment. I felt completely out of my element. "Probably with the parents Luke and I met in the hallway. If Luke and I approach them, we might get further than if all four of us go. We've already built a little rapport with them."

"I agree." Cooper pointed to Adele's laptop on the desk. "We can stay here and start pulling together everything we can find including any contact information on all the missing young women."

I looked at the clock on the wall. It was nearing midnight. "Do you think it's too late to make contact with the parents?"

Luke shook his head. "I'm sure they heard about the body found and are worried that it might be their daughter. I don't think it is though.

I'm sure the media will be reporting her identity soon. At least the media is here and access to information might be made easier because of it."

With that Luke and I left and made it halfway down the hall before he stopped. "We don't know where they are staying." He was used to flashing a badge and demanding the hotel room of whoever it was he was trying to find.

It didn't work that way as a private investigator. "I'm sure that either they have a command room set up in the hotel or the front desk will call them for us. You have your badge on you. You can still flash it although it might not mean much here."

Luke patted down his pockets. "It's in the room."

We headed back to our room so Luke could grab his badge. Neither of us had a gun with us. Because of the amount of paperwork involved in traveling to a U.S. territory with a weapon, neither of us had bothered. We were supposed to be sitting on a beach sunning ourselves.

After we left the room, we kept scanning the throngs of people as we went to the lobby in the hopes that we'd see either Bill or Ava Presley on our way down, but we didn't have such luck. At the front lobby desk, Luke asked the man he had spoken to before if he knew how to reach them.

Surprisingly, the man didn't even flinch. "Right this way. I can show you where we have them set up. As you can imagine, they were quite shaken to hear that a body had been found. We are doing everything we can to make sure they are comfortable and taken care of while they are here. It's been hard for them and I'm sure they would welcome a calming presence."

I wondered why he was so eager to allow us access, but then before he opened the door, he stopped and formally introduced himself. "My name is Vic Hanley and I'm the manager of this hotel. Amani Hanley was my cousin." When he asked if we knew her name, we nodded. "I'm hoping if you find out what happened to this young woman it will answer some questions about my cousin. We were close, more like siblings, and it's been so hard not knowing what happened to her."

Luke laid a hand on the man's shoulder. "We'll do whatever we can to help."

"Let me know if you need anything. You'll have my full cooperation."

Luke offered him a sympathetic smile and thanked him. Vic opened the door for us and told the few people sitting around the table that a detective wanted to speak to them. Hopeful eyes turned to us and then Bill got up from the table and came over to greet us. He introduced his wife again and then the other people who were local volunteers trying to help them find their daughter.

"You didn't say in the hallway yesterday that you were with the police."

"We're not exactly." Luke gestured toward the table. Once we were all seated, Luke led the discussion as we had planned. "I'm the head of the violent crimes division with the Little Rock Police Department in Arkansas. Riley, my wife, is a private investigator and our friends who just got married are also in the same field. We just happened to be here in St. Thomas for their wedding. Cooper and I were on the beach when we heard the woman scream. We did our best to secure the crime scene until the cops arrived, but I'll be honest with you, I don't have much faith in them."

Bill nodded in agreement. "Did you speak to Det. Hanley?"

"Yes. In my opinion, he was too quick to brush off what happened as a routine drowning without any facts to back that up and that's not what the..." Luke paused as if trying to find the right word.

Ava locked eyes with him. "Please don't hold back. I'm a registered nurse. I deal with death and trauma all the time. Det. Hanley told me that it wasn't Laurie who had been found."

"I agree with him, but we won't know for sure until the autopsy or they take fingerprints of the victim. It did not appear to be your daughter." Luke took a breath. "What I was saying is that I don't think based on the condition of the body and what she was wearing that it was a drowning. I don't know her identity. After meeting you briefly yesterday, we learned that your daughter isn't the only young woman missing."

Ava welled up again. "We only learned that when we arrived and someone from the media told us. If I had known there were other missing young women, I'd have never let Laurie and her friends vacation here."

That was probably why it hadn't made the news. I looked over at her. "Unfortunately, that can happen in vacation areas. They try to keep things quiet."

Bill cleared his throat. "If you don't have any updates for us, can I ask why you wanted to speak to us?"

"We want to offer you our assistance in finding your daughter. We'll be here at least another week and think we might be able to help."

"We don't have much money," Bill said with hope in his eyes.

Luke waved him off. "For free."

Ava rested her head on the table and sobbed, thanking us for being so kind.

If I hadn't been on board before, I was now.

CHAPTER 5

We gave Ava a moment to compose herself while the volunteers and Bill thanked us and asked what we needed.

"Information," I said evenly. "We need to get up to speed on everything you know. Cooper and his wife, Adele, are upstairs doing some research on the other young women who are missing. We want to learn everything we can about Laurie."

"You said your friends just got married. Wouldn't they rather be enjoying their honeymoon?"

"I understand why you'd ask that. Cooper is my investigative partner and is an excellent investigator. He used to be a detective." I looked to Luke because I didn't want to disclose anything I shouldn't. The look on his face told me to go ahead. "This is personal for Adele and Luke. Both of their sisters went missing as college freshmen and were later found to have been murdered by the same killer."

A young volunteer snapped her fingers and pointed at Luke. "You're the detective they talk about in the Rock City Killers podcast."

My head turned to Luke. He had been mumbling something the other night when he came home drunk, but I had forgotten by morning and he never brought it up again. I thought he had been kidding.

Luke seemed embarrassed. "I only heard about the podcast recently from a reporter. I didn't even know it existed."

"Well, you're excellent. We are all glad you're here."

Bill had a look of relief on his face. "Tell us what you need."

I was always a little overwhelmed at the start of a case. There was always so much to find out and uncover. It was like throwing a massive thousand-piece puzzle on the table with all the pieces upside down so you couldn't see the image. "Are the other three girls who were with your daughter at home now?"

"Yes," Ava said. "They wanted to stay but had final exams coming up. I told them to go home and finish the semester."

"Is there any way we can speak to them?"

Bill pointed to a laptop on the table. "We can video chat with all of them. Other than an initial statement to the cops the morning after Laurie disappeared, none of them have been formally spoken with." He checked his watch. "Would it be okay if we set that up for you tomorrow? I don't know their schedules and it's fairly late."

"That's perfect," Luke said. He pulled out his phone and made a note as Bill told them the other women's names and information. "Had you heard from Laurie during the trip?"

"She video chatted with us a handful of times," Ava explained, sniffling back tears. "We are a close family and I was worried about her being away from home."

"When did you get the call that Laurie was missing?"

"The girls called us immediately. I wanted to get on a flight that night. It was two in the morning though and the best we could do was a flight later the next day. Bill and I had been hoping that Laurie would turn up by then. Maybe she had gotten separated or met new friends or something. We were here on the island about twenty-four hours after she disappeared. Even then the police wouldn't take a report from us."

"There's been no sign of her," Bill said, putting a hand on his wife's. "We went to the bar where she had last been seen and showed her photo around. People remembered her, but no one knew what happened to her. One guy said he thought he saw her walk outside alone, saying she needed some fresh air, but he wasn't one hundred percent sure it was her. The bartender I spoke to said people often go in and out of the bar because it can be crowded and hot. They have a back deck on the beach but that's normally filled. The girls said they were in and out of the bar all night, but that Laurie had gone to the bar and no one saw her again."

Luke checked a note file on his phone. "You said the hotel had no record of Laurie coming back here that night?"

"Correct," Bill said and gestured toward the door. "The hotel has been amazing. We couldn't have asked for better cooperation or more help from them. Laurie and her friends were seen on video surveillance going out at seven that night and then the three of them return without Laurie around one in the morning when they were searching for her. There's nothing in between. Laurie never came back to the hotel. That's about the only thing we know for a fact."

"It's a starting point," Luke said and then paused as if considering his next question.

I watched Luke and could nearly see the gears turning in his head. It wasn't just cliché that the first forty-eight hours of any investigation are critical. Not that it couldn't be solved after that but time was of the essence. The longer a missing person's case went on with no clues, the less likely the person would be found, alive at least.

Luke drummed his fingers on the table as he considered. "Do you know if all the surveillance cameras were checked or just the ones in the front of the hotel?"

"What do you mean?" Bill asked with confusion on his face.

"We've seen in some cases if someone is familiar with the hotel they might use another entrance other than the front. Sometimes there is a side or back door that can be opened with a keycard. There is a door that leads out to the restaurant patio and bar. Were they all checked?"

"We know that her keycard wasn't used on any doors that night. I don't understand why this is important?"

"Let me explain it this way," I said, leaning into the table. "We want to make certain that it was the bar your daughter disappeared from. That was the last place her friends saw her, but for all we know, she wandered back here, went in a door other than the front, and then went missing. Does that make sense?"

Bill said, "We only watched video surveillance of the front entrance. We didn't see surveillance from any other part of the hotel. We didn't even think of that."

"Bill, it's okay," Luke reassured him. "You're not expected to do the job of the police. I'm thorough in my investigations – probably annoyingly so to some."

"I'd rather have you thorough than not." Bill went to stand but Luke gestured for him to sit back down. "I was going to ask for the surveillance video."

"I'll do that in the morning. I'll sit down with their head of security and ask the questions I have and then one of us will go over all the footage from that night. It will be tedious and time-consuming. While one of us does that, we will still focus on other avenues."

Luke turned to me to see if I had any questions. I had several but knew we were all tired and we'd have a chance to start fresh in the morning. I asked the most important. "Did you bring in any dogs to track her direction?"

Bill shook his head. "We asked Det. Hanley that and he said it would be pointless with so many other people in the bar that night."

"We'll look into that for you too," Luke said with annoyance in his voice. "We won't take up any more time tonight, but let's meet down here at eight tomorrow morning."

As Luke stood to leave, I said, "We need to address what you are telling Det. Hanley. Once we start poking around, he's not going to like it and will probably tell you that we will make the situation worse for your daughter. Detectives have been known to say some wild things to try to keep private investigators away from their cases. They get territorial."

Bill looked down at his wife and then back to us. "I don't care if he wants you to be involved or not. You've done more for us in twenty minutes than he has in days. They barely even took a report. I don't care what he has to say."

I stood, letting my hands linger on the tabletop. "That's good enough for us. We will see you in the morning."

I followed Luke out of the room and thought we would be heading back upstairs, but he surprised me by going to the front desk and asking to speak to the head of security. The woman picked up the phone and placed the call, spoke briefly to someone, and then gave us directions to get to the security office.

As we walked away, I asked, "Isn't it late to do this?"

"It's most likely not the head of security on tonight, and I don't know what kind of relationship he has with Det. Hanley. I figured I'll chat up the security person and see what we can access now."

I hadn't even thought of that. I looped my arm through his. "That's a smart idea."

As we walked down the hall, Luke checked his phone. "Cooper texted and said he found some preliminary information, but they are calling it quits for the night. He wants to meet at breakfast early tomorrow."

"I'm glad they are stopping for the night."

Luke looked down at me and agreed. "I'm kicking myself now for not getting that reporter's name and phone number."

"What was his name?"

"Grady Campbell."

"It's easy enough to find. I'll find some of his articles." I remembered what the volunteer said about the podcast. "You were rambling last night about the podcast. What's up with that?"

"I don't know. Maybe you can look that up too tomorrow."

We went down a long hall, reading off the room numbers as we went. When we reached the office door for security, Luke knocked once. A young man with a head full of dark hair and equally dark eyes answered. Luke explained who he was and what he was asking for.

When the young man hesitated, Luke pressed him. "All we want to know is if she came back here at any point. I have no reason to believe she's missing because of anything to do with the hotel. All I'm trying to figure out is if she ever came back. The family saw footage from the front door and hallway. We know there are other entry ways. We just need to know the last place she was seen." Luke flashed his badge. "I'm out of my jurisdiction. I'm doing everything I can to help this family though, and this would be a huge step in the right direction for us. If you need to call the front desk, ask for Vic. He's been helping me out with this."

He raised his eyebrows. "You spoke to Vic?"

"He told me anything we needed he'd help provide."

"Come on in," he said and stepped out of the way. "What time parameters do you need? I don't have time to sit here tonight and go through it all, but I can make you a copy that you can take with you. Then maybe, we never had this conversation. I don't know that my supervisor would like me to give you this."

I tried to hide my surprise. I gave him the dates and times and then we waited while he made copies of the files and sent them to Luke via a link in his email.

CHAPTER 6

Luke woke the next morning ready to go. It had been a long time since a case had invigorated him the way this one had. Luke uploaded the surveillance video files to Riley's laptop while she was in the shower. He wouldn't have time to go through all the footage right now, but he could start. He had a little over an hour before meeting Cooper and Adele for breakfast and two hours before he met the family again.

It helped that they had narrowed down a short window of time between when Laurie went missing and her friends started searching – not even twenty minutes. The girls last saw Laurie on the dance floor at eleven-forty-five. Just after midnight, they had begun their search.

"Where are you, Laurie?" Luke said to himself as he hit the video surveillance for eleven-forty-five. His computer screen had all three hotel entrances – front door, back patio entrance, and side door – in small windows so Luke could view all of them at once. He hit the slowest fast forward option and then watched and waited. The back door at the hotel didn't have much activity at all, which made sense because the restaurant and bar closed at midnight. The front door had the most activity but he didn't see Laurie. The side entrance came in from a parking lot for guests and didn't have much foot traffic at that time of night.

Luke watched all three entrances and at twelve-ten, a young woman who fit Laurie's description stood at the door fumbling with her keycard. She inserted it into the slot and tried to pull the door open but it wouldn't budge. She tried it three more times and then dropped her card on the ground. She swayed back and forth intoxicated.

Laurie turned sharply as if someone had called her name. She spoke to someone although, with no sound, Luke had no idea what she was saying. She didn't appear to be afraid or upset. It appeared to be a conversation. Then all at once, a hand gripped her right arm and pulled her out of frame.

Luke lurched forward in his chair and yelled for her to stop, forgetting for a moment that he wasn't watching a live-action shot. He hit the rewind button and watched it again, moving his face closer to the screen, and then repeated the action one more time.

Luke froze the frame on the man's hand. He clicked a few buttons and took a screenshot of the image and then enlarged it. He didn't have a printer so he saved the file to Riley's hard drive and a removable drive she had sitting next to her laptop. Before breakfast, he'd need to print the images.

"Riley," he called, not even believing it had been that easy to find. "We got something."

Riley stuck her head out of the bathroom door, her hair nearly dry. She stepped toward him wearing a pair of shorts and her bra. "In the surveillance video?"

He waved her over and then pointed to the screen. "Watch. It's very brief, but I'm sure that Laurie went to that side door at twelve-ten. She fumbles with her keycard and wasn't able to open the door. She speaks to someone who approached but remains out of the shot. Then someone grabs her." Luke backed up the video to the point before Laurie approached the door and scooted the chair back so Riley could have a better look.

Riley leaned down toward the laptop and watched the entire scene play out. She turned to him, surprised. "I think that's her. Play it again for me. I see the hand, but I think I see something else too."

Luke did as she asked and then waited while she stared at the screen once more. She instructed him to back it up again and then told him when to freeze the frame.

"Right there," she said, pointing toward the bottom of the screen. "He grabs her with one hand but for about a second his other hand pops into the frame. He's wearing some kind of ring. Do you see it?"

Luke hadn't seen it before, but that area of the video hadn't been what drew his attention. He had to focus on the area where Riley had her finger on the screen. Once he saw it though, he asked, "What is that ring?"

"You'll have to enlarge that section. He must have his sleeves rolled up or is wearing short sleeves. We can make out his hands but that's about it. It's definitely a man though." Riley went back into the bathroom to finish getting ready.

Luke put all the files he needed on the removable drive and then yelled to Riley that he was off to print the photos. He told her that he'd meet her at breakfast and then headed toward the hotel lobby, hoping someone at the hotel could print the photos for him.

Nearly an hour later, he scanned the hotel restaurant for Riley, Cooper, and Adele. He found them sitting on the patio outside even though the sky looked like it might drop a deluge of rain at any moment. "Risking it, aren't we?" he said as he pulled up a chair.

Cooper looked toward the sky. "It will hold out. I figured we'd want to talk and there's hardly anyone out here. It's too crowded in there to discuss anything sensitive."

Luke slid a manila eight-by-ten file folder across the table toward Cooper. "I was able to print these from the hotel surveillance."

Cooper looked at him in amazement and shock. "I can't believe you were able to get access already."

Luke gestured toward the lobby. "The hotel manager, Vic, has been tremendously helpful. You saw him briefly last night when we asked him to take the woman inside after finding the body. It turns out he's the cousin to Amani Hanley, but we can get to that later. Take a look at those."

Cooper pulled the photos out of the file and leaned over so Adele could look at them, too. They studied each of the photos and then slipped them back into the file. "That's Laurie Presley without question. Where was this taken?"

Luke realized he hadn't given them much context. "This is the side door of the hotel the night she disappeared. The last known sighting of her is not the bar, it's this hotel. We need to identify that man and see what he knows. We also need to see who else might have been a witness in the hotel parking lot that night."

"How do you plan on going about that?"

"Vic. I already spoke to him about it." Luke paused while the server came over and took their order. He didn't realize until he looked at the menu how hungry he was. Scrambled eggs, pancakes, and bacon would hit the spot. When they were done with their orders, Luke explained, "Vic said that he'd make up a new missing person's flyer with the photo her parents provided and the surveillance video of her at the door and my phone number. He said he'd add the close-up of the man's hand with the ring, too. Then he will deliver it to every room in the hotel. Some people might have already checked out, but it's the best we can do right now."

Adele reached for the photo that Luke mentioned and studied it. "This looks like a family crest. It's hard to make out though. Looks like a horse rearing back on its hind legs and then a knight's helmet."

Luke agreed with her. That was the only thing he could make out of the ring as well. "I don't even know how to begin searching for something like that."

"They sell them on Etsy," Riley said, taking a sip of her juice. "Unless that thing is a real coat of arms and someone recognizes it, I don't think that it's going to be much help."

Luke agreed. "We have to be careful because it doesn't mean this man did anything to her. For all we know, he was a good Samaritan trying to help. We don't know what happened after that point."

Adele leaned back in her chair. "If he was a good Samaritan and was helping her, then she would have made it to the front lobby or he could have helped her with her keycard right there. I'd be looking at this guy like a potential suspect."

"Definitely not ruling it out," Luke said, agreeing with her. "What did you and Cooper find in your research last night?"

Adele turned to Cooper and he grimaced. "There's not a lot of information out there. We have names and dates from a few reports that Grady did in the *San Francisco Chronicle*. I searched for each victim's name and came back with all the basic details Grady had already provided. What's most striking is the absence of information. None of these cases were investigated. It's like these young women went missing and the parents accepted the word of the detective on the cases who said they ran off with someone. Grady noted that was the response Det. Hanley gave for each case."

"As we said last night, it's been going on because it's not getting much publicity and the victims are all from different countries," Riley reminded them. "I'm glad the Presleys called the media. It's the only thing that's going to warn people."

Luke took a sip of water. "Who are the victims?"

Cooper pulled out his phone and read from the list. "Gia Tibbitts was in April of last year. She's from Colorado and came here with friends on a spring break trip. Ruby Wallis is from Toronto and was here during the summer with her friends. Daphne Powers is from

London and went missing over Christmas break, and Freya Reid from Edinburgh went missing in early February. Now, we have Laurie Presley following in late March."

"The parents didn't follow up at all?" Luke asked, not believing that could be the case.

"I'm sure they did," Cooper said, "but there's no account of it in the news. The local news reports indicate that each of the girls' parents is doing everything they can to find their daughter. Nothing specific as far as action is detailed though. We are going to need to reach out to all of the parents."

Their food arrived and they dug in, chatting between bites. Luke knew they needed a game plan and mulled it over as he ate breakfast. The food tasted so good that it was hard to concentrate on anything else. When they were done, Luke checked the time. It was about a quarter to eight and they'd need to meet the Presleys soon.

Dropping his napkin on the table, Luke said, "Feel free to tell me no and suggest other ideas if you like. I don't want to take control over this whole thing, but you know that's my tendency."

Riley smiled at him. "Just tell us your plan. I'm sure it will be fine for us."

She knew him too well. "Cooper and Adele, do you mind calling the parents of the other victims and finding out what details we can and anyone else they think we should speak to?" Then he turned to Riley. "After I meet with the Presleys and tell them what we found on the surveillance video, it would be great if you could video chat with Laurie's friends away from her parents. They might be holding back details to not get Laurie in trouble."

Riley set her fork on her empty plate. "I was going to suggest that last night. Not that you're not good with interviewing twenty-something girls, but I feel like they might relate more to me and be more honest. The more comfortable we can make them, the better." She raised her eyebrows to Luke. "What are you going to be doing?"

"A few things," he said with a sly smile. "I want to hunt down Grady and have a chat with him now that we are involved in the investigation. The sooner I can make nice with the media, the better off we'll be. Then I want to connect with the medical examiner."

With all of them in agreement, they paid the bill and promised to meet back at lunch. Cooper had been right, too, the rain held off until they were done. Once inside, the rain pelted against the windows.

CHAPTER 7

I was glad that Luke wanted me to interview Laurie's friends. I was going to suggest that to him but didn't want to step on his toes. This investigation seemed to be his baby and I wanted him to run with it. The only concern I had now was how to ask Ava and Bill for privacy when I made the calls.

The door to the conference room was open. When we stepped inside, we were met with even more volunteers than the night before. I pulled Luke back. "What's the plan for all of them?"

"I don't know," Luke said, shaking his head as if he were as overwhelmed as I felt. There had to be at least twenty people in the room with Ava and Bill. "It's good to see so many people this morning. Before we start, it would be helpful to know what the volunteers have planned for the day."

That was as good a start as any. I went over to Laurie's parents and put my hand on Ava's back. She smiled up at me, but it was clear she hadn't slept the night before or maybe even the night before that.

One of the volunteers stepped forward. "We are going out to hand out flyers and talk to people to see if anyone has seen Laurie or has any information about that night at the bar."

Luke took a seat near one end of the table. "I'm having some new flyers made up. I'd like to speak to Bill and Ava though before you head out." He turned to them and said he had information and wanted to know if they wanted privacy.

"No," Bill said. "These volunteers have been here every day and are waiting for information. They can hear anything you have for us. We wouldn't have been able to accomplish as much as we have without them."

Luke took the photos out of the file and laid them on the table. "Last night, before we went up to our room, I spoke with security and was able to get copies of the videos of the other doors at the hotel. I have an image of Laurie from that night." Luke went on to explain what he had found on the surveillance video including the man who approached her.

Ava and Bill looked over the photos. She sucked back a sob and then groaned when she got to the photo of the man grabbing her daughter by the arm.

She turned to me. "That man took my daughter."

"We don't know anything yet," Luke cautioned. "This might have been someone passing by. He might have seen that she was swaying and couldn't get in the door. For all we know, he escorted her around to the front of the building. This hotel does not have surveillance cameras outside other than at the doors. The only other surveillance is interior so we have no idea what he did after he approached."

With uncertainty on his face, Bill said, "He's considered a suspect, right? If this man was the last person to see my daughter, he must be questioned."

I sat down next to Bill. "We have to find him first. That's why we included an up-close photo of the man's hands and the ring." I pointed to the photo. "Someone might recognize the ring or even his hands. The goal is to get this out there, but we have to be careful about the language we use. If we label him a suspect and he hasn't done anything wrong, he might not come forward. His friends or family might not identify him for us. The goal is to sound like we want to talk to him because he might know something – no more, no less."

"I don't have a choice but to agree with you," Bill conceded.

Luke addressed Bill directly. "I share your frustration. When I saw the video, my first instinct was to assume he had something to do with Laurie's disappearance. Cooler heads have to prevail though. The goal is to get this flyer to as many people as possible. We know Laurie made it back to the hotel, so we need to focus on where she went."

"Okay," Bill said, his face stiff. He didn't look happy about what Luke said, but Ava seemed to understand.

Luke gave them a rundown of the plan for today. "I figured Riley might be better at interviewing Laurie's friends. She might be able to build rapport faster with them than I could. We also want Riley to be able to interview them alone."

"Why is that?" Ava asked.

I put my hand on her arm. "I've found that when interviewing young women in this situation, they can hold back in front of parents for fear of getting in trouble or getting your daughter in trouble. I'm not saying the girls did anything wrong or have held anything back, but it's a precaution."

Bill looked over at Ava. "I told you that before when we talked to them the first time."

"My daughter doesn't hide things from me."

The last thing I wanted was for them to argue. "Ava, I'm not suggesting your daughter hid anything from you. But they were out drinking at a bar and who knows what happened that night. If I interview them alone and their stories are exactly as they were the last time someone spoke to them, great. That's what we hope for. At least, if I interview them alone, I allow them an opportunity to say things they might not otherwise be comfortable saying. It's no reflection on you or your husband or Laurie."

Ava nodded once in understanding. "What do you want us to do?"

I gestured toward the laptop on the table. "Is everything set up for me to call them?"

Ava gave me each of the girl's screennames and clicked a button on the laptop. "The video chat program is open. I'm logged in so you can just click their name. They are available all morning." She and Bill got up from the table, looking to Luke for further instruction.

"Come with me and we can start distributing the flyers." Luke gave the volunteers some instructions and then had them follow him out of the room so they could make enough copies and help Vic distribute the flyers within the hotel before they hit the streets and started talking to people.

Once they were gone, I clicked the button Ava indicated and the video chat program came to life. I called Megan, the first of Laurie's friends. I was a bit surprised by how quickly she answered. I don't know why, but I had assumed the process might be more complicated.

"Hi, Megan," I introduced myself and told her about how we were helping to find Laurie. "Ava and Bill are with my husband, Luke. I thought it might be better if we spoke alone. I know sometimes it can be uncomfortable talking in front of someone's parents."

Megan had short blond hair and a pretty smile. "There isn't anything I'm hiding if that's what you mean."

"Not what I mean at all. I've done enough of these interviews to know that details sometimes get forgotten or things happened that night you might not want to share because of how Laurie might be perceived. It would be helpful if you could start at the beginning and tell me about that night."

Megan sat back in her chair and sniffled. "We had been having a great trip and that night we did what we had been doing. We went to dinner at a restaurant down the street and then we went out for drinks. We had been to the Sunshine Bar before and had a great time so we chose to go there again."

"Is it fair to say that you felt comfortable there?"

Megan nodded. "It had a chill vibe. The drinks weren't expensive and the people were friendly. It was a mix of locals and tourists. They always had good music, and yeah, we felt comfortable there."

"Was there anything unusual about that night?" There were several questions I needed to run through for background before getting up to the point where Laurie went missing. Sometimes witnesses tired of telling the story over and over again and I hoped this wouldn't be the case.

"Nothing unusual. We had met some locals a few nights before and they were there, so we hung out with them on the back deck until the band started playing. Then we went inside to the dance floor."

"Can you tell me about the locals you met?"

Megan shrugged. "It wasn't a big deal. There were a few guys who frequent the bar who were always there. I believe they were friends with one of the bartenders."

"Did you feel comfortable with them?"

"There wasn't a reason not to. Our friend Mackenzie liked one of the guys, but she never went off with him or anything like that. We aren't stupid." Megan had a defensive tone that made me curious.

"I wasn't suggesting you were being stupid," I assured her. "I'm well into my thirties now, but trust me, when I was in my twenties, I did my fair share of drinking. I probably did more stupid things than anyone on the planet. There's no judgment, trust me on that. I'm just trying to sort out where Laurie might be."

Megan relaxed in the chair. "We searched everywhere that night."

"I'm sure you did. It sounds like there was only a short window of time between when Laurie went missing and you started searching. It's remarkable to have such a short window of time to narrow things down."

Megan locked eyes with me through the screen. "We made a pact before we left for vacation that we had to look out for each other. It didn't matter if one of us met a guy or anything, we weren't going to do anything stupid. I feel terrible, like I did something wrong. Laurie said she was walking over to the bar to get us more drinks and the next thing I knew she was gone."

"Did she go to the bar alone?"

"No," Megan said. "She walked over with one of the guys from the group of locals we met. His name is Dylan. I don't remember his last name, but they walked to the bar together. We found Dylan outside when we realized Laurie wasn't in the bar. He said that Laurie had walked outside after they ordered drinks, but that he couldn't find her."

I made a note on a notepad next to me. "Did he help you look for Laurie?"

"Yeah, he and all of his friends did. No one could find her though."

"Did anyone go back to the hotel with you?"

"No. We hadn't told anyone where we were staying."

If Megan was telling the truth, and I thought she was credible, I was impressed that they had a safety plan and stuck to it. "I assume you didn't see Laurie again or find anyone who saw her?"

"There was no one. All we know is Dylan said she went outside for some fresh air and that he lost track of her."

"Had Laurie done that before?"

Megan considered the question for a moment. "She hadn't left like that before. There were a handful of times that she had asked one of us to go outside with her. Most of the bars we went to were warm inside even with air conditioning. St. Thomas is muggy and the places were packed. All of us were warm. Some nights were hotter than others."

I made another note. "It's reasonable then that Laurie walked out front to get some air."

"Not really," Megan said, surprising me. "Laurie had been going to the back deck and she always asked one of us to go with her. She had never gone out the front of the bar alone before."

"Did you believe Dylan?"

Megan seemed to consider it. "I believe that's what he believed. I don't have any reason not to believe him."

We talked for several more minutes about that evening. I could tell there was something that Megan wasn't telling me. I urged her to tell me anything even if it seemed minor.

After several minutes of convincing her, Megan relented. "There were some guys who hit on us and some of them didn't really take rejection well. No one stands out, but it happened to us more than once."

I assured her we'd be looking into everything. The last question I asked was about the man we saw at the hotel. I showed Megan one of the photos of the man's hands but she didn't recognize him. By the time we ended the call, I felt like I had a decent handle on the night Laurie disappeared.

CHAPTER 8

Cooper worried about Adele. She had assured him that she wanted to be involved with the case, she had pushed for it even. Now, Cooper wasn't so sure. A worry line creased her forehead and he worried that she'd be upset later that they hadn't had a proper honeymoon.

They were seated at a table in their hotel suite. Adele had pulled out her laptop and seemed to be concentrating on an article she had found. Cooper watched her across the table as she worked. He didn't want to ask if she was okay because he had already done that at least five times. She had grown annoyed with his concern.

Instead of asking, he simply inquired about what she was reading. "Find anything interesting?"

Adele didn't respond at first. Cooper asked again and she finally raised her head to acknowledge him. "Not really. I was searching about the risk of going missing on Caribbean islands. It seems to be low."

"Is that important?"

Adele closed the lid of her laptop and folded her hands on the table. "I was trying to see if having this many missing young women was normal or not for this area. Certainly, somewhere like Los Angeles or New York City, it would be normal to have this many missing women in a year. Those areas eclipse this number with runaways and missing girls. Five in a year seems high to us because of the circumstances, but I wanted some solid research on tourists running away or going missing. It is abnormal."

Cooper clasped his fingers through hers. "I hadn't even thought to search for something like that. Do you want me to call the families alone? You had that spa appointment for later today. You can still make it if you'd like."

Adele smiled over at him. "It was for a couple's massage. If we split the list and both call the families, we can make our appointment this afternoon. There's no reason we can't enjoy ourselves a little and still help out."

There was no way Cooper was going to argue with that. He readily agreed and then wrote down two names and their respective phone numbers and slid the main list over to Adele. "You take two and I'll take two. Remember to find out who the girls were with on their trips and any contact information for them."

Cooper got up from the table and went into the bedroom and closed the door so they'd not be talking over each other. Thankfully, the suite was big enough to accommodate them both.

For the next two hours, Cooper spoke to the families of Gia Tibbitts from Colorado and Ruby Wallis from Toronto. He hadn't had any trouble reaching their families and they were saddened to hear that another young woman had gone missing. Gia Tibbitts' mother had no idea that after her daughter disappeared, four young women had also gone missing under similar circumstances.

Sharon Tibbitts asked, "Did the police tell their families that the girls ran off with men? That's what they told me and there's no way that happened."

"That seems to be the common response. Have you watched the news lately? This most recent case – Laurie Presley – has been garnering some international news coverage. We are hoping that this will help find answers."

"I haven't watched the news. I haven't done much of anything in the last year since my daughter disappeared." She sighed heavily into the phone. "We didn't have the money to stay in St. Thomas and continue to search for Gia. We went down for a month and then her brother stayed for three months. He returned for another month, but there's no information. The police didn't help us even at the start and the media didn't care."

Cooper felt a lot of empathy for Sharon and her family. He asked about the details surrounding Gia's disappearance and what Sharon described sounded a lot like Laurie. Gia had gone on a trip with three girlfriends. After a night of drinking, Gia disappeared. The friends said that Gia got up from the table where they were sitting and went to the bathroom. A few minutes later, when she didn't return, her friends went in search, thinking she was sick. They couldn't find Gia in the bathroom or outside. She never returned to the hotel that night. It was like she was there one moment and gone the next, leaving no clue as to what had happened to her.

Cooper made notes as Sharon talked. When there was a pause in the conversation, he asked, "Earlier you said that there was no way Gia went off with a man. How can you be sure of that?"

Sharon let out a sarcastic wry laugh. "Well, besides the fact that none of her friends said that she had been talking to any men on the trip, my daughter was a lesbian. She had only told me a short time before the trip and I supported my daughter fully. When I told the detective that, he responded that maybe Gia changed her mind – like that was something one did."

In his head, Cooper cursed Det. Hanley's stupidity. "Do you know if anyone was bothering your daughter or her friends on the trip?"

"Not that any of them said. I've spoken to them a few times. Gia's brother spoke to them a few times and none of them indicated that.

She vanished from that bar."

Cooper knew based on what Luke had found that Laurie didn't disappear from the Sunshine Bar. He didn't know if Gia had ever made it back to the hotel and would likely never know. Hotels didn't keep their security footage that long. He thought he'd ask anyway. "What hotel was your daughter staying in on her trip?"

Sharon told him the name of the place, about a block away from their hotel. "The security cameras have all been checked if that's what you're thinking. Gia never used her keycard and never made it back to her room. Call her brother, Steven, if you'd like. I'm sure he has much more information than I have given. He was there for a few months."

Cooper thanked her for the information and wrote down Steven's name and number. Sharon told him that he should be home now. Cooper hung up with her, promising to call back with any news and then punched Steven's number into his cellphone. It rang a few times and then a man answered. Cooper confirmed it was him and then introduced himself.

Steven groaned when Cooper told him other women had gone missing like his sister. "I'd like to say I'm surprised, but I'm not. The detective was no help at all. I'm sure my mom told you he insisted Gia ran off with a man. Even if my sister was interested in men, there was no way she was running off with one. Gia was a smart kid. She excelled in school and was about to graduate. She already got into graduate school. She was going places. She didn't abandon her life and take off. Besides, she didn't even have her purse with her. Her money and identification were at the table where they were sitting."

Cooper noted that. "What did you find while you were here looking into her disappearance?"

"You mean other than the cops being worthless," he said sarcastically. He paused for Cooper to respond and when he didn't, Steven went on. "Nothing much, man. There were no sightings of Gia after that night. I didn't find one person who had seen her."

"What about anyone she or her friends were bothered by? Anyone harassing them or anyone they found creepy?"

"Yeah, there were two guys. Cousins, I believe. They are locals from over near Smith Bay. They are always at the Sunshine Bar and have been known to hit on tourists for sport. Pick up a girl and bring her home. They keep score with each other. It's like a game. I heard one of them hit on Gia several times and wouldn't take no for an answer."

"Do you know the guy's name?"

"Dylan Carter was the kid who was trying to chat up Gia. His cousin's name is Ollie Carter. They are in their early twenties, and from what I heard, both have been in trouble with the law a handful of times. Not that much ever came from it." Steven mumbled something Cooper couldn't understand. Then said, "Sorry, my daughter needs something. Anyway, I tried to speak to them, but Dylan's parents wouldn't allow it. There wasn't much else I could do. I tried to lay low and watch them for a while, but they knew who I was. After a while, I had to get back home to my job and my family. I wish I could have done more."

"Sounds like you did more than most people could have in your situation." Cooper checked his notes to see if he had any other questions. "Did you by chance ever get dogs to follow your sister's scent?"

"I did. There was a group of volunteers who came out to help me and one of them has a dog who does that kind of thing. Not a cadaver dog though. She said there was a difference. The dog followed my sister's scent out of the back of the bar onto the deck and then down to the road. Her scent disappeared after that. It didn't lead to much."

"No one saw your sister leave the bar that night?"

"Not that I know of," Steven said with regret in his voice. "You know most of the people there are tourists, so by the time I got to St. Thomas most of the people who might have seen my sister were gone. With no widespread media coverage, I bet most of those people don't even know she's missing."

Cooper already felt the weight of the case on him. "I appreciate everything you did to look for your sister and for talking to me. If there is anything else you can think of, let me know."

"Will do." Steven paused before saying goodbye as if he wanted to add something. After a moment of silence, he said, "I hope you find this latest young woman. It's a terrible thing for a family to live with. It broke my mother. It would be better if we knew she was dead and we could bury her. Then we'd know. The not knowing is the hardest."

Cooper wanted to say he understood but he didn't. He had been in college with Luke when his sister went missing, but he had never experienced it within his family and hoped he never did. "I hope you get the closure you need."

Steven hung up and Cooper placed his phone on the bed. He leaned back and stared up at the ceiling. He wasn't sure what else to do other than what he was doing, but still, it felt like he could be doing more.

Cooper gave himself a few minutes break. He went to the fridge in their room and grabbed a bottle of water. Adele seemed to be deep in conversation with someone. He watched her for a moment while he sipped his water. He couldn't make out the full conversation she was having from only her side, but she appeared to be finding out something of importance.

Her brow furrowed and her mouth set in a firm line as she listened intently and then she asked insightful questions. He loved to watch her work. After a few moments, she raised her eyes to him and gave him a sad smile.

Cooper closed the bedroom door behind him and called the family of Ruby Wallis in Toronto. He spoke at length to Ruby's father and then was given the phone numbers of the two women with her on the trip. He made those calls and found that they were more than willing to speak to him.

It was only toward the end of the conversation when Cooper asked if anyone had been bothering them that one of the young women admitted that Dylan Carter had approached them more than once at Sunshine Bar and wasn't good at taking no for an answer.

Cooper went back into the main room of the suite and found Adele leaning back in the chair rubbing her temples. "Headache?"

"Tension probably," she said, waving him over. "What did you find?"

Cooper ran through the calls he made and then pinpointed that Dylan Carter had been mentioned in both cases. "Is that a name you've heard?"

Adele shook her head. "I did find something interesting. Two girlfriends of Freya Reid from Edinburgh said that she was spending time with Lyle Blaylock. He paid for their dinners, took Freya and them out on his boat, and spent a few nights with Freya. He wasn't there the night she disappeared, but it's an interesting fact nonetheless."

Cooper said the name *Lyle Blaylock* a few times trying to figure out why it sounded so familiar to him. Finally, he gave up and asked Adele.

She looked at him in complete shock. "Tech billionaire Lyle Blaylock. He's all over the news and one of the richest men in America."

It hit Cooper like a truck. "He's in his forties. What was he doing chatting up a bunch of college students?"

"Seems like a question that needs an answer," Adele said, reaching her hand to him. "Let's go get those massages and think about this later."

CHAPTER 9

After wrapping the calls, I found Ava and Bill who were waiting in the main lobby of the hotel. I explained that I might have a lead on a name of a young man who was seen with Laurie before she went missing.

"Was Laurie involved with him?" Ava asked, her eyes narrowing.

"No, not at all. He and his friends were hanging out with Laurie and her friends. It all sounded innocent enough, but Laurie was at the bar with him when she disappeared. He said she had walked outside, but no one could find her."

Bill shook his head. "That's not how the girls described it to us. They said they never went anywhere without a partner."

"It was just from the dance floor to the bar, not far at all. In the crowd of people though, Laurie walked off and that's when they lost sight of her."

Bill folded his arms over his chest. "That seems like a stupid thing to lie about. Why not tell us that they were with a group of guys?"

"I don't know," I said, speaking honestly. "That's how these cases go sometimes. These young women also experienced trauma. I'm not sure if they remembered that detail or just didn't want to share information about the guys sooner. None of them indicated that they had any concern about these guys. Megan indicated that it was nice to have them around. They trusted them as much as you can trust a stranger you meet on vacation."

Bill seemed satisfied with that answer. "I wish we had known."

I told them I was going to find Luke and that I'd have an update soon enough. Before I could walk away though, the television in the lobby jumped to life with images of the hotel we were in. Anderson Cooper stood in the back of the hotel and provided an update on the victim pulled out of the water the night before.

"Today we were notified by the police department that the victim pulled from the water has been identified as Daphne Powers from London, England. She went missing just before Christmas while on vacation with her friends. The police do not believe there is any foul play and that Daphne stumbled into the water and drowned. We are still waiting for the medical examiner's official report. Daphne is one of five victims who have gone missing on the island over the last year." Anderson Cooper went on to detail each of the prior victims and hinted that there might be more at play here than a simple drowning.

"She didn't drown. She was killed like my daughter was killed."

Ava screamed and smacked her husband on the arm. "You don't know that Laurie is dead. Stop saying that!"

I touched Ava's shoulder. I didn't want her to have a full meltdown in the hotel lobby. "Let's go back into the conference room."

"No," Bill said, standing. "I can't sit around here anymore. I need to take a stack of flyers and get back out there and start talking to people." Then he turned to his wife. "I'm sorry for saying that Laurie is dead, but I don't have much hope left. At some point, we are going to have to face the reality of the situation."

Ava lowered her head and the tears began to fall. "Today isn't that day."

When Bill walked off, I sat down on the couch with Ava and tried to offer words of comfort. I didn't want to encourage her idea that her daughter was still alive because I believed she was probably already dead.

"Do you think Daphne's death is connected to my daughter?"

"I don't know," I said honestly. "We don't even know the cause of death yet. It could be a simple drowning as the cops said. We won't know anything until the medical examiner's report is released."

I wasn't being truthful with her. While I didn't know any more than what had been reported on the news, there were gaps in the story that made the cop's version of events unlikely. There were too many holes in the story for a young woman who had been missing for three months. Where had she been? Was she being held against her will and recently murdered? Had she gotten away from someone who kidnapped her only to drown in the sea? Had she been killed months ago and the killer preserved her body and then dumped her in the water? None of these questions could I pose to Ava, so I kept my thoughts to myself.

"You don't know?" she asked again, drawing my attention.

"I don't know anything more than what we heard on the news. I've been focused on Laurie. My friends have been calling the other families."

Ava turned to me glassy-eyed. "I'm going to go to my room and try to rest. My brain is starting to feel fuzzy. I can't make sense of anything."

"That's a good idea. You won't be able to do much while sleep-deprived. Get some rest."

Ava stood from the couch and had to steady herself once she was upright. I asked if she wanted me to walk with her up to her room, but she declined. I sat there for a long moment, watching the news, but they weren't providing any other kind of updates.

As I stood to leave, I nearly walked right into Cooper and Adele. "Where are you two headed?"

"Couple's massage," Adele said with a smile.

"Good," I said and meant it. I wanted them to still have some enjoyment from the trip. "You didn't happen to hear the name Dylan in any of your interviews?"

"Dylan Carter?" Cooper asked, eyebrows raised.

"I don't have a last name. Who is that?"

"Gia Tibbitts' brother, Steven, spent some time on the island searching for his sister. During his investigation, he heard about a guy named Dylan Carter. He and his cousin, Ollie, target young female tourists and hook up with them. His name was brought up in two different cases. If it's the same person, this will make a third. It's a lead we need to run down."

"I'll be looking into it this afternoon. Do you know where on the island he's from?"

"The Smith Bay area."

I let them get on their way and headed toward the elevator to go up to my room, but changed my mind and turned around to get some lunch. My stomach growled, and I couldn't think hungry.

I went to the bar instead of getting a table and looked over the lunch menu. I ordered a chicken sandwich and fries. While I was sitting there, the patio filled up with media types.

I walked over to one of the tables with a woman reporter who looked about my age. I introduced myself and noted that I was helping to find Laurie Presley but didn't elaborate on my role. I told her that I was a former crime beat reporter. "Given the number of tourists who probably left the island and might not even know these young women are missing, do you think it's possible to put out their photos and ask if anyone has information, they call into a hotline that we'll set up?"

She readily agreed as did a reporter at another table who had overheard. I told them I'd get back to them when I had the details firmed up. I'd need to check with Luke and get a dedicated phone line, bank of phones, and some volunteers to cover the line. A lot to be done but worth the effort.

I made my way back to the bar and picked up my food. As the guy behind the bar handed me the bag, he said, "I heard you and your friends are investigators and helping to find Laurie Presley. You know she and her friends were down here a lot for lunch. I spoke to them several times."

It occurred to me as he said that, we hadn't made a plan for interviewing any hotel staff. "Did anything seem strange to you?"

He leaned against the back of the bar and shrugged. "Nothing really. Young women that age, you know. They were constantly giggling about some guy or another. They had talked about meeting a group of guys at a bar. That isn't unusual. They come down here to the island to let loose. The only thing that piqued my interest was one of them mentioned Ollie and another mentioned Dylan. The Ollie and Dylan I know are cousins and troublemakers. I warned the girls about spending time with them. They pick up girls for sport. Everyone around here knows that. I told them to steer clear of them."

I pushed my food to the side and sat down at the bar. "The name Dylan came up in an interview I did. He might have been the last person in the bar to see Laurie. He said she went out the front door to get some fresh air. Her friends told me she never did that before and it was unusual."

The bartender shook his head in disgust. "I'm telling you that they are no good. You're not going to be able to touch them. Dylan's father isn't going to let you anywhere near them."

"Do you think Dylan is capable of hurting a girl?"

The bartender folded his arms across his chest and looked me up and down. He had something on his mind and I assumed he was trying to figure out if he trusted me or not. I assured him, "Listen, whatever you tell me can stay between us. You might save me some time and time is not something we have a lot of right now."

He pushed himself forward and then leaned on the bar, getting closer to me. "You didn't hear this from me, but Dylan was accused of sexually assaulting a local girl last year. Nothing came of it because the cops said it was a he-said, she-said kind of thing. It didn't surprise me though."

"How do you know him?"

"My younger brother went to school with him. I've seen him around, but there are very few local bars and hotels that haven't seen or heard of Dylan Carter. Ollie is the quieter of the two. Dylan is full of himself and cocky. Don't underestimate either of them."

I formulated a plan. "Do you think if I go out to a bar one night and happen to meet up with them, I could chat them up and ask some questions?"

"If you do it casually enough and they don't know who you are." He seemed to consider for a moment. "There's already talk that some hotshot investigators are here looking into the disappearance. You're better off doing it sooner than later – like tonight."

I thanked him for the information, left a generous tip, and headed to my room. By the time I sat down to eat, my chicken and fries were cold but good enough to fill me. I grabbed my laptop from the desk and sat down on the couch and propped my feet on the ottoman.

Steadying my laptop on my lap, I started my search on Dylan Carter. I didn't have access to the databases that Luke had for criminal records. What I wanted to see was his social media. Not only did people put everything out for public consumption, they often did so without any regard to spying eyes watching them. I never quite understood people who posted photos of their kids along with the name of their school and the hometown where they lived. Equally curious to me were the people who posted identifying information about their address including pictures of the front of their homes and then told the world they were going on vacation. It all seemed like a disaster waiting to happen.

Luke and Cooper had no social media presence at all. I had one that was locked down tighter than my house, and even then, I rarely posted much beyond favorite recipes to save for later.

As suspected, Dylan Carter overshared. He had Facebook and Instagram and his socials told me his whole life story including where he shopped, worked, ate, who his friends were, and where he socialized. It also gave me a hint of his frame of mind. He was twenty-four, a Leo, and thought he was God's gift to women. He got high frequently and drank like it was the night before Prohibition. I scrolled back a few days and noted all the photos of him and his friends at bars. He had dark hair, looked like he had a perpetual tan, and a lazy smile. His eyes captured me the most. There was something cold and uncaring behind them.

I scrolled back a few days and then a few days more. Right there for all to see was a photo of him with his arm around Laurie Presley. The photo caption read – *I win!* The post was time and date stamped about two hours before she disappeared.

CHAPTER 10

After getting the volunteers new flyers and making a plan of action, Luke hadn't had much luck meeting with the medical examiner or tracking down Grady Campbell. He returned to the hotel frustrated and sweating. He wiped his brow on the back of his wrist and headed for the elevators. Cooper and Riley had texted him about their developments and he was glad that some progress had been made.

Luke jammed his finger against the elevator button again. He had no idea what was taking so long but his patience had grown thin. Just as he was debating taking the stairs up to his floor, the doors slid open and there stood Grady.

"Det. Morgan," Grady said not hiding his shock at seeing him standing there. He stepped off the elevator and Luke let the doors slide closed. "I heard a rumor that you decided to get involved in the investigation. Is it true?"

"It is and I was looking for you today."

"For me?" he asked, pointing to his chest. "I was at the police station for a while and then chasing down some leads. I only got back about thirty minutes ago. I'm about to grab something to eat. Want to join me?"

Luke followed him through the lobby to the back door. He lingered, not wanting to go back out into the humidity. It was like wading through pea soup. "Can we eat inside? I don't think I can take another minute of the heat. We are supposed to get a thunderstorm, too." As if the heavens wanted to confirm the decision, a roar of thunder echoed in the distance.

"I guess that's our answer." Grady turned back and followed Luke to a table away from other people. He sat down and stared at Luke across the table. "I have to admit with all the other reporters here, I'm wondering why you want to speak with me. I'm a local reporter. I'm sure Anderson Cooper or one of them would be more your speed."

Luke appreciated his humbleness. "I'm not looking to do an on-air interview. When you approached me the other night, you said you had done research. I was impressed that you had connected all of the cases. I apologize for blowing you off. It was the night before my friend got married and the last thing he wanted to do was talk about an investigation."

Grady raised his hands. "Say no more. I understand. I'm happy to help you in any way I can."

The server came over and took their order. Once their drinks were dropped off, Luke took a sip of his soda and relaxed back in the chair. It was the first time all day he'd decompressed. "I want to know everything you know starting from the first case – Gia Tibbitts."

"What about Amani Hanley?"

Luke shook his head. Not that he wanted to rule that out. She didn't fit the pattern neat enough to start with her. "We can go back to Amani. Let's start with Gia."

Grady pulled his iPad from his bag and read over his notes. The information Grady provided about Gia matched with what Cooper had texted him earlier in the day. The only thing missing from Grady's notes had been Gia's interaction with Dylan Carter.

Luke listened as he talked but then his mind started to wander. The server came over and dropped off their food, which he didn't touch.

After a moment, Grady said Luke's name, drawing his attention. He raised his eyes to Grady. "Sorry, processing what you said. Could you repeat that last bit?"

Grady dug into his meal and then in between bites repeated himself. "I asked if you saw the news? The body you found yesterday is Daphne Powers. She's the third missing woman on the list. She went missing two days before Christmas."

"I hadn't heard," Luke said, grabbing his fork and digging into his steak salad. "That means she was missing for three months before her body was found."

Grady scrolled to a section of notes on his iPad. "I have a bit of information about her if you'd like to hear it."

Luke told him to continue.

"There's a local guy named Andy Barber who had been seen with Daphne while she was on vacation here. Has his name come up before?"

"That's not a name on my radar," Luke said, trying to keep everything straight. He'd need a board in his room to start collecting all the data they had. Right now, it was a jumble of names he was starting to confuse.

"Andy's name came up a few times when I looked into Daphne's case. They were involved when she was here. He's local but not originally from here. He's Canadian and runs a snorkeling and scuba diving business. I guess his parents came to St. Thomas when he was in his teens and they stayed. He grew up on the island for the most part."

"Do you consider him a suspect?" Luke asked and watched as Grady's forehead creased. "It's okay if you say yes. It doesn't mean it's true. This is a conversation between us. You're a journalist. You must have some gut feeling on things."

Grady's shoulders relaxed and the line in his forehead disappeared. "I'd consider his behavior suspicious. Some of Daphne's friends wondered if the two had met before she arrived, like on a dating app or something, because they met the first night and rarely left each other during the trip. It annoyed most of her friends."

Luke had never been on a dating app or website in his life. He knew that's how people met these days, but the idea of it made his stomach turn. "Did her friends say that's what they thought or is that your speculation?"

"One of her friends said it but wouldn't go on the record. She didn't think Daphne ran off with him because he was seen giving snorkeling tours after she disappeared. Still, though, they questioned the connection. He was with them in the bar the night she disappeared."

"That was from the Sunshine Bar?"

"All of the girls disappeared from there except Laurie."

"What do you know about Andy?"

"I didn't find much. As I said, he moved here when he was in his teens. His parents are both professionals. He's an only child and has never been in legal trouble as far as I can find. His business is booming and he's got great reviews. There's nothing that jumps out at me that he might be responsible, except that he was the last one seen with her and the relationship seemed to move fast. Daphne's friend also said that it was hot and cold. Over the few days leading up to her disappearance, they had argued and Andy got pretty heated. Her friend said that he yelled at Daphne over something stupid at the bar and then punched a wall on the way out. It was a lot for a new relationship – if it was new at all and not something ongoing that she had hidden from her friends."

Luke considered that for a moment. "Do you know whose idea it was to come to St. Thomas?"

Grady broke into a wide grin. "I do. We think alike. It was Daphne's idea to visit St. Thomas. Her friends wanted to go to Ibiza. Daphne was set on coming here and wouldn't consider any place else. She told her friends she was visiting with or without them. I assume it was because she was already having some kind of long-distance relationship with Andy."

That's what Luke suspected. "You never confirmed a preexisting relationship?"

"No. Her friends said she had never been to St. Thomas before, but I have no idea if he visited her in London. The reality is they could have met on a dating app but never met in person before."

"Would she risk that?"

"People do it all the time."

Luke couldn't wrap his mind around that. "What about her parents. Did they tell you anything?"

Grady shook his head. "When I called her parents, they wouldn't speak to a reporter. I asked if I could see her phone or her computer, but they wouldn't even entertain the idea. I offered to go to London. Her father is some bigshot investment banker and he acted like the whole thing had caused a family scandal. Once I found out what he did for a living, I was surprised he hadn't hired an investigator or made more of a push with the media. I understand wanting to protect your brand, but at the expense of your kid? No way."

Luke couldn't imagine it either. It's not something he'd ever do, but he had seen that behavior in other family members of missing people. There was often shame that the person who went missing had brought it on themselves. "Is there anything else you think is important?"

Grady scrolled through his notes but didn't have much else to offer. "I heard earlier today that Riley suggested setting up a tip line so that if people who were here on vacation saw anything, they can report in. That's something I'm interested in and would fully support. I think that's what's been missing in this case. With almost no media attention or anyone connecting these cases, people who were here on vacation might have seen something and probably have no idea these young women are missing. There could be significant information we might uncover."

Riley had texted Luke the question earlier. The only thing pending was logistics. He had already left a message for Vic. Luke said, "I've got people working on that and you'll be the first to know."

Grady thanked him. "Is there anything else you need?"

Luke chewed on the inside of his cheek uncertain if he should share a potential lead with a reporter. He stared over at Grady and assessed him and finally deemed him trustworthy. "We have a tip but you have to promise me you won't go public with it. We need to interview him casually and we won't be able to do that if word gets out. He might even be a flight risk."

"I swear I won't print a word."

"Is the name Dylan Carter familiar to you? It's come up in a few of the cases. He's local to the island."

Grady nodded. "I've heard his name. I didn't mention him because I didn't have any reason to suspect him. I heard he's a local kid who hangs out at the bars where the girls went. They met but I never heard any information to suspect he might have done something to any of them."

"Let me be clear. We have no information right now that makes him a suspect, so that's not something we are saying. He's not even a person of interest. He was the last person seen with Laurie before she left the bar that night and the one who said she went outside. That's new information as of today. He was also mentioned in another case. Given he's connected even loosely to more than one of the missing women, we must interview him. My understanding is that his father shut down an interview before and wouldn't allow his son to be interviewed. That's not the behavior of an innocent person."

Grady grimaced. "That doesn't mean guilt either."

"Of course not," Luke said not wanting to overplay his hand. "It does mean we need to talk to him. It's good nothing jumped out to you that could indicate his guilt. I'm happy to hear that, but this information needs to remain with us right now."

"I promise I won't breathe a word of it."

Luke had one more thing for Grady. He pulled out his phone and showed him a photo of the flyer that had been created. "Since you know Laurie was last seen at the hotel, I'm sure you saw this already. That image shows Laurie at the side door trying to get in with her keycard. She's drunk and can't manage it. Then this man shows up, grabs her by the arm, and leads her away. Again, we can't say he's a suspect, but it does make me wonder. Do those hands or that ring seem familiar to you?"

Grady studied the photo and then raised his eyes to Luke. "I have never seen a ring like that before. I don't know who he is."

Luke pointed to the photo. "This is the story we need to run. Along with the tip line I want to put this out to the public and see if anyone knows who that is. We have to be careful how we frame it so he or someone who knows him might come forward."

"Understood." Grady looked like he wanted to ask Luke a question but held back.

Luke smiled at him. "Are you wondering if I'm going to give you an exclusive?"

"I didn't want to seem presumptuous."

"You can have it. You'll probably need to run it online first if any of the other reporters haven't already seen the new flyers that we've been passing out today. For all I know, that man's hand and ring already made the news without context to it."

"I haven't seen it." Grady picked up his phone and searched news articles. "No, I'm not seeing it. When can I run with it?"

"Let me get back to you this evening. The sooner we can get it out there the better. I need to make sure the phone line is operational first."

Grady said he understood. "Anything else I can help you with?"

"Not right now, but I'll connect with you again as soon as I know more."

They finished lunch getting to know one another a little outside of the case. Luke, who normally didn't like reporters, left lunch feeling he had made another ally in the investigation.

CHAPTER 11

I was deep into background research on Dylan and Ollie Carter when Luke returned. He came over to the desk and wrapped his arms around me from behind, planting a wet kiss on my cheek. "I've missed you today."

I turned in my chair. "I've missed you, too. I think we got a bit accomplished."

Before Luke could say anything else, there was a knock on the door. He went to answer it and then profusely thanked whoever it was. "I don't know what I'd do without you," he said and then invited the person in.

I checked my reflection in the mirror before walking out to the main room. I was as good as I was getting. Luke had his hand on a large dry erase board on wheels and a basket full of markers and an eraser in his other hand. He looked like a kid on Christmas morning.

Vic handed Luke a stack of papers. "These are photos of all the missing women that I gathered from missing flyers and websites. We have the tip line set up and a bank of phones being brought into the conference room the Presley family has been using. Does that work?"

"It does." Luke thanked him and then set the basket of markers on the floor. He grabbed his wallet, pulled out a stack of cash that he didn't even count, and tried to give it to Vic. "I can't thank you enough for all of this. We wouldn't be able to do any of this without your help."

Vic refused the money. "I'm here to help. I was born and raised in St. Thomas and our economy relies on tourism. The people who visit need to be safe. You have the full support of the hotel. Whatever you need, come get me. If I'm not here, you tell them Vic sent you." With that, he shook Luke's hand and left.

Luke put the money back in his wallet. "I'm always glad for the reminder that there are still good people left in this world." He rolled the dry erase board back to the area of our suite that had the desk and small round table. He positioned it up against the wall and then dropped the basket with markers and other items onto the table. He dug around in it until he pulled out some tape. He then taped each of the girls' photos on the board in order of disappearance. Then he jotted down the dates of their disappearance and where each girl was originally from under it. He made another arrow and noted where each girl was last seen – almost all the Sunshine Bar except for Laurie Presley. He stood back and assessed.

He turned to me. "Did you see the news that the body that washed up was Daphne Powers? If I had seen a photo of her before that, I would have known that right away."

I sat down in the chair at the table. "She didn't drown, Luke. Det. Hanley gave another press conference to a handful of reporters and said she drowned and that it was an accidental death. He said that before the release of the medical examiner's report. Where was she for three months because we both know she didn't go into that water three months ago."

Luke ran a hand over his head and then took a seat in the chair across the table from me. "I've been asking myself the same thing since Grady Campbell told me. I met with him and had lunch. That's about the only thing I accomplished today. I promised him an exclusive story after we got the tip line set up. I told him I'd cover the tip line and updates in the Laurie Presley case."

"I bet he loved that." I had worked as a journalist long enough to know that being first was everything in the newsroom. For some newsrooms, being first sometimes was more important than being right. The *San Francisco Chronicle* did not have that reputation.

Luke hitched his chin toward my laptop. "What did you find out today?"

I gave him the rundown on Laurie Presley. "I don't think her friends intentionally lied to her parents. I think they did what most young women do and left out the part about flirting with guys. None of them seemed to have any concern about Dylan and Ollie. I don't like that Dylan's name came up connected to other missing women. The bartender downstairs at the restaurant told me that he had spoken to Laurie and her friends and cautioned them about Dylan."

"Why would he do that?"

"Dylan picked up girls for sport." I grimaced, hating to think of young women coming on vacation and having to deal with that. "I understand men in their twenties are out there sowing oats or whatever you guys do, but I hate to think of the girls being taken advantage of."

Luke leveled a look at me. "Not all of us are like that."

I smiled at him. "I didn't say you were. I wouldn't be married to you if you were. There are men like that though and it's terrible if that's the experience they had while on vacation. I found most of Dylan's exploits on social media for the world to see. There's a photo of him and Laurie the night she went missing. We knew they were together so it doesn't mean anything right now." I pointed to the board. "We need to note his name under the women he was known to be involved with."

Luke stood and went to the board. I read him the names – Gia Tibbitts, Ruby Wallis, and Laurie Presley. "The Americans and the

Canadian," he said, looking over his shoulder at me.

"I guess if you want to put it that way. I'm more inclined to look at the timing of their visits rather than the location where they are from." I checked my notes. "Spring and summer break. Daphne and Freya went missing during the winter. Jot that down too for reference."

Luke stared at the photos for several moments, hung the photo with the man's ring, and then sat back down. "I'm wondering if three of the women were more his type and the others not, but they all look about the same to me. All are about the same age, attractive and blond or light brown hair."

I had already considered that and agreed with him. "This killer has a type."

"You think they are all dead?" Luke asked, a hint of sadness in his voice.

It was the first time we both acknowledged their probable fate. "They have been missing a long time, Luke. Daphne's body was already found. They are dead unless he is holding them someplace."

"It's possible." He turned back to the board. "I was also thinking about human trafficking. Do we know much about that on the island? I've got a good handle on it happening inside the United States and in Europe but haven't seen much hard data on the Caribbean."

I went to my laptop and brought it to the table. I pulled up a file I had been working on earlier. "In 2020, St. Thomas University School of Law in Miami, Florida held a conference on human trafficking. There are some twenty-five million people trapped in forced labor in industries including agriculture, construction, domestic work, and manufacturing around the world. That's directly from their website. The university has an entire human trafficking academy. They covered the Caribbean at the conference and even held specific workshops on the region, and it's been a problem."

"St. Thomas University in Miami? That isn't here?"

"No. It's the University of the Virgin Islands here. A bit confusing but the data is still sound." I considered the question further but wasn't sure it was what we were looking at. "If the young women were trafficking victims, Daphne's body wouldn't have washed up on the beach here. She'd be long gone."

"Unless she fought her kidnapper and died in the process."

"Three months after being taken? They would have moved her right away."

"True," he said, frustrated. "I guess we can put a pin in it for now and keep it as a consideration for later." Luke took a breath and had a far-off look that made me think he was lost in thought.

"Are you okay?"

It took him a moment to answer. "Yeah," he said finally. "It's a lot to take on while we are supposed to be on vacation, particularly when I don't have resources here."

"Have you called Captain Meadows or Det. Tyler?" Luke had worked with Captain Meadows and Det. Bill Tyler, his partner, for years. I was sure being thrown into an investigation without their help was more than a little daunting for him.

"I haven't. Captain Meadows gave me strict instructions to take a break. Tyler warned me not to let you get involved in any criminal cases. I don't want to call and tell them I went charging into this."

"Aahh, you're scared of getting into trouble." I laughed and reached for his hand. "Everything will get sorted. I want to go to Sunshine Bar tonight and try to interview Dylan. By all accounts, his father won't let anyone speak to him."

Luke agreed it was worth a try. He changed the subject to Daphne Powers. Grady had given him information during their lunch meeting. Over the next twenty minutes, Luke filled me in on Daphne's relationship with Andy Barber. He added in Grady's commentary as well as his own about the case. "Bottom line. You're right that it was a homicide. I knew that the moment I saw her in the water. I didn't know at the time she had been missing for three months. That puts a new spin on it entirely. We are going to need to hunt down Andy Barber and figure out how he knew her and when."

I agreed with him and started explaining my earlier interaction with Ava and Bill when I was interrupted by another knock on the door. "Expecting someone else?"

Luke shook his head as he stood to answer the door. He came back in with Cooper and Adele. Both looked well-rested and had smiles on their faces.

"You look like you enjoyed the massage." I got up and hugged Adele.

"It was amazing. You and Luke need to schedule yourselves one before we go home." She released me from the hug and went to the board. "This is a good setup. I was going to ask if we could get something like this."

Luke walked over to the board. "I need everything visual. There are five victims and info we need to keep track of and it's too much to remember."

Adele pointed to the board under Freya Reid's name. "I can fill in some missing information about this case. You better sit down there. It's going to knock your socks off." She looked down at my flip-flops and giggled. "Okay maybe not your socks."

It was clear she was excited about what she had uncovered.

"Riley, I wanted to tell you when I saw you in the hallway earlier. I could barely keep it in."

Luke and I watched her on the edge of our seats. "Well, tell us. You're keeping us in suspense."

"I know," she said, her smile beaming. "It's that big! Freya Reid had captured the attention of Lyle Blaylock while on vacation. She was seen with him right up until the time she disappeared. He has a house on the island and splits his time between here and his home in

Mountain View, California."

"You've got to be kidding me?" I said not containing my shock. I looked over at Luke but he seemed to have no clue. "Lyle Blaylock is not only a tech mogul but he's known to be a playboy. He has a string of girlfriends and is always in the newspapers for his flamboyant lifestyle. How could you not have heard of him?"

Luke shrugged. "You know I don't keep up with stuff like that."

"He is a billionaire, Luke," Cooper said, stressing the point. "We have no idea how he came to meet her."

I asked, "You don't think he had something to do with her disappearance, do you?"

Adele shrugged. "We don't know. It's suspicious to me though."

I turned to Cooper to see what he thought. He confirmed he felt the same way as Adele.

"I guess we can add him to our unofficial suspect list," I said, not even believing I was saying such a thing. It was hard to believe that Lyle Blaylock would risk everything he had accomplished.

Luke seemed to have a hard time believing it too. "Why would he kill a young woman when he's wanted by so many? He'd have to be crazy to risk his whole career and reputation."

Cooper shared a look with me and then turned to Luke. "Crazier things have happened. Look at how many powerful men have been taken down over sexual harassment and sexual assault. It doesn't mean he's immune."

Luke lost that round and gestured toward the board. "Put him up there. He's one more person to interview if we can get anywhere near him."

I told Cooper and Adele the plan for the night and they were in.

CHAPTER 12

I walked into Sunshine Bar later that night on a mission. I had no solid information that Dylan Carter would show up at the bar that night. Call it a gut feeling. I knew in my bones that he'd be there, and I was as ready as I was ever going to get. Adele came with me while Luke and Cooper remained at the hotel. They were going to interview as many hotel staff as they could. We decided that I was the best person to approach Dylan.

Cooper could bro it out with the best of them, but he had years on Dylan and would most likely come across as a bit desperate to connect. At least, that's what he told us even though Adele and I disagreed with him. If we failed tonight, we had Cooper as a backup for another night.

Luke was becoming known on the island. He had given Grady an exclusive, and after his story was published, Luke held an impromptu press conference with the others. He expected fall-out from Det. Hanley. He didn't care though. He knew he was doing what had to be done. Before the press conference, he had called Captain Meadows who gave him not only permission but encouragement to keep working on the case.

I stayed away from the spotlight and so did Adele. The more we could work out of the spotlight the better. Adele and I were three months apart in age. I'd be thirty-eight in two months and she'd follow later in the summer. Neither of us quite looked our age, which we were hoping would give us an advantage.

I had on a strapless shirt and mid-thigh shorts with a pair of wedge heels that while cute would negate my ability to chase after someone. Adele was dressed similarly.

"Let's go to the patio. That's where the crowd is right now," Adele said. "There's a nice breeze out back we might as well enjoy while we are eating dinner."

Luke and Cooper were opting for work and a late dinner at the hotel. I had asked if they wanted us to bring anything back and they assured us they were fine. I followed Adele to the patio, which was much bigger than I had anticipated. It had probably fifty tables and gave a nice view of the beach and evening surf. It was plausible that someone could stumble out of the bar, onto the beach, and into the water – if they had the wherewithal to climb over large boulders that separated the bar's property and the beach. It was possible, but still not probable, that's what happened to the women.

"This place has a young vibe," Adele said as she sat down at the two-seater table. She sat facing the water and allowed me to view the whole patio and inside the bar from my side. "If I were in my twenties and I was looking to chat up some young men, this is where I'd come."

The way she said it made her sound sixty rather than nearing forty. I scanned the crowd of young college-aged men and women and didn't see Dylan or Ollie. "It has that pick-up vibe like a college bar or a bar you'd go to on spring break."

A few minutes after sitting, a young woman in a tight white tee-shirt and shorts arrived at our table. "What can I get you, girls?"

Girls. That was a good start. We'd be done had she called us ma'am. I ordered a whiskey sour and Adele decided a fruity concoction on the menu sounded good. We both ordered water with it. When the server gave us a funny look, I fanned myself. "I'm not used to it being so hot and we haven't eaten anything yet. Don't want to get drunk too fast." I giggled for good measure.

She winked at us. "Good thinking. Besides, give it a min and some of these guys should start buying you drinks. That's how it works around here. They will give you a few minutes to get acclimated before they pounce."

I smiled up at her and went to toy with my wedding ring but found the finger bare. Luke had held his hand out to take the ring before I left. "No one is hitting on old married women," he had teased. I was rarely without mine and it didn't feel right without it on my hand.

We surveyed the scene and chatted until our server dropped off our drinks, took our dinner order, and left again. The air hung heavy around us and was filled with the scent of alcohol, cheap heavy-handed cologne, and the sea.

We remained focused on finding Dylan and Ollie but neither had made an appearance yet. By the time we finished dinner and another drink, we were so deep into conversation that we didn't see the guy approach.

"I'm Teddy," he said by way of introduction, startling us both. He brushed strands of sandy brown hair off his forehead and acted like his mere presence at our table should cause us to swoon or whatever it is young women did these days.

We each introduced ourselves and Adele asked where he was from. He wanted us to guess and we couldn't be bothered, which only made him more intrigued about us so he grabbed a nearby chair and sat down with us uninvited. "What do you do?" he asked.

We had worked out a plan ahead of time. Private investigator and criminal defense attorney weren't going to work for us tonight. Adele offered him a smile. "I'm finishing law school."

"Oh, so you're smart then," he teased and then looked at me. "What about you?"

"Working towards a Ph.D. in forensic psychology."

He squinted. "What's that?"

"Criminology."

He sat up a little straighter. "Like an FBI profiler?"

"There are lots of jobs I could do but sort of."

"What do you think? Am I a serial killer?" He held his hands wide and turned his head showing me a profile view of his face. It was a bizarre question, but I didn't get the vibe that he meant any harm.

I shook my head, tossing my hair back from my shoulder in a flirty move. "It's not quite that easy to figure out. You don't strike me as someone who'd kill anyone though."

He caressed my shoulder. "Only to save a woman like you."

It was a cheesy line and I had to hold back a laugh. "That's good to know. We might need you. We heard a few women are missing."

"Yeah, I heard that too. I've only been here a few days."

We talked for a few more minutes and Teddy asked if he could buy us a drink. We declined but told him it was nice to meet him. He got the hint we were blowing him off and he went from nice guy to annoyed. He stood and grabbed himself lewdly. "You really want to turn me down? I've got a Ph.D. of my own."

I groaned. "That's a terrible line. Tell me that doesn't work with girls."

"Sometimes," he said and then sauntered off.

"Ph.D.?" Adele asked with a quizzical expression on her face.

"Pretty huge..." I pointed to my lap and mouthed the last word.

She slapped her hand down on the table, laughing at the ridiculousness of it. "That's terrible. I've never heard that before."

"Liv is on dating apps." My single sister had thrown herself back into the dating pool. "Some of the stories make me cringe."

"No. No. No." Adele wasn't having any of it. "I cannot tell you how grateful I am for Cooper even if he leaves a trail of clothes from the bedroom to the bathroom sometimes and he snores. If we ever broke up, I'm choosing to be single forever."

"I feel exactly the same way." We toasted to single seniors and then scanned the place again. It had grown more crowded now. "Let's head inside and see if we can find Dylan."

It didn't take us long once inside to spot him. He looked exactly like the photos I had found on social media. His muscles bulged under his shirt. He'd be physically able to restrain a girl on his own. With Ollie, I wasn't so sure. He was shorter, hung back a little more from the crowd, and his eyes darted around like he wasn't so sure of himself.

I nudged Adele and nodded my head toward them. She got a look at them and made the same assessment I had. "We can rule out Ollie doing it on his own."

"That's what I think. We shouldn't underestimate him though."

We hung back by the bar and watched them laugh and joke with their friends. I stared at the back of Dylan's head almost willing him to turn. When he finally did, I caught his eye and smiled. I had no idea if I was his type. I didn't look anything like the victims, but I assumed that if I flirted enough, he might think I was an easy mark. After a few more times making eye contact and smiling, he said something to Ollie and then walked our way.

"You've got a great smile," he said as a way of introduction. He told me his name and that he was local. He asked a few questions of us and we chatted for several minutes before he asked what I did. When I told him what I was going to school for, he seemed impressed. "I've been studying criminal justice. What made you get into that?"

"It's always been an interest. I like knowing why people do what they do."

"Right on." He smiled and leaned against the bar. "You must be interested in all the missing girls then."

"Missing girls?" I asked, letting my voice raise an octave. I looked to Adele and she shrugged and sipped her drink.

"Yeah, it's been crazy," he said, his face growing animated. "Five girls over a year have gone missing. One of the girls' bodies washed up down the beach the other day."

Adele and I shared a look. He connected all five when even the cops and the media hadn't done that until recently. "I hadn't heard much on the news about that. I saw all the reporters around but didn't know why. How'd you hear about it?"

He pointed down to the floor. "They all went missing from this bar. My professor thinks there's a serial killer on the island."

"So scary," I said, my mouth hanging open a little. I breathed heavily in fear.

"What do you think?" Adele asked, drawing his attention to her. "Do you think there's a serial killer?"

"It would be easy enough."

I raised an eyebrow in a question. "How so?"

"We are surrounded by water and ocean life. It's the easiest place to get rid of a body."

Adele set her drink on the bar and waved off the bartender who offered to refill it. She turned to Dylan. "The girl whose body was found didn't stay hidden. How long ago did she disappear?"

Dylan stiffened his smile. "Umm, a few months ago, I think." He stalled and looked at us, clearly growing uncomfortable. "I guess I don't know as much as I thought I did. You see in movies that when a killer dumps the body in water, it washes away the evidence. That's what I was thinking of."

I changed the subject to lighten the mood and keep him talking. We covered his life on the island, his friends, and even his cousin, Ollie. Dylan explained that Ollie was two years younger and they were more like brothers.

"Ollie seems shyer than you," I said toward the end of the conversation.

Dylan looked back at him and then back at us. "Don't let him fool you. He comes out of his shell at the right time. How about we go back to your hotel and you can get to know us a little better?" He reached out and tugged a strand of my hair.

I yawned and then excused myself. "I'd like that, Dylan. Not tonight though. Do you think you'll be around tomorrow night?"

"I might be. You'll have to take your chances." He pulled me close for a hug. "Do you want to take your chances? Women don't usually say no to me."

Given I wanted to build rapport and see him again, I didn't knee him in the groin. I pulled back and gave him my best smile. "I'm sure they don't. I've had a long day. I promise I'm worth the wait." I let my hand linger down his chest while I pulled away from the hug. Adele and I walked toward the door and I gave him a wink over my shoulder before I left, pleased with how the night had gone.

CHAPTER 13

Luke and Cooper finished dinner in the hotel restaurant and were figuring out a plan of action for the rest of the night when their discussion was interrupted by a man shouting Luke's name. Expecting another reporter, his face fell when he saw Det. Hanley standing there with his hands on his hips, flanked by two uniformed cops on each side.

He strutted over to the table and glared down at Luke. "I could arrest you right now for obstruction of justice."

Luke angled his head to look up at the detective. "How do you figure that?"

Det. Hanley snorted. "Some detective you are if you don't know what that means."

Luke stood to his full height, looking down at him. "I know what it means. I asked how is the charge credible and possible. I haven't obstructed justice."

"You are interfering in my investigation." Det. Hanley puffed out his chest like he had scored a point.

"You're not doing anything to help the Presley family and they turned to private investigators, which they have every right to do. I just happened to be here with my best friend and my wife who were willing to let me lend a hand. I'd think since you can't be bothered taking it seriously that you wouldn't mind the help."

Det. Hanley gestured toward his officers. "Arrest this man right now."

"He hasn't done anything wrong," Cooper said, his voice loud and booming as he sprang to his feet. "We were hired by the Presley family and have a right to help them find their daughter."

"Not if it interferes in my investigation."

"You have no investigation," Luke said, looking to his left and right. The last thing he wanted to do was cause a scene and he didn't want to pull rank on the detective. His officers made no move to put Luke in cuffs. "What do you want us to do?"

"Enjoy the rest of your vacation and go home and let me do my job." Det. Hanley looked at Luke as if daring him to say something else or worse, defy him.

Cooper wasn't having any of it. "There's still time for you to save face if that's your problem. The media is right here. We can say that you were involved in setting up the tip line and we'd be happy to have some of your staff running it if you have the people available for that."

"There's no need for a tip line. I have everything under control."

Luke took a step toward him, trying to control his temper. He had faced cops before who didn't do their jobs. "You haven't even taken the disappearances seriously. Gia Tibbitts has been missing for more than a year. What have you done to try to find her?"

Det. Hanley scoffed. "She ran off with a boyfriend."

"She's a lesbian," Cooper said, not controlling the anger in his voice. "She left a table at the Sunshine Bar and went to the bathroom. She was never seen again. She left her purse with her identification and her money at the table."

Det. Hanley shifted his eyes to Cooper. He didn't say a word. His breath came hot and heavy and it was clear they were poking a bear. "You will leave this island right now. Understand me? If I have to come back or hear one more report that you're interfering, I will arrest you."

"I thought you came to arrest us right now?" Luke said, knowing he was pressing his luck.

A crowd of reporters had started to gather around them, and out of the corner of his eye, Luke saw a man with his camera on his shoulder filming the whole thing.

Grady stepped toward them. "Det. Hanley, are you saying that you are refusing to allow the Presley family to hire investigators to do everything they can to find their daughter? Is that your official statement?"

The detective turned only slightly to acknowledge Grady's presence. "Finding Laurie Presley is a priority for us. All I was saying is that visitors should be assured we are doing everything we can and focus on enjoying their vacation."

A television reporter stepped forward. "Det. Hanley, you've refused to answer any of our questions. You've put out official statements that all of the young women ran away. You said that again now about Gia Tibbitts. You've come out in front of the medical examiner's report and said that Daphne Powers drowned. The medical examiner released a statement not even twenty minutes ago saying that she was strangled. How do you respond to the fact that Ava and Bill Presley have lost confidence in your ability to find their daughter?"

Luke had to bite the inside of his cheek to keep from smiling. He had never been so happy to see the media in his life. Emboldened, Luke pressed him. "It seems you might need help, after all, Det. Hanley."

The detective's nostrils flared and he glared at Luke. Det. Hanley would learn the hard way that Luke did not intimidate, especially when it came to homicide cases. Luke sat back down and Cooper followed. He folded his arms across his chest and stared up at the man. "We will not be leaving and we will be moving forward with our investigation and the tip line. We are more than happy to hand over any viable leads to a detective who is willing to investigate them."

Luke left that hanging in the air because it certainly wouldn't be Det. Hanley. Luke didn't even know how the man still had a job.

"You'll hand over all viable evidence to me," Det. Hanley said through gritted teeth while pointing at Luke. "Do you understand me?"

"What's your supervisor's name?"

Det. Hanley didn't respond. He glared down at Luke and then turned on his heels and left, taking his uniformed officers with him. Luke had won that round. He didn't want to have to keep getting in the ring with him because it took up valuable time.

When Det. Hanley was gone, Luke gestured for Grady to sit down with them. "I hadn't heard about the autopsy report. Do you have a copy of that?"

Grady shook his head. "The whole report wasn't released. It was snippets of the report that indicated the victim had been strangled and then dumped in the water. That's about all we've been told."

Luke would have to visit the medical examiner. He only hoped that the office would be more helpful than the police. They sat talking for a little while longer and then Luke excused himself and Cooper for the evening. Before he walked away, Luke said, "Grady, let's look for each other tomorrow and we can chat again. I'd like to give you all of our exclusives of information we are planning to release."

"I won't say no to that." Grady smiled and waved as Luke walked out the front door of the hotel with Cooper right behind him.

"Where are we headed, Luke? It's late." Cooper followed Luke down the hotel's front entranceway until they were on the sidewalk in front of the hotel. Groups of tourists passed by them heading in both directions.

"I want to go to the medical examiner's office." Luke checked his watch and it was nearing nine-thirty. "If they released a statement a short time ago, I assume someone must be in their office. If I catch them this late, then maybe they will be willing to talk, or at least someone will be willing to talk."

"Let me text Adele and tell her where I'll be. They should be back soon." Cooper pulled his phone from his pocket and sent the text while Luke hailed a cab.

Not even twenty minutes later, they stood at the door to the medical examiner's office. Luke pulled open the front door, surprised that it wasn't locked. He entered an office that looked nearly identical to every medical examiner's office he'd ever been in. The sterile white walls, tiled floor, and smell that was a mix of cleaning supplies, antiseptic and slight hint of death.

"I'll be right there," the melodic voice of a woman called from behind a double door.

Luke had no problem entering the medical examiner's building, but he wouldn't be rude enough to go traipsing through the office uninvited. A moment later, a short black woman, a little round in the middle, with a pleasant smile pushed open the double door.

"Can I help you?" she asked looking up at him through dark brown wide eyes.

Luke placed her age anywhere from forty-five to fifty. He introduced himself and Cooper and then said, "We're sorry to bother you so late. We were hoping to speak to the medical examiner about the Daphne Powers case."

She planted her hands on thick hips. "On what authority would you be doing that? I don't speak to reporters in here."

Luke pulled his badge from his pocket and handed it to her. "I'm out of my jurisdiction. I'm the head of the violent crimes division in Little Rock, Arkansas. I'm here on vacation and we are looking into the cases with the missing women. Ava and Bill Presley are staying at our hotel. I was there when Daphne's body washed up on the beach and believe the cases might be connected."

The woman glanced down at the black leather holder that held

Luke's badge on one side and his identification card on the other. Then she raised her eyes to him. "I'm Dr. Gloria Wheatly, come on back to my office." When they stared at her without moving, she added, "I know the website doesn't say my name or have my photo. The last medical examiner retired a month ago. I was his assistant for more than ten years. I didn't make any top billing on the website and haven't had time to change it. I have identification if you need it." With a hint of a smile she handed Luke's badge back to him.

"Not at all," Luke said, sliding his badge back in his pocket. "I apologize. I was anticipating meeting a man who seemed rather surly from the website. I was geared up for a fight I'm not going to have."

She chuckled. "We can go a few rounds if it makes you feel better."

Luke liked her already. "Please, lead the way and we'll follow." Once back in her office, they took the two seats across from the desk. "Dr. Wheatly, I don't know what information you're willing to share with us, but we'd appreciate anything we can learn."

"First off, call me Gloria or even Dr. Gloria if you won't drop the formality." She eased herself into her chair. "Does Det. Hanley know you're here?"

Luke debated only for a moment how much he'd share. If he had any hope of winning her trust, he'd need to be honest. Luke told her the interactions he'd had with the detective including what had happened right before he arrived at her office. "Needless to say, no, he doesn't know I'm here. I have no plans on interacting with him at all."

"Good. He's a boob," she said definitively. "He tries my very last ounce of patience. I told him before he made that statement today that the victim didn't drown. What does he do – goes out and says it's a drowning."

"Is there a reason he's so..." Luke wasn't sure of the word – difficult, incompetent. Nothing seemed to fit.

"He's in the mayor's pocket. All they care about is tourism. Det.

Hanley would like to be the chief of police one day and the current chief is Det. Hanley's father – who should have retired about twenty years ago."

That certainly explained a lot. "We'd like to help in any way we can."

Gloria leaned back in her chair and assessed them. She was quiet for several moments and let the uncertainty hang in the air. Finally, she pointed between Luke and Cooper. "I trust you two."

"I wouldn't do anything to break that trust. You can call my captain back in Little Rock if you'd like to check me out."

Gloria waved him off. She pulled a report out of her desk and slid it across the top to Luke. "Everything you want is in there. You'll need to read it here. I can't have it leave the office. I knew by the third missing woman that something wasn't right here. We are a quiet community for the most part. We don't get the same rowdy crowds as some of the other islands. When those young women started going missing, I knew something was wrong."

Luke took the report and flipped it open. Cooper inched his chair over to read along with Luke. It contained all the basics. The toxicology wasn't back yet but the information available told the story. Daphne had been dead two days before her body was found. She had been strangled, probably manual strangulation, and her hyoid bone was broken. She had defensive wounds on her hands and her legs and there was a good deal of bruising on Daphne's body.

"I don't think she was in the water long before she was found," Gloria said, drawing their attention. "I know she's been missing about three months. I have no idea where she was before being found in the water, but she put up a fight. Other than the bruising, her body wasn't in bad condition. She's been fed and taken care of. There were no signs of sexual assault or torture. It's a strange case. Definitely homicide."

Luke handed her back the file. "We assumed it was homicide when her body washed up. That much was obvious. The rest of the report helped to fill in the blanks."

"I'm here if you need anything else. Good to see someone doing their job."

By the time they left her office, Luke felt like he had a real resource on the island. There were still more questions than answers, but Luke had met an ally and for that he was thankful. He promised he'd keep her in the loop with anything he found.

CHAPTER 14

The next morning, I woke before Luke. I had one leg out from under the covers, his arm thrown across my middle, and yawned before I even opened my eyes. I had come back the night before and Luke and I stayed up late going over the cases.

I was happy Luke connected with Dr. Gloria Wheatly. I knew it had been bothering him that he didn't have a solid contact within the criminal justice system in St. Thomas. It wasn't how he was used to working, and no matter how much Luke said he was okay with it, he wasn't. Calls were already coming into the tip line too.

We had also made enough headway with Dylan Carter to satisfy me. After all, it wasn't like I could walk into the bar and start questioning him about being a serial killer. He had been more open with me than I had anticipated and it left the door open for more.

After discussing the case, we fell asleep snuggled up together. His soft snores filled the room and he pulled me closer as he felt me inch away. I patted his hand and slid out of the bed. I stretched my arms overhead and went to the bathroom. On the way, I passed by the door to our room and noticed the white corner of what looked like an envelope poking underneath the door. I tugged at it and it slid inside.

The outside of the card-sized envelope was addressed to Det. Luke Morgan, so I tossed it on a nearby end table. I went through my morning routine wondering what was in the envelope. Luke had talked about scheduling us a couple's massage so it could have been about that.

It also might not have anything to do with us. I hadn't stopped to consider that he might have given Ava and Bill Presley or Grady our room number and hoped he hadn't. I wanted a small bit of privacy when we were in our room.

I finished towel drying my hair and applying a small amount of makeup to make me presentable for the day and then came out with a towel wrapped around me to find clothes for the day.

Luke whistled too loudly for a man who was still lying prone in bed. He had his head angled to look at me. "Why don't you come back to bed and we can continue what we started last night?"

"We can't. We have to meet Adele and Cooper for breakfast."

Luke winked. "We can make them wait."

"I showered already," I said and watched his face fall. "Later, I promise."

I carried over the envelope that had been under the door and handed it to him. He sat up in bed and adjusted the pillows to support his back. "I don't know if it's important. It was under our door." I went to the closet and pulled out some clean clothes and got dressed while he opened the envelope.

"Who left this?" he asked, his voice tight. He held the index card up for me to see it.

"I don't know. As I said, it was under the door this morning." I wiggled into my shorts and turned to him. "I can't see from here. What does it say?"

"British Diplomat Samuel Fletcher."

"Never heard of him."

"Me either." Luke examined the front of the card and then the back. "I'm not sure what this is supposed to mean."

I ran my fingers through my damp hair and headed toward the

vanity to finish fixing it. "My laptop is on the desk if you want to search for him. You need to hurry up and shower."

I focused on drying my hair, turning the roll brush with each section of hair, and drying it so my auburn locks would become soft waves instead of the half wavy, half straight mess my hair would be if I didn't fix it. I checked my watch again and called for Luke but he didn't respond. I finished what I was doing and then went back into the room to find him hunched over my laptop. His face was inches from the screen.

"What are you doing? We are going to be late."

Luke called me over to him. "I texted Cooper and told him we'd be late. Look at this."

I stood behind his chair and leaned over him to see the photo on the screen. The caption under the photo of the handsome dark-haired man wearing a suit and a cheesy grin was Samuel Fletcher. "I guess he is a British diplomat."

"That's not what I'm looking at, Riley." Luke pointed to the man's hand, which was visible in the photo. "Look at the ring. Doesn't that look familiar to you?"

I rested my hand on his back, leaned over, and focused my eyes on the spot at the end of Luke's index finger. There it was – the ring with the crest that was on the hotel's surveillance video. "A British diplomat grabbed Laurie Presley the night she disappeared?" I could barely believe what I was saying because it was hard to believe it was true.

Luke angled his head over his shoulder. "We shouldn't jump to any conclusions or tell the Presleys until we understand what we are looking at here. We don't even know who left the note."

After Luke showered and changed, we headed to the front desk. We waited while Vic finished his phone call. Then he looked at us with his eyes wide. "What can I help you with this morning?"

Luke held the envelope in his hand, shaking it towards Vic. "I need to know who left us this note. They know what room we are in."

Vic stared at him with confusion on his face. "I left that note. It was here on the desk when I came in this morning and I brought it up to you thinking it would be important. It was so early I didn't want to knock and wake you."

Relief came over me that some random person didn't know what room we were staying in. "Do you know who left it for Luke?"

"No idea, sorry. I found it this morning right here." Vic patted his hand on a stack of mail. "I go through this every morning and it was addressed to you. I figured you'd want to know right away."

Luke blinked several times, seeming unsure what to say. "Is there any way to know who left it there?"

"I can ask the person who ran the desk last night. It's possible someone dropped it in the pile of mail or left it right on the counter there." Vic held his finger up for us to wait. He grabbed the phone, punched in a number, and then asked the person on the other end about the envelope. He nodded a few times, said thanks, and then hung up. "She has no idea. It was on the stack of mail she didn't get a chance to go through. She had no idea who put it there or when."

Luke cursed and then apologized to Vic. "It's not your fault. I need to speak to the person who left it and it's clear they don't want me to know."

Vic stared at the envelope. "Do you mind me asking what's in it? I might be able to help."

Luke looked down at me and I shrugged. It was his call. He had formed a relationship with Vic and either he trusted him or he didn't. Luke pulled the index card from the envelope and handed it to him. "There's a man's name on that, and when I looked up this person online, he's wearing the same ring as the person who grabbed Laurie Presley's arm the night she disappeared."

"It's incredibly unbelievable that this person would have something to do with her disappearance," I added, noticing that the hotel lobby was starting to fill up with people heading to breakfast. "You better look fast. We don't want every media person here to get ahold of this name."

Vic lowered his eyes and read the name and then said it twice more. He handed the card back to Luke. "It might not be as unbelievable as you think."

"Why is that?" Luke asked, putting the index card back in the envelope.

Vic shifted his eyes around to see who was watching them. Then he stepped around the counter and gestured for us to move off to the side with him. "I could get fired for telling you this. Samuel Fletcher is a frequent hotel guest. He's been living here on the penthouse floor for some time."

Given that Samuel Fletcher was a frequent guest meant that his interaction with Laurie could have been completely innocent.

Luke stepped even closer to Vic. "Can you print me out a report or jot down the dates of when he's been in the hotel over the last year?" When Vic balked, Luke explained, "The last thing I want to do is spark some international incident and drag a British diplomat into a murder investigation. I want to see if he was here during the other disappearances. Once we know more, we can figure out how to proceed."

Vic looked over at the counter, which had a few people already lined up waiting to speak to him. "Let me get through the morning rush and then I'll get something to you this afternoon."

It would have to be good enough for now. Luke and I walked over to the hotel restaurant and grabbed a table out on the patio since the weather was nice and there was an ocean breeze. As we sat, Luke raised his eyes to me. "I scheduled couple's massages for us late this afternoon. We deserve some relaxation on our vacation."

I couldn't help but smile. Even in the middle of all the craziness, Luke wanted to take some time out with me. "I regret not crawling back into bed with you this morning."

He laughed. "I knew you would. I'm going to make you keep your word later."

Cooper and Adele joined us a moment later, both of them looking well-rested and happy. They sat down still holding hands and then they smiled at each other when they realized. "If we are a little much, we can sit someplace else," Cooper teased and then glanced over at Adele with so much love on his face, it made my heart hurt.

I lowered my menu. "It makes me happy to see you so happy."

We ordered what was becoming our usual breakfasts and then chatted casually while we waited for our food. Luke held back the information about Samuel Fletcher so I didn't bring it up. I told Adele we were going for the couple's massages that afternoon and she told me again how amazing they were.

When we finally got our food and dug in, in between bites, Cooper said, "Adele said you did well with Dylan Carter last night. Does he seem like a viable suspect?"

I had already filled in Luke the night before. This was the first Cooper and I talked about it. "I don't know much of anything right now. We made some initial contact that I think will lend to more conversation. He seemed far chattier about it all than I anticipated. It's not like he gave off a killer vibe or anything."

"That's a fair assessment," Adele echoed, popping a bit of bacon in her mouth. "It's too bad you can't get him alone someplace and geek out on crime stuff with him. I think you'd get him talking then."

Luke took a sip of his coffee and then set the cup down. "That's not happening. I don't want either of you alone with him."

I wasn't going to argue with Luke. I didn't want to be alone with him either. "I understand what you mean, Adele. Maybe tonight you can hang back a little or chat with Ollie. He seems like he might be the weak link in the whole thing if they are involved in the disappearances."

Cooper finished off the rest of his breakfast and then looked to Luke and me. "What's the plan for the day? We've spoken to the victims' families, interviewed a good deal of hotel staff last night, and looked at surveillance video. I assume the hotels where the other victims were staying won't have surveillance footage saved."

"They don't," I explained. "I made a few calls yesterday while I was doing some background research. I didn't bring up the cases but told them I was doing research and asked how far back they keep the video. Only a couple of months if it's not requested otherwise."

"That's about standard," Luke said, taking another sip of his coffee. "Thanks for making those calls. I had no idea you did that."

"Everything is happening so quickly. I wanted to nail down what evidence we might have or not have access to." He reached for my hand and squeezed it. "We are all in this together. The sooner it's solved the better. What's your plan?"

Luke opened his eyes wide. It probably wasn't fair to put all the pressure on him. He was used to being the leader though. "I want to go talk to Lyle Blaylock and see what he knows. Since you stumbled onto his name the other day, it's been on my mind. I'd like to rule him in or out quickly before the media gets ahold of his name."

He turned to Cooper. "How do you feel about going to interview Andy Barber? He has a direct connection to Daphne Powers. Since her body was recently found, he might be a bit on edge. Riley, you could go with him."

"What about me?" Adele asked. "Am I supposed to sit around looking fabulous while you all work?"

We all laughed at the funny infectious tone of her voice. Luke said, "I was thinking you might connect with some of the volunteers who are covering the phone lines. Sort through any credible tips and such."

"That works for me."

As we were getting up to leave, Grady approached the table. "I heard from another reporter that you're looking into Samuel Fletcher. He's a British diplomat."

Luke sucked in a sharp breath; annoyance was written all over his face. He turned to a shocked Cooper and Adele. "I'll handle this and connect with you later."

I leaned down and kissed him before I left the table. He looked ready to explode, and I couldn't blame him. It was the first real leak in our case.

CHAPTER 15

"Where did you hear that name?" Luke asked, not bothering to get up from the table. Cooper had thrown money down for breakfast and he still needed to grab the check. When Grady didn't respond right away, Luke asked him again.

"You seem upset that I have this guy's name." Grady pulled out a chair and sat down. "I heard it from another reporter. I wasn't digging around where I wasn't supposed to."

Luke relaxed his posture. "Sorry. It was a name I recently received. I don't have any information about it and wanted to figure it out before it was released to the media. It's a big deal and I wouldn't want to tarnish someone's reputation for no reason. We don't even know what we are looking at yet. Can you point out the reporter who told you?"

"I'll do better than that. I'll take you to him."

Luke paid the check and then followed Grady down the hallway of the first floor of the lobby, past the room that they had set up for the tip line, and entered another conference room filled with media. Familiar reporters sat around a large conference table and cameramen fussed with their equipment against the back wall. Luke's heart raced. It was like walking right into the lion's den. Grady pointed out a young reporter sitting at the far end of the table and gestured for him to come over.

Grady introduced the reporter as John from the *Washington Post.*

Luke shook his hand, introduced himself, and then asked if he would follow him out of the room. Once they were outside and out of earshot of the other reporters, Luke asked him how he had obtained the name Samuel Fletcher.

John ran a hand through his blond locks, seeming nervous. "I had a note slipped under my door this morning. I had to look him up. I had never heard the name before."

"Have you mentioned him to anyone else?"

John swallowed hard. "My editor and Grady. I asked Grady if he had heard the name and if he was connected to the case. I didn't understand the note."

It sounded like what Luke had dealt with earlier that morning. He couldn't be angry with the young reporter for being handed a tip any more than he could blame himself. Someone was trying to make sure the information about Samuel Fletcher got out one way or the other. He softened his tone. "I received the same note under my door. I want to interview him before the information is made public."

John held up his hand. "I understand and my editor wouldn't let me run with it even if I wanted to, which I don't. I don't know what it all means. When I looked him up online, I noticed he had a similar ring as the surveillance image you released. That didn't mean anything to me though. A lot of people could have a similar ring. I don't have any confirmation right now one way or the other and we aren't running speculation."

While Luke was glad to hear that, he didn't know, and therefore, didn't trust John. "I'm hoping to speak to Fletcher today. Please don't share the information. I have no idea if or how he connects to these cases."

"Understood." John walked back into the conference room without looking back.

Luke could have made a mistake by making a bigger deal out of it than needed. He wanted to err on the side of caution. He turned to Grady. "Thanks for alerting me on this. I'll let you know what I find if it's relevant. Keep your ears open for me in case you hear anything else." Luke slapped him on the back and then headed for the front desk.

Vic saw him coming and held up three printed pages for him. He handed the pages to Luke. "I got to this sooner than I expected. I went back five years since Fletcher started coming to the hotel. I should have mentioned this sooner. Samuel Fletcher was a British diplomat in Antigua. He vacationed here and wouldn't have any diplomatic immunity here. To be honest with you, there have been rumors for years that Fletcher was relieved from his post for some relationship with a woman. I don't know all the details though."

Luke took the pages and thanked Vic. He went back upstairs to his room and sat down at the desk. He thumbed through the pages, noting the dates that Fletcher had been in town. He checked the board and each corresponded to a date that a young woman disappeared. It didn't mean anything. Vic was right. Fletcher had been staying more frequently. Instead of weekend trips, Fletcher had been in St. Thomas for eight of the last twelve months.

He set the pages down on the desk and opened Riley's laptop. He plugged in a few search terms and came back with troves of information about Fletcher, more so than he had seen earlier that morning. Vic had been right about the rumors, too. Fletcher had been the British diplomat in Antigua but had been removed from his post close to fifteen months ago.

Luke scanned through several stories and they all reported the same information. Fletcher had been accused of sexually harassing several women at the embassy and had been quickly removed from his post. The British government wasn't about to get caught up in the scandal. Fletcher hadn't defended himself in any of the news reports, had never given a statement that Luke could find, and had taken off for St. Thomas and was hiding out from the public eye – until now.

Several news reports speculated about where Fletcher had gone. None of them seemed to have confirmation. Another news report gave Luke the background on Fletcher he had been searching for. He was forty-two years old, never married, had no children, and his parents came from considerable wealth.

Fletcher's father came from old British wealth with ties to the royal family. It was presumably why Fletcher got his diplomatic position even though he lacked any real credentials. Luke couldn't even find a work history on the man.

Luke restacked the pages and noticed that Vic had written a note on the back. It was a floor number and elevator key number to access the floor.

Luke grabbed his belongings, leaving the pages behind. He went to the elevator, hit the button for the penthouse floor, and then had to type in the code Vic had provided to get the elevator to move. Luke had no idea what he was expecting.

At the penthouse level, the elevator door opened to a short hallway and a door straight ahead. He half-expected to see hotel staff but the floor was empty of people and noise. He knocked and waited.

"Leave the towels out there and I'll grab them myself later," a man with a posh British accent said.

Luke knocked again, wanting to force Fletcher to answer the door.

"I said to leave the towels!" Fletcher shouted, this time with growing frustration in his voice.

Luke cleared his throat. "Mr. Fletcher, I need to speak to you."

A moment later, Fletcher answered the door wearing blue shorts and a white tee-shirt that was damp around the collar. His mess of dark hair stuck to his head as beads of sweat ran down his face. He looked Luke up and down. "Who are you?"

Luke explained who he was and how he was helping the Presley family. "I need to speak to you for a moment."

Fletcher held out his hand to prevent Luke's entry. "I have nothing to say. I don't know anything about that girl's disappearance or any of the others."

The others. That struck Luke as an odd thing to say for an innocent man. "You're going to want to speak to me."

"Why is that?" Fletcher asked, his tone indicating he was humoring him rather than being serious.

Luke pulled his phone from his pocket and held up a photo that was used in the flyer. "Because that's your hand grabbing Laurie Presley the night she disappeared. I'm certain you're the last person to see her." He put his phone away and then pulled out the envelope with the index card and handed it to him, forcing him to take it in his hand. "Someone slipped me that note with your name on it. Whether you talk to me or not, someone thinks you're involved. A reporter got the same note."

Fletcher kicked the door and spit a string of curses. "I don't want to be involved with this. I've had enough scandal."

"I'm here trying to prevent more. I've spoken to the reporter and told him I was speaking to you. They are willing to hold off on the story – for now." Luke didn't care that he was lying. The reality was the media could run the story at any point. By the look on Fletcher's face, the ruse was working.

Fletcher stepped out of the way resigned. "At least, let me take a shower before I speak to you. I just got off the treadmill. Have a seat in the living room."

Luke followed Fletcher through the main foyer of the penthouse suite past a small kitchen and dining room and into the living room, which featured floor-to-ceiling windows and a wraparound balcony that overlooked Harbor Cove. Fletcher went to a room off the right of the living room and closed the door behind him. Luke took a seat on a plush tan couch and waited as the shower turned on. He resisted the urge to snoop around the suite.

Fletcher didn't have any personal belongings within sight. The small kitchen looked like it hadn't been used. There were no newspapers or magazines or clothing scattered around. Only one pillow on the couch seemed slightly askew. Luke assumed Fletcher kept his wallet, cellphone, and laptop in the bedroom. Luke relaxed back into the couch and waited.

Fletcher came out twenty minutes later freshly showered with damp hair, wearing tan shorts and a blue V-neck tee-shirt. He hadn't bothered to put anything on his feet. He offered Luke something to drink. When Luke declined, he poured himself a Scotch.

With a drink in hand, he slouched down into the chair across from Luke and toyed with the glass as he spoke. "I know you're here because of the women back at the embassy. I didn't sexually harass anyone. I had sex with a few women and you know how they are. Consent at the moment and regret later and suddenly it's sexual harassment."

Luke resisted the urge to debate the merits of a case he hadn't been involved in. "I'm not here about that. I'm here because you are seen on surveillance video grabbing the arm of a missing woman. That's it. No more. No less."

Fletcher took a long sip of his drink and then rested the half-empty glass in his lap. "She was drunk and couldn't get her keycard to open the door. I didn't grab her. I tugged on her arm so she'd come around the front of the building with me. I walked her to the lobby door and then left for the evening. I didn't wait around to see if she made it in."

There was one thing that had struck Luke as odd. "Why escort her to the front? You have a keycard and she had hers. If she was as drunk as you said, why not just swipe it and let her in the door where she was standing?"

Fletcher stared over at Luke with his mouth slightly agape as if he were on the verge of responding. He didn't though. He took another sip of his drink and stalled. "I don't know," he said finally. "That's a good question that I don't have an answer to. I was headed toward the front of the building and I took her with me. To echo your words – no more, no less. Seems stupid now, but it's the truth."

Luke remained calm even though he knew Fletcher was lying. "What were you doing on the side of the hotel?"

Fletcher smirked and raised his eyes to Luke as if daring him. "You want to know the truth?"

Luke opened his arms wide. "It's why I'm here. I much prefer the truth so I can get on with the investigation. Makes no difference to me if I bring you into the cops or clear your name. I'm only after the truth."

"Hookers and blow, man," he said, mocking a California surfer accent. He changed back to his normal voice. "I'm stuck up here exiled and occasionally have a little fun. If I'm paying for it, they can't say they didn't want it. I met my dealer at the side of the building and then took a cab to spend a few hours with a terrific shag."

Luke knew he was looking for a reaction, so he gave none. "I still don't understand why you didn't open the side door."

"She walked right past me in the middle of a drug deal. The last thing I was going to do was show up on surveillance at the side of the building corroborating anything she saw."

"Why even help her then?"

That seemed to stump him for a moment. "Why do anything? I don't know. She seemed to be struggling and I didn't want to leave a woman in distress."

Luke's mouth remained set in the same firm line it had been, showing no emotion. He didn't believe him but he wasn't going to stress the point right now. "I'm going to need the name and contact info of your dealer and the prostitute."

"No," Fletcher said adamantly, shaking his head for emphasis. "There is no way I'm giving you that."

Luke shrugged and stood. "Then enjoy the media attention in the morning. They are going to need something and a disgraced British diplomat admitting to buying cocaine and visiting a prostitute will be a fairly juicy story." Luke started toward the door and as expected Fletcher called him back. With the threat of media attention, Luke had the name of both the drug dealer and prostitute in a matter of seconds.

He wasn't at all surprised by the drug dealer's name, but if it checked out, it meant Laurie Presley's friends were lying.

CHAPTER 16

Andy Barber's one-floor blue house sat back from the road and had a long dirt driveway. The place was well-kept and unassuming. Cooper asked the cab driver to loop around the single-lane road once and then drop them off three houses down.

He handed the driver a wad of cash and asked if he'd be willing to wait for them. The driver flipped through the bills and then put the car in park and let the engine idle. He told them he'd sit there for no longer than thirty minutes. Cooper assumed that would be long enough.

"What's the plan?" Riley asked as they stepped out of the car onto the road that hadn't been paved for many years. Potholes and gravel littered the path to Andy's house.

"I don't even know if Andy's home. I didn't want to have to wait out here for another cab to find us." Cooper had been thinking they should have rented a car. Unfortunately, he only thought of that after they had made most of the trip by cab. It wasn't that it was far, only a few miles, but the slow pace of island driving had made the trip longer than it needed to be.

They stood back and assessed the house from the road and didn't see any signs of life. There was no car in the driveway, the drapes were drawn, and the windows and doors were shut. Cooper pointed toward the back of the driveway at a garage that looked like it was barely standing. "He might have parked in there."

"If he did, I'd assume his car is what's holding up the structure."

Cooper laughed because Riley was right. "Only one way to know for sure." They walked up the driveway and once on the small concrete front step, Cooper rapped his knuckles against the door. He was taken aback when a man yelled that he'd be there in a minute. "I guess he is home."

A man with short dark hair thinning on top answered. He stood about five-nine and had an average build. There wasn't anything particularly memorable about him as far as Cooper was concerned. He'd blend perfectly into any environment.

The man wiped his hands off on his jeans that looked like they'd seen better days. "Can I help you?"

"Are you Andy Barber?"

"I am. What's this about?"

Cooper introduced himself and Riley and explained their involvement with Laurie Presley's case. "Would you be willing to speak to us?"

"I don't have any information about Laurie, but you're welcome to come in." Andy stepped out of the way and let Cooper and Riley enter the house.

A blast of cold air hit Cooper in the face as he entered. He assumed Andy had the drapes drawn and windows closed to keep it cool. The house had a tidy appearance and a comfortable-looking couch and chair facing a television that was mounted on the wall. Beyond the living room was a large eat-in kitchen. Andy gestured toward a square four-person table and then went to the stove and shut off one of the burners.

"We shouldn't take up too much of your time." Cooper sat down in the chair that faced the rest of the kitchen. "Had you met Laurie Presley or had any contact with her?"

Andy leaned against the kitchen counter. "No. I never met her that I know of. I run a scuba and snorkeling business so I come into contact with too many people to keep track of. I heard about her disappearance on the news. Have you found anything?"

Riley folded her hands on the table. "We have a few leads we are running down. If you saw the news reports, you know that the media is connecting several other disappearances to Laurie's. Had you met any of the other women?"

Andy turned to the sink and washed his hands, then he dried them on a towel. He came over to the table and sat down with them. "You're not here about Laurie, are you? You're here about Daphne."

Cooper and Riley shared a look. "We are, Andy," Cooper said evenly. "We were given information from Daphne's friends that she spent time with you before she disappeared."

"It's true. I won't deny it." Andy shifted his eyes away from them. "I didn't kill her if that's what you're here to ask me. I know they found her body washed up on the beach at Harbor Cove. I saw it on the news."

"Tell me about your relationship with her," Riley said.

He looked back at her and sighed. "I don't know what to tell you. We met long before Daphne visited St. Thomas. I had wanted to see her in London but she told me that her parents didn't approve of me. A small business owner wasn't good enough for them. I make a great living. Daphne came to visit me with her friends who I guess didn't know about me."

"They told me they suspected that you had talked before her trip and that it wasn't a spontaneous meeting."

Andy nodded and blew out a breath. "None of that was my plan. It was what Daphne wanted."

Cooper didn't understand that. "Do you know why that is?"

"Money. Daphne said everything is about money to her father.

I didn't make enough of it to give Daphne the life he deemed she deserved. She was a boarding school kid and I'm an island guy." Andy inched his chair back from the table and stretched his legs out. "I don't even know why I'm telling you all this now. It's not important. Daphne's dead."

"It matters because Daphne was murdered." Cooper stared over at the man not understanding how he could be so unfeeling.

Andy shook his head. "She drowned. I saw it on the news."

"No, Andy. That detective got it wrong. I saw the medical examiner's report myself. Daphne was murdered and she fought her attacker. I'll save you the gory details, but she was strangled to death."

Andy's face distorted in horror and then shock. "How did it happen? That can't be."

This wasn't what Cooper had been expecting. "Andy, when was the last time you saw Daphne?"

Before Andy could answer, Riley asked, "May I use your bathroom, please?"

Andy gestured toward the living room. "Down the hall to the left." He turned his attention back to Cooper. "I don't remember the exact date. She had a day or two left of her vacation. I don't even know when she disappeared. I heard it later when her father called to ask me when she didn't come home from the trip. I had no idea what he was talking about."

Cooper didn't believe him. As soon as they had started talking about Daphne, Andy stopped making eye contact. His body language had stiffened and he was on edge. "We have a problem, Andy, that I'm hoping you can help me figure out. Daphne was on vacation, three months ago. She never returned to London and her body was found a few nights ago. Where was she for three months?"

"I don't know," Andy said, rushing the words. "I don't know anything. I think you should leave." Andy stood from the table and his demeanor started to change from defensive to angry. Red crept up his neck and face. "I want you to get out of my house right now. How dare you come here and accuse me of anything."

Cooper remained seated and calm. "Andy, we didn't accuse you of anything. You seem like you cared about Daphne. Enough that you were willing to be a secret in her life and pretend you met her when she came on vacation. I'd think you'd want to know who killed her."

"There's nothing I can do about it now." Andy turned away from him, looking across the room toward where Riley had gone. "Where is she? She should be back by now."

"She'll be back in a minute. Talk to me." Cooper snapped his fingers in the hope of drawing Andy's attention to him. "I'm trying to help you, Andy. Did the cops or anyone talk to you after Daphne disappeared?"

Andy turned his head to Cooper but seemed to stare right past him. "No. It was her father who told me. No one came here. You're the first."

"Weren't you concerned when you heard that Daphne never returned home from her trip?"

Andy finally locked eyes with Cooper. "No. I knew Daphne wanted to run away. She hated her father and hated living with him. He controlled every aspect of her life. She told me she didn't want to go back."

Cooper thought that was the first truthful thing he had said. "Where did she go? She must have stayed on the island, and St. Thomas isn't that big, Andy. You were the only person she knew here."

"You need to go." Instead of anger, Andy had resignation in his voice. "There's nothing I can tell you that will help."

"I think there is, Andy," Riley said from the kitchen entrance. She was holding a hairbrush and a woman's pink bra. "She was staying here, wasn't she? Daphne didn't want to go home, so she staged her disappearance and moved in with you. That's why you never seemed concerned she was missing. You helped hide her."

Andy's face crumbled and tears ran down his cheeks. "I begged her not to do it. I loved her and there wasn't anything I wouldn't have done for her. She stayed here and we never went out. Daphne said it would blow over eventually and her parents would stop looking for her and then she'd show up one day and all would be fine. Then, they'd be so happy she was alive that they'd let us be together."

It sounded like the craziest plan Cooper had ever heard. By the look on Andy's face, he had thought the same. "If she never left the house, how did she die – unless you killed her?"

"I didn't kill her. I could never hurt her." Andy sat back down in the chair and held his face in his hands, hiding the emotion on his face. "Daphne was as hot-tempered as I am. We got into arguments all the time. It wasn't as easy to keep up the plan as Daphne thought it would be. She wasn't happy here. She hated it after a month. I told her to call her parents or go home. She felt trapped by her own decisions."

Cooper reached his hand over and put it on Andy's shoulder. His only goal was trying to seem like an ally rather than trying to elicit a confession. "That doesn't answer my question. What happened to Daphne?"

Andy raised his head to Cooper. His eyes were red and watery. "Don't you see? I don't know. We got into a huge fight a few nights ago and she left the house. I begged her not to go. I told her I'd buy her a plane ticket back to London. I told her I'd go stay in a hotel for the night. I did everything I could to keep her here outside of holding her prisoner. She insisted on leaving. She said she called a cab and then she was gone. The car that picked her up wasn't a cab though. I have no idea where she went."

Riley looked around the kitchen. "Do you have a house phone? When I spoke to Daphne's friends, they said her phone was off. Her father contacted her phone company and tried to ping her location.

They said the phone was off and that the battery was probably out."

Andy nodded. "We took the battery out of her cellphone so it couldn't be traced. Daphne said her father would search for her that way. I don't have a house phone but I bought her one of those prepaid phones. She left it here."

Cooper got up from the table. He needed to see that phone, but he also didn't trust Andy not to have a weapon stashed someplace in the house. It was one thing to be unarmed but another to be outgunned. "Take me to the phone. I might be able to figure out who picked her up."

"There's only one number. After she was gone, I looked through it and realized she had been calling the number a lot. No one answers and there's no voicemail set up. I haven't been able to figure out who it is." He stood with Cooper and they walked to a back bedroom and grabbed the cellphone from the dresser.

Cooper scanned through the recent calls and then jotted down the number in his cellphone. He had another question for Andy. "Let's finish our discussion."

Once back in the kitchen, Riley asked the question before Cooper had the chance. "Why didn't you call the police when you saw on the news that Daphne's body had been found?"

Andy let out an incredulous laugh. "Are you kidding me? It's only my word that Daphne wanted to stay. I can see the headlines now – scuba instructor kidnaps rich Londoner and then murders her. I wasn't going to risk it. Daphne made her choices."

They asked a few more questions, and when they were satisfied that Andy wasn't going to say any more, Cooper glanced over at Riley. They'd need to call this in to the cops but he wanted to talk to Riley first. "You ready to go?"

"That's it?" Andy asked. "You're not going to arrest me?"

"We aren't cops," Cooper reminded him. "We'll be in touch."

With that Cooper and Riley walked out of the house to their waiting cab.

CHAPTER 17

Cooper and I discussed the merits of calling Det. Hanley on the ride back to the hotel. Cooper insisted we needed to call him and I was on the fence. I didn't think Andy was a killer and didn't see any point in getting him mixed up in the case until we knew more. Besides, I figured telling Det. Hanley that he'd been right about Daphne running away with a guy would only confirm his bias about the other missing young women. He wasn't doing much to investigate. I didn't want to run the risk of him closing his investigation entirely.

I convinced Cooper to see my side of it. He and I both agreed that convincing Luke would be another matter. It didn't look like that would be the most pressing thing for the day though. Luke had started texting me while we were still at Andy's house asking when we'd be back. I texted him once we got to the cab to give me thirty minutes. He sounded hyped up in the text but didn't give me enough detail to understand what he had found. He'd only say that there had been a break in the case and that he needed Cooper and me to run down some leads.

We checked on Adele first and she seemed to be getting on well with the volunteers. Nothing had come in yet that she deemed important enough to send our way. She seemed relaxed though chatting away with a few of the women. She told us that Ava and Bill had checked in once and then left to pass out more flyers.

By the time we made it up to my room, Luke had practically paced a path in the carpet. "What's going on?" I asked, giving him a quick hug. "You said it was urgent."

He stopped pacing long enough to zero in. "I spoke to Samuel Fletcher. He's a piece of work and I can't rule him in or out right now. He was fired from his diplomatic post for sexually harassing women, and he doesn't seem to have learned his lesson. You're not going to believe the story he told me."

"Well," Cooper said, sitting down on the couch, "don't keep us in suspense. We have information about Daphne Powers when you're done. It's been an interesting day for us, too."

I joined Cooper on the couch as Luke stood in the middle of the room with his hands on his hips.

"Fletcher told me that he saw Laurie on the side of the building because he was buying cocaine and then left to spend the night with a prostitute. I have both names and contact information so we need to run down those leads to confirm." Luke raised his eyes to me. "You're never going to believe who he named as his drug dealer."

I had no guesses.

Luke pulled back. "Dylan Carter!"

"I don't understand," I said, trying to work the timeline in my head. "If Laurie was already at the side door when the drug deal happened then she couldn't have gone up to the bar with him as her friends said."

"That's exactly what I'm talking about," Luke confirmed with excitement in his voice. "Something in her friends' story doesn't make sense. Tell me again what Megan told you."

I took a breath, trying to remember her exact words. "They were all on the dance floor and then Laurie went with Dylan up to the bar to get more drinks. They lost sight of her at that point. They found Dylan outside. He said that Laurie had gone out to get some fresh air, which even her friends thought was strange since they never went out the front."

Cooper turned to me. "Is it possible that because they were drunk, they had no idea how much time lapsed? Could Laurie and Dylan have been gone far longer than they thought?"

"I'm sure anything is possible." I tried to work out the situation in a few different ways. I raised my eyes to Luke. "Where was Laurie when he got there to make the drug deal?"

"Fletcher said she passed by them when the deal was happening. He was concerned about that because she might have seen the exchange. Then he saw that she was fumbling with the door."

I held a hand up to make him wait. "So, Dylan got there before Laurie did that night?"

Luke ran a hand over his head. "He'd have to. Fletcher said they were in the middle of the deal when Laurie walked by. Assuming this checks out with Dylan."

"Maybe she followed him," Cooper suggested and we both turned to him. He gestured with his hands as he explained his theory. "It's possible Dylan and Laurie went up to the bar together and he got a call for drugs, so he takes off and she follows him. Realizing she's back at the hotel, Laurie decides to call it a night and go inside only she is so drunk she can't get her keycard to work."

I didn't understand how Fletcher got involved in the first place so I asked Luke a few questions and he explained how and why he didn't let Laurie in the side door.

Cooper had another theory for us. "It's possible that Fletcher got freaked out that Laurie saw the drug deal and went over to question her about what she saw or threatened her not to tell anyone. He realized she was too drunk to notice anything and then walked away as he said. We don't even know for sure that he walked her around to the front of the building as he said."

Luke nodded in agreement. "There are definite holes in the story. If Megan and her friends found Dylan outside the bar, then he could have been on his way back. Why not just say she went back to the hotel? Even if he didn't want to admit to being at the hotel, he knew she was back there."

That was the bigger question for me. "I'd say all roads lead back to Dylan. Fletcher isn't going to pull that name out of thin air so I'm sure Dylan sold him drugs. I agree with Cooper that it's possible Laurie followed him out of the bar. It sounds like she was pretty drunk that night. If Fletcher's story about the prostitute checks out then we are back to Dylan."

"Except for one thing," Luke said, holding up his hand. "If we know that Dylan went right back to the bar because that's confirmed from Laurie's friends, how could he have kidnapped or killed her? You're talking a matter of maybe five minutes."

Cooper looked over at me. "Was his cousin at the bar, too?"

"Megan said Dylan and his friends. I didn't ask specifically about Ollie. I'll have to check."

Luke sat down in the chair across from us. "I'll follow up with the prostitute to confirm the rest of Fletcher's story. Riley, will you check with Megan today?"

"I'll do it as soon as we are done. She provided me with her phone number when we video chatted. Ideally, I'd like to get her back on video chat and nail down the details again. Interviewing someone twice doesn't hurt for confirmation." I hadn't told him that she had been defensive on the first call so I added it now. "She could have been tired of telling the story or someone suggested they had been lying. I want to get to the root of that, too."

"What about me?" Cooper asked, looking between Luke and me.

"Take Adele to lunch and enjoy some time together." I checked the time on my phone. "I have enough time to call Megan and then Luke and I have massages. Cooper, you and Adele should relax. We can meet up tonight for dinner. Then, I'll take another crack at Dylan."

"Sounds good to me." Cooper got up, stretched, and headed for the door. Before he left, he said, "We didn't tell Luke about Andy Barber."

It had completely slipped my mind. "Could you do that while I call Megan?"

Luke and Cooper stepped out onto the balcony and left me alone to call Megan. I texted her first and she told me she was available for a quick video chat. I sat down at my desk and called her. When she appeared on screen, I said, "Thanks for being available so quickly. I have a quick follow-up question based on information we came across today."

Uncertainty fell over her face. "I'm not sure what more I can tell you."

"You mentioned Dylan was there the night Laurie disappeared. What about Ollie? Was he there with you?"

Megan pulled back. "You can't possibly think that Ollie had something to do with Laurie's disappearance? He's such a sweet guy. A little awkward but sweet."

"I don't suspect anyone. I'm only trying to confirm who was in the bar with you and when they were there." The same defensive tone Megan had before was still present. It hinted at secrets that she wasn't telling me. "You said that you didn't know Dylan and Ollie well. I'm surprised that you'd be that protective of them."

Megan shifted her eyes away from me. "I'm not being protective. I don't think Ollie had anything to do with this."

"That wasn't my question. Was he in the bar with you that night or not?" I wanted to go right to the source and ask about her relationship with Ollie because she was behaving like she was protecting him. I didn't think that would bode well for the interview right now.

Megan took a breath and let it out slowly. "No," she said stiffly.

"Ollie wasn't at the bar that night. He said he was at home."

"You've spoken to him since then?" I asked, not hiding my surprise.

"Only a handful of times. He's been supportive knowing that Laurie and I were close."

Supportive or trying to figure out what she suspects. I hated to have such cynical thoughts. "Did you tell him Laurie was missing that night?"

Megan nodded. "I texted him but he didn't respond until morning. He said that he'd been asleep. He had worked all day out in the hot sun and hadn't felt like meeting us out. He works construction, so it's a demanding job."

The Ollie I saw didn't look like he'd ever swung a hammer in his life. I asked a few more questions about Ollie but didn't make much headway. Toward the end of the call, I had to address the elephant in the room. There was no other way than directly. "Did you know that Dylan sold drugs?"

Megan paused and bit her lip. In that one look, she gave herself away. Slowly, she confessed, "We had bought some weed from him one night. That was the second night we saw him before we got to know him and Ollie. He doesn't do it all the time he said. Just once in a while."

"So, a once in a while drug dealer?" I asked sarcasm dripping.

"It's not like that."

"What's it like then? Every time I talk to you, Megan, you share more information." I pounded my fist down on the desk for emphasis. "Every day wasted is another day that Laurie's life hangs in the balance."

"She's probably already dead," Megan said evenly with nearly no emotion. "That sounds cold, I know. We have been talking about it and that other girl's body was found. I don't have a lot of hope she's alive."

I said the only thing I could. "It's probably better for you to be realistic in this situation. That said, if Laurie was murdered, don't you want to find who killed her? Doesn't she deserve justice?" Megan stared back at me not saying a word. I pressed on. "I understand that you may not want to trash your friend's reputation or yours. I'm not taking this information and running to tell the media or her parents. I'm using it to find out what happened to Laurie. Is there anything else you're not telling me?"

Megan didn't say anything for several moments. "We were pretty wasted the night Laurie went missing. Everything I told you is the truth based on what the three of us could piece together. We might not have been as quick to search for Laurie as we said."

I had already assumed that. "Did you see Dylan outside the bar? Was that part correct?"

"Yes. We searched the back deck and the bathroom for her first. Then when we headed out the front, we saw Dylan. Laurie kind of liked him. She had a boyfriend and nothing happened between them, but we gave them some space when they left to go up to the bar together. We did start to get worried when we saw him outside alone and he said Laurie had walked out the front door. All that was true."

I asked Megan a few questions about Dylan's demeanor from what she remembered. There was nothing that stood out to her. I was dealing with the memories of three drunk young women who had gotten together to go over their statements. At that point, I had to take everything with a grain of salt. I cautioned her about not telling Ollie or Dylan the things we were asking. I even asked if she had told them about me and she assured me she hadn't. I didn't put much stock into that answer either.

CHAPTER 18

Luke walked out of the spa feeling like a new man. Every muscle ache had left and the tightness in his shoulders was completely gone. More than anything, he had enjoyed the downtime with Riley, who he sent back to their room to take a nap or go to the beach or do whatever she wanted that wasn't connected to the case. She'd be working later that night trying to connect with Dylan again. He wanted her to relax for a bit that afternoon.

Luke left her with a promise that he'd be back soon. Riley had offered to go with him to the prostitute that Samuel Fletcher had visited, but after speaking to Vic, the address wasn't in the best part of St. Thomas and he wanted to spare Riley that conversation. He took a cab to that side of town while the cab driver gave him a raised eyebrow and a knowing look.

"It's not what you think," Luke said, catching the look in the rearview mirror.

"It never is." The cabbie chuckled to himself.

"No. I'm a detective and I'm working on the case with all the missing women. The woman I'm going to see might be able to provide an alibi for the night Laurie Presley disappeared."

That got the cabbie's attention. He stopped at a red light and looked over his shoulder at Luke. "Who are you asking around about? We know lots of things. People take cabs a lot on the island and we see more than people think we do."

Luke hadn't thought of that. He assumed it would be like any big city. They were never able to get much cab information and when they did, it took hours sifting through fare data. "Samuel Fletcher..." Luke started to say before the cabbie cut him off with a laugh.

"We know about him. Boy, do we know about him. He's got all kinds of women on the island. Ones he pays for and ones he doesn't. That one's up to some shady business. It wouldn't surprise me if he had something to do with those girls being missing. A few of us have said that."

"Why would you say that?" Luke inched closer to the back of his seat and leaned his arm over it. "Did you see something that made you think that?" He needed to know if it was speculation about Fletcher's past or something recent he had done on the island.

"I saw him with one of the girls."

"Which one?" Luke tried to regulate his tone and not sound so frantic for information.

"Pull up some pictures and I'll tell you who it was. I'm not good with names, just faces." Luke did as the cabbie asked and kept scrolling through photos until they landed on Gia Tibbitts. "That's her. She didn't look too happy to be around him either. Fletcher said he was sharing a cab with her but he got off at the same spot."

"Where was that?"

"Sapphire Beach. I picked them both up outside of the hotel where you're staying and dropped them off at the same place." The cabbie shook his head as if recalling a memory. "They didn't seem like they were together though. She had called for the cab and then there he was. He asked if they could share and she kind of shrugged but didn't make any conversation with him. It was an odd pairing. He kept trying to talk to her and she showed no interest. That's why I remembered it. A night or two later, I heard she went missing from the Sunshine Bar.

Don't even get me started on that place."

Luke sat back amazed at the flow of information. He didn't know what to ask first. "I have questions about the Sunshine Bar, too. Let me ask more about Fletcher first. Did you ever see him again with any of the missing women or hear about him with any?"

"The one from Scotland. I don't remember her name and don't know that I'd remember her face. Another cabbie I work with said that he saw Fletcher one night at a bar across town trying to get her to leave with him. She didn't want any part of Fletcher so he left her alone and went back to the hotel. She went missing, too." The cabbie grunted. "So many beautiful young girls come here on vacation and lose their heads. They see the surf and beautiful blue water and nice hotels and forget that real people live here. Real bad people, too. People that prey on girls on vacation. I try to tell them when I get them in my cab. I'm an old man, like their fathers, they don't listen."

Luke asked a few more questions, but the cabbie didn't know much more. He said he'd ask around and get back to Luke if he heard anything. "You said you didn't like the Sunshine Bar."

"It's not the bar. It's the locals who go there. All young men trying to pick up girls for the night. It's what they call a hook-up bar. Drinking, drugs, casual sex – all the things these young girls shouldn't be getting up to, especially so far away from home."

"What about the people who run the bar? Do they do anything to keep their patrons safe?"

The cabbie laughed. "They do everything they can to keep their patrons drunk and buying more booze. That's the only goal. I don't know the owner well, but we all know the Sunshine Bar."

The cabbie pulled up in front of a ramshackle house that was desperately in need of new windows and a paint job. A thin wire fence ran around the perimeter of grass that looked like it hadn't been mowed in a while. The exterior matched that of other houses on the street. "Do you want to wait or should I call when I'm done?"

The cabbie waved him off and cut the meter. "I'll take a break now so you don't get charged for doing good work. We need more people like you instead of the idiot cops we have. Go ahead and be safe. Yell out if you need anything." The cabbie reached over to the glove box and opened it, revealing a small handgun. "To do this job, you have to be prepared."

Luke thanked him and told him that he'd hurry. The cabbie told him not to worry that he wouldn't even be thinking about another fare for thirty minutes at least. Luke exited the cab and walked up the dirt driveway to the door and knocked. He couldn't imagine a British diplomat, even a disgraced one, coming here for sex. Luke waited for several moments but as he turned to walk back down the driveway, accepting he wasn't going to get an answer today, the front door opened and a woman in her thirties stuck her head out.

"Can I help you?"

Luke turned and explained who he was. She nearly slammed the door in his face when he said he was a detective. "I'm not here to cause you any trouble. I'm looking for a woman named Charmaine."

She raised her eyebrows at him. "You're not here for sex. What's your angle?"

"Are you Charmaine?"

"Maybe."

"All I want is information." Luke pulled cash out of his pocket. "I can pay you for your time if you're willing to speak to me."

Charmaine pointed toward the cabbie. "He gonna wait for you?"

"He's on a break. He'll wait though." She stood back and let Luke come inside her home, which was a little like night and day. Charmaine must have saved all the renovations for inside because it was updated with nice furniture, a slate blue color on the walls, and nice tile flooring. She didn't offer him a seat or anything. She closed the door and stood right there in the small foyer.

"Well, get on with it," she said, "I don't have all day."

"Samuel Fletcher. He said that he was with you on the night that Laurie Presley disappeared." Luke gave her the specific date and time. "All I need to do is confirm that he was with you when he told me he was."

Charmaine roamed her eyes up and down Luke's body. "Sam was here. He spent the whole night with me. If he says he was here, he was here."

Luke had believed her right up until that last part. "Do you know he was here because he told you he was or do you remember him being here? It's a distinct difference."

"Don't question me. He was here." Charmaine stalked off down the hall and slipped into a room on the right. Luke waited right where he was standing. This was not a woman he trusted in any way. She came back with a black leather book. She flipped open to the date and jabbed her finger into it, showing Luke the page. "Right here. See his name. That means he was here."

Luke would have to take her word for it. "While I'm here, let me check a few other dates."

Before Luke could get the words out of his mouth, Charmaine flipped through her calendar showing Luke every date he was about to request. Then she snapped the book shut. "Sam told me that the police might come asking one day if he was with me on account of his past."

Luke pulled back. "When exactly did Sam have this conversation with you about the police coming to ask?"

"Today. I make a note of every client I have. He told me you were snooping around asking about those missing girls. Given his past, he said you were looking at him. He was with me every one of those nights." She dropped the book on a nearby stand. "Sam isn't a killer. He might like women too much, and like most men, has trouble hearing the word no, but he didn't do anything to those girls."

"Most men don't have trouble hearing the word no," Luke said with emphasis, wanting to drive home the point. "Are you afraid of Sam?"

"I ain't afraid of nobody, understand?"

Luke wasn't sure if he believed her. There was something twitchy in her eye and the clipped way she spoke made him uneasy. "If you say so. If you change your mind or remember that Sam wasn't here with you on every one of those nights, call and ask for me." Luke gave her the number of the hotel. "We can protect you."

Charmaine shooed him out of the house. "I don't need your protection." She slammed the door shut behind him.

The sun hit Luke square in the face as he stepped out of her house onto the porch. He raised his hand to shield his eyes and looked over at the cab. The cabbie sat watching him with a broad grin on his face and then waved him over.

As Luke slid into the backseat and slammed the door shut, the cabbie gave him a knowing look. "Did Charmaine give you a hard time?"

"You know her?" Luke regretted not asking the cabbie about her before he went into the house.

"Everybody on the island knows Charmaine. She took over her mama's business a few years ago. This house is infamous."

"Can I trust her?" Luke asked, looking back at the house.

"That's hard to say. If she likes you, she'll be straight with you. If she doesn't, you don't have a shot. She'll lie straight through her teeth as if she believes it herself."

That's what Luke was afraid of. He sighed. "It was worth a shot at least. I don't think I'm any further ahead talking to her than I was before I bothered."

The cabbie finished the last bite of his apple and then threw the core out of the window. "What did you want to know?"

Luke repeated the question he had asked her and then explained in detail her response, including knowing exactly what dates he was going to ask. "I knew immediately that she had been tipped off that I was coming. It makes me think Fletcher told her what dates he needed an alibi."

"That's what I thought as you said it." The cabbie turned around to face Luke. "I'm James, by the way. I should have told you my name earlier. I'm willing to help you out. Missing girls on the island aren't good for tourism, and what's not good for tourism, isn't good for my livelihood. I know Charmaine. She trusts me. I'll come back and try to talk to her. It can't do any harm. If she sticks to her story, she sticks to it. If she tells me something different, I'll tell you."

Luke couldn't thank him enough. He offered him cash but James refused. "I told you, finding out what happened to those girls and making sure it doesn't happen again is good for my business. I have a family to feed. You keep your money in case you need it for something else."

"I appreciate that." They chatted on the way back to the hotel. Before getting out, Luke paid him for the fare along with a generous tip. Then it occurred to him to ask one more question. "We heard about the disappearance of Amani Hanley. Do you know anything about that?"

James nodded his head slowly. "Terrible thing. You're at the right place though for answers. You want to know about Amani you ask her cousin, Vic. Those two were thick as thieves. I don't think he's ever gotten over it."

"I'll do that." Before closing the door, Luke reminded him, "You find out anything give me a call day or night." James gave him a thumbs-up before he drove off.

CHAPTER 19

The stakes were getting higher the more we learned about Dylan Carter and his cousin, Ollie. Luke and Cooper didn't want Adele and me to go to the bar alone. They went ahead of us and found a table. When they were settled and saw Dylan come into the bar, Luke texted us.

We didn't acknowledge Luke or Cooper when we arrived, but I gave Dylan a flirtatious smile and waved as we walked into the bar. We went to the back patio as we had the night before and ordered dinner. We settled in for a longer night than the last. Luke figured this would be our last shot talking to Dylan before someone told him who we were. I wasn't even convinced that he didn't already know.

Dylan let us get through our dinner before he made an appearance at our table. "You ladies are looking beautiful tonight. I'm glad to see you back here."

"Dinner was great last night, and it's a chill atmosphere, so why not?" I smiled up at him. "Are you here every night?"

"Just about. I'm friends with the bartender and it's the best spot in town. I've been coming here for a few years. I know most of the locals and it gives me a chance to make new friends with tourists who are visiting."

"Where's Ollie?" Adele asked, taking a sip of her drink.

"I'm not good enough for you? You want my cousin, too," Dylan teased and then pulled up a chair and sat down uninvited at our table. "He's home. Not feeling great tonight."

Ever present in the back of my mind was the fact that Ollie hadn't been there the night Laurie disappeared either. I glanced over at him. "What do you have planned for the night?"

"I was hoping to run into you girls. I have to run out to meet a few people a little later, but then I'll be back."

Adele wiggled her finger at him to come closer. She lowered her voice. "Do you know where we can get some weed? It's been a long time since either of us has gotten high and we figured no better time than at the beach on vacation."

We had talked about one of us asking and I was glad Adele ran with it. She was more natural undercover than I was. I smiled and nodded in agreement with her. "We thought it would be fun."

Dylan frowned. "You have to be careful who you buy from on the island. You only want the best of the best."

"That's why we are asking a local," Adele said, winking at him. "We figured you had a hookup. You seem like the kind of guy who knows everyone and everything. Who better to ask?"

Dylan puffed out his chest. "It usually takes longer for people to figure out I'm that guy. I'll tell you what. I can get it for you."

"Really?" I asked, surprised. "That would be great. Do you have anything a little more daring?"

"Like what? Ecstasy? Coke? I can pretty much get it all."

I let my mouth hang open agape. "Not anything like cocaine. That seems a bit scary. You know what's funny though, you're the second person to mention that to us."

"Who else offered you some?"

I looked over at Adele as if I couldn't remember the guy's name. "I'm good with faces, but Adele's good with names."

Adele paused just long enough to make it seem legit. "Steve? Sam?

Fletcher or something like that. He's a British guy who is staying at the same hotel as we are. He's up in the penthouse."

A broad smile spread across Dylan's face. "He got it from me. I can't believe he's trying to sell what I sold him."

"I don't think he was trying to sell it to us. He was trying to get us to do it with him."

Dylan nodded slowly. "I can see that. You're both his type."

That took me a bit by surprise. "You know him well enough to know his type?"

Dylan shrugged. "I've seen him around with women. That's what I meant."

I wanted to push the envelope a little, but I didn't want to spook him. "As Adele said, we are staying in the same hotel. We've heard rumors about him getting in trouble for his behavior with women. Do you know much about him?"

Dylan glanced away from the table and then back at us. "He has some unusual tastes. I don't discuss my clients. Bad for business."

"Sure," I said casually. "I get it. There's something that struck me as odd though. I haven't said anything to anyone and I'm not even sure that I will."

"What's that?" Dylan asked, his tone implying that he wasn't at all interested. He kept looking around and not meeting my eyes.

"When we were talking to him the other day, I noticed he was wearing a ring similar to the man in the flyer of the missing girl, Laurie Presley. Her parents are staying at our hotel, too. I guess that's where she stayed the night she went missing."

Dylan furrowed his brow. "What do you mean the same ring?"

Adele held up her finger and wiggled it. "The ring he wears has a similar crest on it like the guy who grabbed Laurie Presley on surveillance that night. You can't see his face in the video, but his hand is visible."

"I'm sure it's a coincidence. I heard Laurie disappeared from this bar." Dylan stopped looking around and zeroed in on us. "I wouldn't go around spreading that rumor. He's a powerful guy, and if I were you, I wouldn't want to make him angry."

I took a sip of my drink and remained quiet for a moment. "I don't think either of us had any intention of creating trouble. It was interesting that they were both staying at the same hotel and he has a similar ring. For all I know, maybe he was trying to help her that night."

As soon as I gave Sam an out, Dylan relaxed back in his chair. "That's true. I didn't think of it that way. I bet that's what it was. Sam is a decent guy so maybe he was helping her after she left the bar. Nobody knows where she went after she left here. I bet she went back to the hotel."

Adele let her eyes drift to me and she gave me a look. I nodded for her to go ahead. If Luke was right and this was our last chance, we might as well push a little. Adele turned to him. "You said last night that you knew Laurie. Did you see her that night?"

Dylan took a sip of his drink. "Yeah, for a little while. Then I had to leave the bar and when I came back, she was gone. I don't remember her that well though."

I knew all of that wasn't true. "What about the other women? I heard several of them disappeared from this bar, including Gia Tibbitts, the other American who is missing."

Dylan sighed like he was bored with the conversation. "I don't know, ladies. There are so many young women in and out of this bar, I could have met them. I only talk to a select few."

"The lucky ones." I forced a giggle and held up my glass in a toast.

"Exactly." Dylan locked eyes with me. "Come on, don't you want to talk about something nicer than a bunch of missing girls? I know this is what you're studying, but you got to give it a rest sometime."

"Oh, sorry," I said. "I had no idea the subject bothered you so much. Last night you acted like you were into it. I find it fascinating. I feel horrible for Laurie's parents as well as the parents of the other missing women."

Dylan's features tightened and he bounced his leg up and down. "Don't you think these girls are responsible for what happened to them?"

I drew back in surprise. "Why would that be?"

"They come down here, get drunk, flirt with random men. They go off with strangers…" He let that hang in the air and when neither of us agreed with him, he said, "I'm just saying that they engaged in risky behavior and it could lead to something bad happening, which it did."

I took a deep audible breath and let it out slowly like I was seeping steam from a tea kettle. I tried to control my temper. "I don't think the consequence to any of the things you mentioned is murder. If someone targeted them, then nothing they did or said while they were here would stop a predator."

Dylan scoffed at me. "You think it was so dramatic as someone targeted them?"

"Why not? It's someone who knows what they are doing. Look at how long they have gotten away with it." I took another sip of my drink. Adele knew I was on the edge of losing my cool. Either Dylan was involved or he simply didn't care what happened to these girls. I set my drink down. "I would think you'd care because if women are missing and St. Thomas gets a reputation as being unsafe, it would hurt your business."

Dylan said nothing as the seconds ticked by. Then he laughed and shrugged, releasing all the tension at our table. "I didn't think of it that way. Do you guys still want weed? I'm going to have to go but I'll be back."

I pursed my lips. "I'm feeling a bit tired so not tonight. Maybe tomorrow night."

"Yeah," Dylan said, standing. "That would be great. I'd like to see you guys again. Maybe next time you can come back to my place. Ollie and I live together."

I raised my eyes to him and couldn't help myself. "Didn't you tell me that young women who go off with strangers set themselves up for bad things happening? I don't think it would be smart to go to your place. We'd be happy to meet you here."

That seemed to stump him for a moment. Then he pointed at himself. "You're safe with me. If you're implying you're not, that's insulting."

"Not my intention," I assured him all the while trying not to look at Adele who seemed to be on the verge of laughter. "I was only echoing what you said about the missing girls. Poor attempt at a joke."

"I am someone you can trust." He said it with emphasis.

"I believe you." I let the words hang in the air until he saluted us and then went back into the bar. When he was gone, I leaned across the table. "Was that too much?"

Adele finally let the laughter go. "He's not the brightest. I don't know that he killed anyone. I'm not sure that's the vibe I get from him."

I wasn't ready to go that far. "I don't think he's going to admit anything to us. He got defensive about Sam Fletcher. I'm surprised he admitted he sold him cocaine. At least we know that much of Sam's story is true. I don't think Dylan will admit to seeing Laurie back at the hotel though because that places him at the scene. He doesn't even seem to want to admit to interacting with her much the night of her disappearance or any of the other women for that matter. I'm not sure what more we can do."

"I'm glad you said we aren't going back to his place." Adele looked over my shoulder. "Luke's right there. I think he might be signaling us to go."

"That's fine. I'm ready to leave. I don't know that we accomplished all that much tonight." We had to wait until our server came back and we paid the check. Then we got up and walked into the bar. Cooper and Luke were nowhere to be found. I assumed they had walked out ahead of us. I was surprised to see them standing on the corner of the road. Luke hitched his chin forward when he saw me. I wasn't sure what he meant at first.

"Over there," Adele said, gesturing across the road.

I turned my head in the direction they were all looking and there was Dylan with a young woman no older than Laurie Presley. He stood there arguing with her. She tried to walk away and he pulled her back. It was hard to tell what was happening. The young woman didn't look particularly afraid of him, more annoyed and frustrated.

She turned abruptly and started to walk off and he chased after her, grabbed her by the arm, and then said something to her. She turned around and nodded once. Whatever the fight, she didn't put up much resistance. A moment later, a cab pulled up and both of them got in, driving off in the opposite direction of our hotel. "I guess we lost them for the night."

"I've got a plan," Luke yelled over to us. "Come on, let's follow them."

CHAPTER 20

A cab pulled up to Luke. I had no idea how he could summon a cab that quickly. I hadn't even seen one on the road. Adele and I rushed over as Luke got in the front passenger seat. Cooper, Adele, and I squeezed in the back.

As we slid in, Luke turned around to us. "This is James. I met him earlier today and he's offered to help us out by being our driver for the trip. Plus, from what I learned earlier today, James knows everyone."

Luke always had something up his sleeve. I asked, "What made you think we were going to need that?"

He shrugged as a sly smile spread across his face. "Gut instinct maybe."

James looked in his rearview mirror at me and winked. "He's stealing my thunder. Luke asked me earlier today to keep my ears to the ground. He hadn't mentioned Dylan Carter but he mentioned the Sunshine Bar and the two are one and the same. After the first few girls went missing, a few people thought it might be Dylan. Luke didn't mention his name to me but I wondered. Tonight, when Dylan reserved a cab, I called Luke and asked if he wanted to follow him. When Luke said yes, I sent Dylan's fare to someone else and offered to take Luke."

I furrowed my brow. "Luke, why didn't you tell us sooner?"

"I swear I didn't know," he admitted. "James called me while you were having dinner. The plan got pulled together quickly. I couldn't interrupt you to tell you that we were going to follow him."

Cooper tapped my arm. "Did you get much from him?"

I hesitated to say anything in front of James until Luke assured me it was fine. "Not much. Even if he knows something, he's not going to talk." I went on to explain how he got weirdly defensive about Sam Fletcher. "It made me feel like there is more to the relationship than being his drug dealer. The fact that he said Adele and I were both his type made me pause. How would Dylan even know such a thing?"

James slowed at the red light right behind the cab with Dylan and the young woman. "Dylan is not a good kid. Always in trouble in school and now in trouble doing bad things. He sells drugs, started fights. He robbed a store a few years ago and his father paid off the cops to clear his record. These aren't good people – too much money and power and not enough brains."

Adele leaned forward. "What about his cousin, Ollie?"

James wiggled his finger in the air. "Don't underestimate that one. He comes across as quiet and sweet, but he's got a mean streak. He got in trouble in school for tormenting one little girl so badly that her parents pulled her out of school, moved across the island, and put her in another school. The whole family is rotten fruit."

Luke looked over at him. "Was it verbal harassment?"

"No. Ollie would corner her when no one else was around and hurt her physically. He bit her, punched her, kicked her. The final straw was when he put her in the hospital with a broken arm."

"Did the police do anything?"

"Boys play too rough was the excuse. The parents were furious, so were the teachers. Cops didn't see it that way. Of course, the payoff from the family helped smooth that over. The little girl's family was poor and had no power in the situation." James lurched the car forward. "I'm glad they changed schools. I wouldn't have been surprised if Ollie had killed her. They never figured out why he didn't like her or bullied her so badly."

I added Ollie to the suspect list. James put him in a whole new light.

We followed Dylan's cab along a winding road outside of the tourist area that was marked with thick lush vegetation. The ocean sat off to my left and it grew darker the farther we went. The cab turned off to the right and James hung back.

"The driver will let me know where he dropped him off. I assume you don't want him to know he's being followed."

"If we can help it," Luke said and then reconsidered. "I didn't like Dylan's interaction with that young woman, so I'm likely going to confront him. You're right to hang back though for now."

We waited for several minutes idling at the side of the road until the cab returned. He stopped in the middle of the road, put down his window, and leaned out. James did the same and they exchanged a message I couldn't hear. When the cab drove off, James said, "The girl didn't want to go with Dylan. They argued most of the way. It's a small house about a half-mile down this road. Should I take you there?"

"Definitely," Luke said and turned to look back at us. We all agreed.

"Okay." James didn't put the car in drive. He leaned over across the console and opened the glove box. He pulled out a handgun and handed it to Luke. "Take this with you when you go inside. You don't know what you're walking into and you shouldn't go unarmed."

Luke thanked him and my heart raced. The whole setup of confronting a potential killer in a strange area and having to trust a cabbie even if he seemed to have the best of intentions – it was a lot to take in.

Cooper sensed the tension. "Maybe Riley and Adele should wait for us in the cab."

"No," I said, raising my voice. "I'm the only one with rapport built with him and I'm going in."

Luke turned his head to me. "Are you sure, Riley? I think Cooper is right."

"We're sure," Adele said, speaking up. "It's better if we are all together."

"Go ahead," Luke told James who put the car in drive and navigated down the dark two-lane road with confidence. "You'll wait for us, right?"

"Of course. I'd never leave you here. There's not much out this way except residences."

"Is this the area where Dylan Carter lives?"

"I don't know." James pulled over to the side of the road. The lights to the houses were visible through the trees. "His parents live over near Frenchtown, west of Charlotte Amalie. It's a nicer part of the island where people with money live and dine. We aren't anywhere near there."

Luke tucked the gun into his side waistband and then got out of the cab. The three of us in the back followed. He walked ahead of us with a confidence I didn't feel. Maybe it was because he'd been a homicide detective for so long that he was used to walking into completely unknown situations with potential violence. I usually try to have a better situational analysis when doing private investigation work.

We ended up walking single file along the road, with Luke in the front and Cooper covering our back, right up the driveway of the house. I could see right into the living room. There were lights on and no window coverings. Dylan stood in the middle of the room and had his hand on the arm of the young woman. They were angled in such a way that it looked like they were arguing with someone sitting on the couch.

We walked up to the small wooden porch and no one seemed to be the wiser that we were there. All I wanted was to get the girl out of there if she didn't want to be with them. Nothing else mattered to me at that point.

Luke knocked once rattling the metal screen door. Dylan snapped his head in the direction of the door. The girl pulled loose from him and Ollie stood from the couch, assuring Dylan that he wasn't expecting anyone. Now that we were close, it was easy to see and hear what was happening inside. The whole ramshackle house seemed like it could be knocked over with a stiff breeze.

Ollie pulled the door open. He looked at Luke and then at Adele and me who he seemed to recognize. He couldn't seem to register what was happening. He looked directly at me when he spoke. "What are you doing here? Did you follow Dylan? That's not cool at all."

Feeling slightly more confident, I stepped forward. "We followed Dylan because we saw him grab a woman by the arm and get in a cab. With so many young women missing, we wanted to make sure she was safe."

Ollie didn't seem to have a response. At that point, Dylan marched over toward the door. "You need to leave," he barked. "You have no right to be here."

Luke pointed to the girl. "Let me talk to her."

"No," Dylan said, posturing for a fight. "None of you belong here. Riley, who are these guys?"

"My husband, Det. Luke Morgan, Adele's husband, and my business partner, Cooper Deagnan. We're private investigators who are looking into the cases of the missing young women."

"You played me." Dylan stepped back as if shocked anyone could play him. "I told you I don't know anything about that. You have no right to be here."

"You're right," Luke said, putting his hand on the door. "We have no right to be here, so you can call the cops if you'd like. I'm not leaving here until I speak to the young woman inside."

Ollie and Dylan shared a look and I knew that neither would call the cops. I was more concerned that they'd call Dylan's father and then it would be all over. That didn't happen though. Dylan stepped out of the way and let us enter.

Once we were all inside the small living room that had remnants of take-out and smelled of weed, Dylan pointed to the young woman who stood at the far end of the room clutching her purse and looking as if she wanted to be anywhere but there. "That's Marissa, Ollie's girlfriend. They were fighting and Ollie asked me to bring her here. She didn't want to see him and it took some convincing."

"I still don't want to be here. I have nothing to say." Marissa didn't make a move though. Her eyes flicked to Dylan, then to Ollie, and finally settled on me.

I waved her over to us and nodded my head hoping she'd understand that we were the only rescue coming for her tonight. "We can drive you home. There is a cab waiting for us."

She started to walk toward us and Ollie stepped into her path. "If you leave, I'll make you regret it."

Cooper, who had been quiet until now, stepped around Luke. "She's not going to regret anything because you're not going to lay a hand on her. I heard that was your kink, hurting women. That's not going to happen anymore." He reached his hand past Ollie, who seemed uncertain how to respond, to Marissa and she took it. He walked Marissa over to Adele and asked her to walk her to the cab.

"I swear you'll regret it if you leave," Ollie said again.

Cooper turned to him. "If I hear you did anything to hurt her, you're going to regret it. The cops may not do anything about it. Your family may protect you, but you'll have to deal with me."

It was an empty threat since we weren't going to be on the island forever. Cooper was intimidating enough that Ollie stepped back and clarified himself. "I didn't mean that I would hurt her. I meant that she'd regret it because I'm not taking her back."

Before she stepped outside with Adele, Marissa turned to him. "I don't want to get back together. I tried telling you that a thousand times." She left without saying another word or hearing Ollie's retort, which was to call her vile names.

Cooper took a step toward him but Ollie backed off. "Can you go now?"

"No," Luke said evenly. "We have a few questions for you both while we are here."

Dylan narrowed his eyes and pulled his cellphone from his pocket. "I'm calling my father."

"I wouldn't do that if I were you," Luke cautioned. "This might be your only chance to clear your names. You've been tied to a few of the missing women and this is your only chance of helping us out. If not, I'll be forced to go to the cops."

Dylan smiled. "The cops won't touch me."

Luke stood with his stance wide and looked over at him. "Maybe not the local cops. All it will take is one call and the FBI will be here investigating. There are two missing women from the states and three from other countries. This is international now. The person responsible could face criminal charges internationally."

That wasn't true, but I knew what Luke was doing. I pressed him. "All we want is the truth, Dylan. I tried talking to you earlier in a way that didn't come across so forceful. This is your last chance."

For the first time since I'd met him, Dylan's eyes got wide and beads of sweat formed at his brow line. He knew this could be serious trouble.

"Fine," he said with a tone of defeat. "Ollie and I will talk to you."

"Good choice." Luke pointed to Cooper and me. "Take Ollie to another room and speak to him while I talk to Dylan."

"You won't talk to us together?" Ollie said, looking over at Cooper with his features tightening in fear.

Luke shook his head. “No.” That’s all there was to the discussion.

I walked over to Ollie and let him lead us to a back room of the house.

CHAPTER 21

"Is Ollie going to be okay with him?" Dylan asked Luke once they were alone. "He seems..."

"Angry. Dangerous. Like he might break Ollie in two." Luke smiled over at him. "Yeah, that's possible. Most real men don't like violence against women. He's serious that if he hears that either of you bother Marissa again, he'll be trouble for you."

"He's not going to be in St. Thomas forever."

"No. That doesn't mean our reach isn't that far though." Luke sat down on the edge of a chair. "Don't even get me started on who Riley's father is. That man would sooner shoot you than have a conversation with you. Frankly, you'd be better off going to the cops right now and talking to them than dealing with Riley or Cooper. You're lucky it's me who chose to speak to you."

Dylan took a deep breath. "Okay. What do you want to know?"

Luke wasn't going to waste any time. He wanted to knock Dylan back with the first question. "Tell me about selling cocaine the night Laurie Presley went missing. You told her friends that she left the bar through the front door and you never saw her again. We both know that's not true. So, let's start there. Don't waste my time or yours. I'll know when you're telling the truth."

Dylan started to tell Luke he didn't know what he was talking about. Luke informed him he had already interviewed Samuel Fletcher whose story he believed. In truth, Luke wasn't sure if he believed Fletcher, but Dylan didn't need to know that.

Luke looked over at him. "I think you should assume I already know the true answers to every question I ask. This is your only opportunity to explain yourself. That might help us get to the truth a little quicker. So, start with leaving the Sunshine Bar before you went to sell Fletcher drugs."

Dylan sat down on the couch across from Luke. He leaned forward and clasped his hands at his knees. "Sam is a regular customer. I get him drugs and other things he wants."

"What other things?"

Dylan blinked rapidly several times. "He hires prostitutes sometimes. He's gone to strip clubs on the island. He has different needs and he pays me to find him what he needs."

"Young college-aged girls?"

Dylan shook his head. "Never that. At the bar that night, Sam texted me and asked if I had any cocaine. I told him I did and that I'd run it over to him. We always met around the side of the building away from the camera. I never went inside because people would get suspicious and Sam is a regular at that hotel. He told me he couldn't have people questioning him there. I met him outside that night."

"Back up," Luke said, slowing him down. "You were at the bar and got the text. Then what?"

Dylan looked away. "I was hanging out with Laurie and her friends and I told them I was going up to the bar to order us drinks and that I'd be back. I figured it would give me enough time to slip out and come back without them asking questions. Laurie said she'd go with me so I pretended to go to the bar with her and then I told her I had to go. That I'd be right back. She was standing there ready to order. I figured it was a good time to leave, so that's what I did."

Luke had a feeling where the story was going. "She didn't stay at the bar though, did she?"

Dylan shook his head and looked back over at Luke. "I didn't think she'd follow me but that's what she did. I made it over to the hotel and was standing there with Sam and she passed by us. I didn't think she saw us so I didn't say anything to her."

"What did you do after you sold him drugs?"

"Nothing. I walked back to the bar."

"You left Laurie there struggling at the door?"

"I didn't know she was struggling." Dylan held his hands up. "I swear to you. I sold Sam the drugs, he handed me cash, and I got out of there. From where I was standing, I couldn't see Laurie at the door. I honestly thought she went inside."

Luke locked his gaze on him. "She didn't say anything to you as she walked by?"

"No. I don't even think she noticed us." Dylan scratched at the top of his head. "She was wasted that night. Not in her right mind at all. She stumbled through the parking lot and headed for the door. I was a bit relieved that she was going back if I'm being honest with you."

Luke noticed that he said the word honest a few times, which usually meant the person was being anything but that. "Why were you happy she was going back to the hotel?"

Dylan held his arms wide and offered a slick smile. "She was all over me at the bar before she left. Laurie was a nice girl but not my type. I couldn't shake her loose. I wanted to go back to the bar and have some fun."

Luke didn't have anything to say about that. He remained quiet for a moment while he considered the other questions he needed to ask. When he was ready, he jutted his chin forward. "If you were all about being a good guy that night, why didn't you tell her friends where Laurie was when they were looking for her? You never mentioned that you saw her back at the hotel."

"You really do know everything," Dylan said with sarcasm in his voice. "All right, man. I saw Sam walk over to her before I walked away. He said she was cute and I figured he was interested, so I let him do his thing. As I said, I wasn't interested in Laurie like that so I went back to the bar. Her friends were as drunk as Laurie. I figured they'd go back to the hotel and find her. I had no idea Laurie was missing until later."

"When you realized her parents were involved and that they had gone to the police, why didn't you come forward then? Surely, you had to know it was serious. And all the initial reports said she was last seen at the bar when you knew the truth. Why not tell them?"

Finally, Dylan relented. "I was selling drugs. I'd have to admit to that to admit to seeing Laurie at the hotel. As my father told me, it's better to keep my mouth shut so that's what I did."

There was one thing that Riley had told him earlier that confused Luke now. "Laurie's friends said that you and a few of your friends helped search for Laurie that night. Is that true?"

"No. We said we'd search for Laurie to get them off our backs. After they left the bar, we went right back to drinking."

Dylan's blasé tone indicated to Luke that he had no remorse for anything. He didn't care one bit that Laurie was missing. "What about the other young women? You've been tied to others."

Dylan held his hands open wide. "I meet a lot of people. I can't say one way or the other if I met the other girls or not." He pointed at Luke, his anger seeming to grow. "I know one thing for certain. I didn't have anything to do with the disappearances and I didn't have anything to do with their murders."

Luke raised his eyebrows. "I didn't say anything about murder."

Dylan didn't seem to know where to look or what to do with his hands. He stood and shoved them in his pockets. "I saw that one girl was found on the beach. The medical examiner said she was murdered.

I assume the rest of them have been too."

Luke wasn't so quick to stand. "What about Ollie? Where was he that night?"

Dylan shrugged. "At home."

"We heard that he had gotten physical with a classmate. Is that true? Could he be involved with the disappearances without you knowing?" It was Dylan's chance to shift the blame and Luke would let him if he chose to.

Dylan refused to say anything else. He reached for the phone and Luke assumed he was calling his father. That was his cue to exit. Luke got up from the chair and went down the hall where Riley and Cooper had followed Ollie. He knocked once, opened the door, and waved them out. Ollie was seated in a chair with a smug look on his face and Riley appeared to be frustrated with the whole thing. The three of them left the house without incident and walked back to the cab.

"Let's wait until we get back to the hotel," Luke said before getting into the cab. He climbed into the front passenger seat and then turned to the back. "Where are Adele and Marissa?"

James hitched his thumb over his shoulder. "I called another cab to take them back. Adele said she'd be happy to go with Marissa and then meet you back at the hotel. They left probably ten minutes ago. Ready?"

Once everyone was in the cab, James drove them directly back to the hotel. James didn't ask how it went. Luke assumed he sensed that it hadn't gone well given the looks on their faces. Cooper and Riley didn't say much from the backseat and Luke couldn't wait to be back at the hotel.

Once they were back in Luke and Riley's room, Cooper shook his head as he sat down. "Ollie didn't tell us anything. He told us that he wasn't even there the nights of the disappearances. That he was working and then at home."

"He was able to tell you that right off the bat?" Luke asked, taking a seat. "How does he remember? I don't remember what I was doing most nights two weeks ago let alone months ago."

Riley sat on the arm of the chair and looped her arm across Luke's shoulder. "That's what I wanted to know. He didn't have a response for us. We didn't get far at all with him."

Luke filled them in about what Dylan had to say. "In the end, he admitted to being there when Laurie went back to the hotel and confirmed that Fletcher was seen talking to her. That's about it. We know he went back to the bar soon after meeting with Fletcher. That's not up for debate. And I couldn't pinpoint any details with the other missing women. The only thing that struck me as odd was at the end when he said he wasn't involved in their murders."

Cooper ran a hand down his face. "Don't we assume that they have been murdered? I don't think that's a stretch for others to assume."

"I agree that these are probably homicide cases like Daphne Powers," Luke agreed. "He got squirrely though when I asked him why he was assuming they were all dead. He brought up Daphne but not until after looking like he messed his pants. It was an odd reaction, to say the least, and made me suspicious. I can't make the timing work though to consider him a suspect."

Riley nudged his arm. "Are you telling me you believe Dylan's version of events?"

"I don't have a choice right now. He admitted to lying to Laurie's friends about not knowing where she was. He also admitted to lying to them when he got back to the bar that he and his friends would help search. As far as I'm concerned, I don't believe anything that I can't confirm. We know that the rest of his story matches Fletcher's. I don't have anything else to go on right now."

The conversation was interrupted by a knock on the door. Riley got up and went to answer it and let in Adele. They were all interested in the conversation she had with Marissa and spoke at the same time.

"Sorry," Luke said once they all quieted. "I'm anxious to hear what she had to say."

"She wouldn't tell me much," Adele said as she sat on the couch and reached for Cooper's hand. "I don't mean to disappoint you. I tried to build some rapport with her but she wasn't talking. All she wanted to do was go home."

Riley asked, "Did she say anything about Ollie being abusive?"

"Not in so many words." Adele paused as if trying to collect her thoughts. "She said that he was mean to her, cheated on her several times, and she didn't trust him. I've seen women coming out of domestically violent relationships and she had all the hallmarks. I don't want to speak for Marissa or say things she didn't say."

Cooper turned to her. "What's your gut feeling on it?"

Adele didn't even hesitate. "That she was most likely verbally abused and there's a strong potential she was physically abused. That's not what strikes me as odd though. Why was Dylan bringing her there when Ollie could have gone after her himself? If anything, I would have assumed earlier that Dylan was the leader and Ollie the follower. I'm not so sure now. They are an odd pairing."

Luke agreed with that although he hadn't had much interaction with Ollie at all. "You didn't happen to ask Marissa if she thought Ollie or Dylan was involved or capable of kidnapping and murdering young women, did you?"

Adele sat back and crossed her legs. "I didn't ask that specifically. I asked if Marissa knew where Ollie was the night of Laurie Presley's disappearance and she wouldn't answer me other than to say he wasn't with her. She asked me if I thought Dylan and Ollie could be involved."

Luke raised his eyebrows. "She asked you that?"

Adele nodded. "That was probably the most telling part of the drive back. She genuinely wondered if her ex-boyfriend and his cousin could be involved. That says to me she thinks they are capable."

As much as Luke wanted to clear someone on their suspect list, no one was giving them that opportunity. They were all making themselves look guilty.

CHAPTER 22

Luke and I got up before the sun rose the following morning. Cooper and Adele hadn't stuck around long the night before. We planned to get together after breakfast and see what more we could do. I was feeling frustrated by the lack of progress and knew Luke was feeling the same. He planned to meet with Bill and Ava around noon and had promised them an update we didn't have. We had uncovered some information but not enough to give them a definitive answer one way or the other.

After quick showers, we hit the beach and watched the sunrise together. Luke thought getting out and getting some exercise might help clear our minds. After we put in a mile, my brain finally started to feel like it was firing on all cylinders. "What are you going to tell Bill and Ava later today?"

"The truth as we know it." Luke stared down at the sand as he walked. "That's all I can tell them. I have to tell them that we know Laurie made it back to the hotel and that Samuel Fletcher was the last known person to see her. The chips are going to have to fall where they fall. I need to follow up and see if we can get the dogs in. I made the call the other day but haven't heard back yet. That was something that should have been done the first day. I don't know if the dogs will be able to pick up her scent, but it's worth attempting."

"If you don't get a chance to call, let me know and I'll follow up. If the dog picks up her scent, we might get another lead. All we know for sure is that she didn't go back into the hotel that night."

Luke grunted an okay but watched his feet sink into the sand as we walked.

I stared at the surf as the waves rolled in and then out again. I struggled to feel like I had a grasp on this case. Without access to forensic evidence, few witnesses, and no law enforcement power, there wasn't much we could do other than what we were doing. As the sun peaked above a cloud, a thought struck me. "What if instead of continuing to focus on Laurie Presley, which we seem to have tapped out of leads on right now, we focus our attention on Daphne Powers."

Luke raised his head and met my eyes. "Why?"

"She was technically the last one to go missing." I reminded him what Andy Barber had told us. "I know you said that you were okay not going to Det. Hanley right away about the fact that Daphne stayed on the island with Andy, but this gives us a whole new timeline to work with. She didn't go missing from Sunshine Bar. She went missing after leaving Andy's house. Let's try to find out who else she knew here or had been involved with that night."

Luke nodded but didn't say much and I wasn't convinced he thought it was a good idea. I persisted though. "At the very least, let me run with Daphne's case while you continue with Laurie's. I know Adele tried to speak with her family but I can try again."

Luke stopped dead in his tracks. "You want to be the one to tell Daphne's father that she faked her disappearance and remained in St. Thomas with a guy her father disapproved of only to disappear and turn up dead in the water strangled to death? That doesn't sound like anything anyone would volunteer for."

"He deserves to know the truth, Luke," I argued gently. "I don't know if her father will believe me or care. He deserves to know."

"I don't know. That case is an active homicide investigation. We might be pressing our luck getting involved in that."

I didn't think Luke was wrong but he was looking at it from a cop's perspective. "If Daphne's father gives me the go-ahead, there's nothing Det. Hanley can do. Given Det. Hanley hasn't gotten as far as we have, he might be open to giving us a shot – especially when I tell him we are working for free. You said the medical examiner wasn't impressed with Det. Hanley and gave you information. She might be happy that we are taking it on."

Luke started walking again, this time at a slower pace. "If you want to investigate Daphne's murder, then go for it. I still need to speak to Lyle Blaylock about Freya Reid and follow up with Vic about his cousin, Amani."

"Let Cooper and Adele talk to Blaylock and you talk to Vic." I looped my arm through his. "You don't have to do all the work." He didn't agree or disagree, but I was sure he was considering it. We got out to the two-mile mark and then turned around to head back to the hotel. It was peaceful that early in the morning. It was nothing but gently rolling surf and white sand beach for as far as the eye could see.

We were nearly back to the hotel when two women walking towards us passed by and then called to our backs to wait. We stopped and turned to them. Luke raised his eyes. "Morning, ladies."

The taller of the two smiled and extended her hand. "I'm Barbara and this is Helen. Are you two investigating the missing young women?"

"We are," Luke confirmed. "Do you know something about that?"

"I called the tip line last night, but I wasn't sure that the woman who answered took me seriously. Will you go through the call information at some point?"

"We will, but if you want to tell me right now, I'll do what I can."

"Good," she said, eyeing Luke up and down. If she hadn't been nearing seventy, I might have been jealous of the way she seemed to devour him with her eyes. "Helen and I live here in St. Thomas in a condo just down from the hotel where Laurie Presley was staying. I don't know anything about her, but that other one from Canada. I forget her name."

"Ruby Wallis."

"Right, right." She smiled at Luke and put a hand on his chest. "I knew you were a smart man just looking at you. Well anyway, we saw Ruby on the beach one night with that tech billionaire on the island. Lyle something or other. You see him on the news all the time. He likes those girls young, too young if you ask me."

Luke shifted his eyes to me. "Did you see them interacting?"

"A few times. They looked like they were having fun splashing around in the water. She didn't look to be in any distress, but it didn't sit right with me. She might have been in her twenties, but she looked like a little girl barely out of high school. Sick. Sick. Sick. That man is old enough to be her father."

I hadn't spoken to any locals about the cases, other than those we thought might be involved. I took this opportunity. If Barbara was focused on me, she might also take her hand off my husband's chest. "What do you think of the disappearances, Barbara? Have locals been talking about them much? I know Det. Hanley brushed them off as runaways."

She shifted her attention to me, but let her hand linger on Luke for a moment longer. He stepped back when she finally disengaged. "We all knew when the first girl was gone – Gia Tibbitts, if I recall. Her brother was here and made a big stink of it to anyone who would listen to him. It divided people that's for sure. Some people thought Det. Hanley was right that she ran away and others, like Helen and me, knew that something didn't smell right. You don't go to the bathroom in a bar and disappear. It's like aliens took her or something."

I smiled at her. "I think we can probably rule out aliens."

"Let's hope so," she said dragging out the words. "Anyway, by the second disappearance even those who once trusted Det. Hanley started to lose their patience. He was doing nothing about it other than getting on the news and running his mouth. Of course, you know why he did that?"

Luke looked at me and we both shrugged. No one had speculated why Det. Hanley had done anything. I assumed he was incompetent and had only gotten the job because his father had been in charge when he was hired. I told Barbara as much.

She clicked her tongue. "His brother-in-law is the head of the Department of Tourism. That's all this island cares about. Rightly so, maybe. It's a good part of the economy but not at the expense of young lives. I can't argue that Det. Hanley isn't incompetent, but he has a motive to be if you catch my meaning."

"Who do you think is involved in their disappearances?" Luke asked what I had been thinking.

Helen spoke up for the first time, interrupting Barbara who had started to speak. "Possibly sex trafficking. I'd also look at all the rich powerful men we have running around here. Too many of them spending time with these young women."

Barbara seconded that. "Any one of those old geezers might be a suspect. I'd start with the Lyle guy first."

Luke asked them a few more questions but they didn't have much to add. When it was time to go, Barbara smiled up at Luke. "If you'd like a homecooked meal while you're here in St. Thomas, I can give you my number. I'd be more than happy to have you stop by."

It was like I was invisible. "That's kind of you. My husband and I are well taken care of though."

Barbara pointed between the two of us, shock on her face. "You two are married?"

I looped my arm around Luke's back and pulled him into me. "Only a few months but we've been together for a while. We are here for our best friends' wedding."

"I would have never guessed this handsome man would be married to you."

As my face burned red and anger rose in my belly, Luke thanked her and scooted me away before I could say anything I might regret later. As soon as our backs were turned, I let the steam out. "What was that supposed to mean? Am I a troll? She went on and on about older men and younger women. She had to have been about seventy! I have never in all my life—"

"Been so good at not losing your temper. I'm proud of you," Luke teased, not letting me finish my sentence. He dropped a kiss on the top of my head. "I thought you were going to explode when she ran a hand down my chest."

"Why would you let her do that?" I asked, my voice full of irritation.

"Because she was an older woman and at first, I didn't think it meant much. When I realized she was flirting, she was giving us good information. If she had taken it further, I would have stopped her."

I seethed as I walked back to the hotel. The comment stung and was something I had considered more than once. Luke was an extremely attractive man who could have had his pick of women. It's not that I wasn't attractive. I had my fair share of men look my way, but my flyaway untamable auburn hair and curvy hips and backside weren't everyone's cup of tea.

By the time we were walking the path up to the hotel, Luke broke the tension in the air. He pinched my side. "You're adorable when you're angry and jealous over a woman older than my mother."

"I'm being silly." I didn't know why I got so jealous. I sat down on one of the patio chairs that overlooked the beach. "What do you think about what Helen said. Could it be sex trafficking?"

"We started there but you convinced me otherwise when Daphne's body washed up. Given we know that she stayed on the island and we haven't ruled out Andy Barber, maybe her murder isn't connected to the others and we should revisit it."

I had biased thinking when it came to sex trafficking. I knew it existed, but lately, everything on social media was about sex trafficking – made-up stories about people being approached in stores, any man that looked at a woman strangely, and a whole host of other things were all labeled as suspected sex trafficking. It was like the people suddenly woke up and realized that it was a thing and then everything that happened was blamed on sex traffickers when the reality was usually something different. It was like stranger danger when I was a kid. Sure, kids got kidnapped but they were far more often taken by someone in the family or someone close to the child.

"Before I start looking into Daphne's murder, I'll find an expert on the island who can give us the data on how prevalent sex trafficking is here and where to start looking into that angle."

Luke sat down beside me and tipped his head back. "I hate that we might leave here and not have any resolution."

"We did more than most people would, Luke." I wanted it solved but didn't take it as personally as Luke did, which I understood. "Let's make the most of the time we have left. I'm sure we'll have a break in the case."

CHAPTER 23

After meeting Riley and Luke for breakfast, Cooper and Adele set out to meet with Lyle Blaylock. At breakfast, Luke had asked them if they'd be willing to track Lyle down and see if he'd speak to them. Cooper and Adele were on board with the idea since they were the ones who had uncovered his connection at the start.

It took a little research to figure out exactly where Lyle lived on St. Thomas. They had asked Vic at the front desk, but he had no idea. Neither did any of the other hotel staff. Once Cooper got ahold of some real estate records, they were on their way. They called James and he picked them up in front of the hotel.

Lyle Blaylock lived across the island, outside of the tourist area, and his property had a private beach. They traveled up a winding road that passed Blackbeard's Castle. That was one tourist spot Cooper wanted to see before they left for home. The road climbed to a peak and then they came down on the other side. Finally, James drove them along a narrow road with swaying palm trees lined with gated mansions.

James pulled to a stop in front of a heavily tree-covered property where only the white stone peaks of the house were visible through the trees. "Here you go. Do you want me to wait or will you call me when you're done?"

Cooper waved him off. "We will call you. After we finish here, we might stick around and explore this area of the island for a bit." They had passed a restaurant with ocean views, and Cooper wouldn't mind having a romantic lunch with Adele.

He tried to hand cash to James but the man refused. "Luke paid me for the duration. We are all set." He wouldn't take the tip Cooper tried to give him either.

They waited until James drove off and then pushed the intercom button for the gate. A man's voice came over the speaker and asked them to identify themselves. Cooper explained who they were and why they were there. He didn't want to trick somebody and get inside only to be kicked out again. He didn't expect they'd get much further than the gate, so he was taken aback by the friendly response and the gate that swung open.

"That was easier than I thought it would be," Cooper said as they walked down the crushed shell driveway. The home was probably one of the most impressive Cooper had seen in a long time. It also fit his taste perfectly. All he needed was a few million dollars and he'd be all set. He knew from the real estate documents how much Lyle had paid for the seven-thousand-square-foot home with four bedrooms and four and a half baths. There was also a pool deck, private beach, and ocean views from every room in the open concept home. Reading it on paper was one thing. Witnessing it in person was entirely more impressive.

Adele hip-checked him as they walked. "Give me a few more years in private practice and this could be ours."

Cooper laughed, not minding one bit that Adele would probably make a million far sooner than he ever did. "I'm going to hold you on that. I could easily see us retiring to beach life."

"Forget retiring. We can do this before we are fifty."

Cooper did not doubt that Adele would accomplish anything she set her mind to, and if it included a house like this with her, he couldn't ask for anything more. "Babe, I'd take a straw hut with you as long as we were together." He meant that as cheesy as it sounded.

She smiled at him. "I can't live in a hut."

They walked right to the front door which had been left slightly ajar. Cooper had expected servants or a housekeeper or someone other than Lyle to come to the door. He knocked on the door, which only caused it to swing further open and Lyle was standing there in board shorts and a white tee-shirt. He was barefoot and his hair looked like it hadn't been combed in a few days.

"Come on in." He extended his hand to Cooper and then to Adele. "I'm Lyle. Good thing you caught me when you did. I was down at the beach on the paddleboard and going to head back out again soon. Can I get you something to drink?"

Cooper stood there momentarily shocked into silence. He wasn't sure what he had been expecting but this wasn't it. "I'm sorry," he said finally, stumbling over his words. "I'm surprised you'd be willing to speak to us."

"Why?" Then he laughed and showed off a row of perfectly straight white teeth that looked even more so against his tanned face. He had a ruggedly handsome quality that shone through in the magazine photos Cooper had seen of the man. "I know you're probably expecting some stuffy business suit guy or the cocky tech whiz they make me out to be in the media. It's all for show. Mostly, I hang out here and fly to Cali when it's necessary but never more than that. I much prefer the outdoors, but we all have to make a living some way."

"You've certainly done that," Adele said, sneaking a peek around him at the rest of the house.

"Would you like a tour before we talk?" They declined but Lyle insisted and walked them through the home. He even explained some of the renovations he had done himself. They finally settled on the back pool deck.

Lyle relaxed back in a chair with his legs kicked out in front of him and his arms hanging loose at his sides. All of his body language screamed that he had nothing to hide. "What can I help you with?"

Cooper took in the moment, sitting on the pool deck of a tech billionaire overlooking gorgeous blue water while gearing up to ask him about five missing young women. It was a surreal moment, to say the least. "As I said, we are looking into the disappearances of the young women that have happened over the last year. We heard that you were spending time with Freya Reid and your name came up during the investigation."

"I knew Freya," he admitted. His eyes flickered up as if recalling the memory. "She was a sweet young woman. I met her while I was out for dinner one night. She was the quiet one among her friends. I don't know anything about her disappearance though."

"When was the last time you saw her before she disappeared?"

Lyle pursed his lips. "I don't know that I can say for sure. I don't know when she disappeared. I know that the last time we saw each other, she went out on my boat with me. Her friends were getting annoyed that she was spending so much time with me, so she told me she needed to focus more on them. She said she'd call me before she went back to Scotland and maybe we could hang out before she left. I never heard from her again. It was a few days later that her friends called accusing me of all sorts of things. I kept the voicemails if you want to hear them."

Adele leaned forward slightly in her chair as if she didn't believe what she was hearing. "You kept the voicemails?"

"My lawyer advised me to." Lyle took a deep breath and then waved his hand in the air dismissively. "I meet a lot of women here – older, younger, all legal though. I know my reputation is a bit of a playboy. I'm in my early forties and like to have fun. I've never married and don't have kids. I work hard and play even harder. I met someone whose company I enjoyed and all of a sudden, her friends are calling me to accuse me of taking advantage of her, kidnapping her, and killing her. I was blown away by the accusations. I called my lawyer immediately. He told me to save the voicemails."

Adele raised her eyebrows. "Were you concerned for Freya?"

"Of course. Before her friends left me all the voicemails, I had answered the phone and when they told me she was missing, I offered to do whatever I could to help find her. They wouldn't give me any information though. They didn't tell me where they last saw her or anything I could go on. I was going to offer to meet them or go with them to the cops, but then they started accusing me of being involved and I backed off."

"You were worried about your reputation?" Cooper asked but he knew the answer.

"Yeah," he said his tone even. "I had to be. I have several companies and it's not just my reputation I have to worry about. I'm an entire brand, and if my companies suffer, my employees suffer. I know I seem carefree, but that's a lot riding on my shoulders. I knew Freya for a few days. This wasn't a relationship that was going on for months or even weeks. I distanced myself because I felt I had to."

Cooper took a moment to see things from his perspective. It made sense to Cooper why Lyle would distance himself. He hadn't come here thinking the man was guilty and maybe he was being swayed too easily. He didn't think this was the killer though. He hadn't been the one to speak to Freya's friends, it had been Adele. He turned to her. "Based on your conversations with her friends, do you have questions?"

"Did Freya say anything about anyone bothering them? Did she express any concerns to you while she was here?"

Lyle bit on his bottom lip. "It's hard to say. I didn't know her that well. She seemed to drink less than her friends. She didn't get high like the rest of them either. Freya seemed a bit more mature than the young women she was with. As I said, quieter too. I think that's what attracted me to her. She was an intelligent young woman." Lyle looked over at them. "I'll tell you a surprising fact. I never had sex with her. I wanted to. Any red-blooded man would, but that wasn't my interest in her. Once she was away from her friends, she was funny and outgoing, and smart. I enjoyed her company for a few days and that was that, no more or less."

"So, you have no idea what happened to her?" Adele asked.

"I don't. I wish I did. I hate to think that something bad has happened to her. I just don't know."

Cooper would hate it if he was wrong later, but he believed him. It wasn't just Freya that he had been seen with though. There had been Ruby Wallis too, according to the witness who spoke to Luke that morning. Cooper shifted gears. "Freya isn't the only reason we are here. It's come to our attention that you were also seen with Ruby Wallis – one of the other young women who disappeared."

Gone was Lyle's affable demeanor. He pushed himself up in his chair. "I did meet her. I'm not going to sit here and deny it. There's no point. My involvement with Ruby was much shorter than my time with Freya and much different. I met Ruby at a bar near the beach and we had a one-night stand that turned into the next day. We went to brunch together and then hung out on the beach and my boat that afternoon. That was it. I didn't see her after that day. Ruby and I didn't have much in common… besides, well you know."

"Sex." Adele was never one to mince words.

Lyle looked over at her and nodded. "I don't have an explanation for this if that's why you're here."

"*This* being your connection to two missing women spaced several months apart?" Adele looked to Cooper when she spoke. "Ruby went missing first over the summer and then Freya in February, is that correct?"

Cooper said those were the facts before turning to Lyle. "As you can see, you either have the worst luck in the world or there is something more going on here."

Lyle shrugged as if he had no other explanation. "Worst luck in the world I'm afraid."

Adele wasn't satisfied with that answer. She pushed harder. "Is there a reason you didn't come forward and speak to Ruby's family after she went missing?"

"I did," Lyle insisted. "Her father came here to speak to me just like you are today. I had been out of the country for a time and hadn't heard that Ruby was missing. When he showed up here, I let him in and told him what I knew. I offered him a place to stay while he was here in St. Thomas looking for her. He slept in one of my spare bedrooms."

Cooper was shocked. "I spoke to Ruby's father and he never mentioned your name."

"Probably because he knew I had nothing to do with his daughter's disappearance. He was staying in a rundown hotel, which was all he could afford, and then when he got my name, he moved up here with me. He ran out of time, leads, and cash. I offered to give him money to stay, but he felt like there was no point. There was nothing more for him to do."

Cooper digested what he was hearing. "Where were you the night Ruby disappeared?"

"With friends who were staying with me at the time. I gave Ruby's father their names and numbers and it checked out. I don't know what more I could do at this point. I have no idea what happened to either Ruby or Freya." Lyle stood from the chair and shoved his hands in his pockets. He looked out at the ocean and then back at Cooper and Adele. "I've been with more women than is probably sane. I wish

I could help, but I don't know anything."

Cooper stood along with Adele. "Not that we don't believe you, but do you mind if I call one of those friends and check it out for myself?"

"I'd expect nothing less from a good investigator." Lyle walked past them into the house and then went to the kitchen. He jotted a name and number down on a notepad and then ripped off the page and handed it to Cooper.

He thanked Lyle. "One last question. Did you meet or have any interaction with any of the other missing women?"

"I've been watching the news and I didn't meet them that I remember. I can't rule out that I didn't say hello or buy someone a drink. I can say with certainty that I don't remember any of the others."

With that, Cooper and Adele left Lyle Blaylock's home with only a little more information than they went in with. If anything, Cooper left feeling like they had crossed one suspect off the list.

CHAPTER 24

Before Riley left to track down a known researcher on sex trafficking at the local university, she had followed up with a dog handler who promised Luke they'd be there by eleven that morning. He moved up the meeting with Bill and Ava and explained to them he needed an article of clothing belonging to Laurie.

Ava provided him a tee-shirt from Laurie's suitcase. It was one she had worn in St. Thomas and Ava found tucked away with other laundry from the trip. Ava didn't want to meet the dog handler or be involved in the process. She thought it would be too hard to bear, which Luke understood.

Luke assured Bill he didn't need to be involved either, but he stoically said that he had to be there. At ten-fifty, the two of them walked to the front of the hotel and met with Margaret, the dog handler, and her dog, Gus.

When she was done explaining the process, Bill asked, "Do you think this many days after her disappearance that the dog will be able to pick up her scent?"

"We will do our best and if for some reason it's not working, we will discuss other options."

Luke assumed that the other option was a cadaver dog and he didn't want to go down that road with Bill and Ava right now. "As Riley might have told you, the last place Laurie was known to be was a side door to the hotel. Would you like to start there?"

"That's a great place to start." Together they all walked to the side of the building to the door Laurie was seen at on surveillance video. Margaret held out the tee-shirt so Gus could get Laurie's scent and then he went to work. He indicated that Laurie had been at the side door, which they knew. Then Gus took off toward the front of the hotel, exactly where Samuel Fletcher had said he directed Laurie. Instead of going into the hotel's front door or the scent ending, Gus went clear around to the other side of the hotel and down a narrow gangway.

Luke had never been in this area before. It was so small that only one person could walk at a time, so he and Bill followed behind Margaret and Gus single file all the way.

"I don't understand," Bill said as they were walking. Luke had no idea either so there wasn't much he could offer. Margaret assured them that Gus was hot on the trail and by his behavior, the scent was still strong.

They kept going until Gus encountered a side door. He sat down right in front of it and looked up at Margaret. She tugged at the door and opened it to reveal a small industrial-looking hallway that led to another door.

Luke, who hadn't known the door was there, was surprised that the door had opened at all. He stepped inside the hallway behind Margaret and saw a door up ahead that said staff only. "Wait here for a second," he said and then stepped around Bill and went back outside.

He needed to get his bearings. Directly across from the door was a high wooden fence with a latched door. He unlatched it and pushed it open to reveal a wide parking lot. Luke assumed that this was the trucking entrance where supplies were brought in and trash was taken out. He hadn't considered that before. The hotel was such a huge resort and the staff only areas were tucked so far away from guests that it was out of sight out of mind.

Given Gus went into the hotel instead of toward the gate and side parking lot, he latched the gate closed and went back into the hotel. Once inside, he met up with Margaret and Bill who remained standing at the staff only door. "Let's follow wherever Gus leads us."

Margaret gave Gus a command and then opened the door for him, which led to another hallway. This time the sounds of pots and pans slamming around and people barking orders at one another echoed through the hallway. The aroma of food wafted through the air.

As they passed by one door, Luke opened it and stuck his head inside. A man standing over a pot on the stove looked his way. "You're not supposed to be back here."

Luke explained who he was and what he was doing back there. "Is that door to the outside always unlocked?"

The man called someone else over to take his place and then came to Luke. He shooed him back into the hallway. "It's generally unlocked during the day, why?" He saw Margaret with the dog and grew visibly upset. "You can't have animals back here. What do you think you're doing?"

"This is a search dog following the scent of Laurie Presley, the missing young woman from the hotel," Luke told him again. "We are following her scent and she came through that side door."

"No. Impossible," the man said. "No one but staff comes through that door."

Luke ran a hand over his head and blew out a frustrated breath. "We came through that door and you said it's unlocked most of the time. Laurie appears to have come to that door the night she disappeared. Does anyone lock that door at night?"

The man shrugged. "I don't work late, but I assume they are supposed to. We all have a key though."

"Everyone who works back here has a key to that door?" Luke asked, not understanding what he meant.

The man confirmed. "Every supervisor or anyone opening or closing the kitchen has a key. The kitchen opens at four in the morning to start preparing breakfast and room service closes at ten. Most staff are gone by eleven and the door should be locked. Whether it is or not, I have no idea." The man waved Luke off with his hand. "I have things to do. Finish up and then get out of the staff area."

Luke pointed down the hall. "Where does this hallway lead?"

The man turned his head. "There is a stockroom, administrative offices, and a small staff quarter with some rooms for those who may need to spend the night." He didn't finish explaining even when Luke started to ask another question. He turned back to the kitchen door and disappeared.

Luke wasn't in the mood to press his luck. He walked back to Margaret and Bill who were waiting for him. "Let's proceed and we can circle back and ask questions if we need to."

Gus started following the trail that led down the hallway, past all the offices that the man from the kitchen had indicated, and then they followed the hall to a dead end. They had no choice but to turn left and follow the hall. They came to another door and Gus waited until Margaret opened it.

The hallway widened beyond the door, more like the hallways on the upper floors of the hotel. There were rooms on either side with doors that were shut. Luke tried one and found it locked. He tried another and it too was locked. Gus walked past five doors on both sides and then stopped on the right at the sixth. He sat and looked up at Margaret.

"Laurie was here," she said to Luke. "Gus indicates that she was here and he is never wrong."

"Why would my daughter be here?" Bill asked, seeming as confused as Luke.

"I don't know." Luke had no idea what was behind the door. The last thing he wanted was to open the door and find Laurie's body with her father standing there with them. "Bill, come with me and we can find Vic who can explain this area of the hotel to us."

Bill turned to the door, tried it even though Margaret had, and when it still didn't open, he followed Luke back out of that section of the hallway. It took Luke a moment to find his way back to the main lobby. Once there, he asked Bill to take a seat while he tracked down Vic.

At the front desk, Luke asked for him and was directed to a back office behind the desk. Luke knocked on the door. "Vic," he said, opening it without waiting to be invited in. "I need to speak to you."

Vic was sitting behind the desk staring at the computer. He raised his eyes to Luke and took in his concerned expression. "Did something happen?"

"We have the search dog here today and it followed Laurie's scent from the door she was last seen on surveillance around the front of the building to the side staff entrance. The dog then led us past the kitchen and administrative offices to another hallway that looks like it might be rooms. Help me understand what that area is."

Vic stood from his desk, concern now on his face. "That's exactly what it is. Sometimes we have staff working double shifts or split shifts and we provide them a room to stay. We've had storms too and I've stayed here instead of going home to be on site in case anything happened. I don't understand why Laurie would be back there."

"I don't understand either but the dog stopped right at a room. The door is locked and we need to get in there now."

"Of course." Vic opened a drawer and took out a key. "It's a master key. I can get in anywhere in the whole hotel. I'll let you into the room right now."

Luke backed out of Vic's office and walked to the lobby where Bill waited. "Vic is going to let us in that room. I don't know what we might find there," he cautioned. "If you'd rather stay here until we know more, I understand. I can't keep you here but I advise it."

Bill got to his feet. "No. I need to see for myself."

Luke nodded once. He would have done the same thing in Bill's shoes. "Let's go then."

With Vic leading the three of them, they walked the distance back to the hallway and to the door where Margaret stood holding the leash. Gus sat right in front of the door, turning his head between it and Margaret.

"He's determined to get in there," she said. At the sound of her voice, Gus stood and put his nose right to the door.

Vic nudged him aside and unlocked it. He pushed open the door and then stuck his hand inside the room and flicked on the light.

Luke had no idea what they'd encounter but felt confident that he hadn't been hit with the smell of death. Gus entered right behind Vic and went to the small couch that sat along one wall, then he went into the bathroom and then to the side of the bed. He sat and then laid down.

"The trail ends here," Margaret said.

They stood there all staring down at a freshly made queen size bed. Other than the scent which only the dog could smell, there was no evidence that Laurie had been in the room. Luke turned to Bill and then to Vic. "We need to clear out of here, seal off the room, and call the local cops and get a crime scene unit in here."

They did exactly as Luke asked of them. When they got back to the lobby, Vic called Det. Hanley and Luke asked Bill to wait in the conference room until after he spoke to the crime scene unit. Bill argued that he wanted to be there. It took some convincing from both Luke and Margaret that it was better to let the professionals handle it at this point. He finally relented and went to tell his wife.

When he was gone, Luke turned to Margaret. "Det. Hanley is not going to be happy to see us."

She smiled at him knowingly. "Det. Hanley is never happy to see me. I offered my services to search for each of the young women who went missing and he denied me each time. I was surprised and happy to get your call the other day. I was in St. John's for a few days or we could have done this sooner."

"Better late than never. I just hope that we finally have some answers."

"You know Det. Hanley isn't going to tell you what he finds."

Luke knew that. He also knew that he didn't need the specific crime scene evidence to know that all traces led right back to the hotel. "You said that you might have some other options if Gus hadn't picked up the scent today. I assume you meant that you also have a cadaver dog."

"I do," Margaret said and then raised her eyebrows. "I've worked with detectives long enough to know that look. You have a theory."

"I do," Luke said, a hint of sadness in his voice. He hadn't wanted the case to end like this. "I think Laurie was taken to that room and sexually assaulted and murdered. I don't have anything to back that up right now. But I've seen enough to believe that might be what we're looking at."

"I wish I could disagree with you. It's what I first thought too when I saw the bed."

They waited there until Det. Hanley arrived with a crime scene team in tow. He got one look at Luke and then at Margaret and Gus and shook his head in disgust. "You can't just mind your own business, can you."

Luke shrugged. "Someone has to be doing your job. We'll be accompanying your team to the room or I'm calling in the FBI. It's your choice."

Det. Hanley bit the side of his cheek, leaving an indent. He huffed. "Fine but stay out of the way."

CHAPTER 25

I had called Professor Adelaide Smith on the cab ride over to the University of the Virgin Islands in Charlotte Amalie. After searching the university's website, I found her name and her bio. She taught several human rights courses and indicated that she'd been at the conference on human trafficking in 2020. I figured she was the best person to speak to.

I had hoped to schedule an impromptu meeting with her but I got her voicemail. I left a detailed message with my number and told her that I was headed to campus now and hoped she'd have a few minutes to speak to me.

When she didn't return my call by the time I made it to campus, I had no choice but to try to track her down. I headed right for the administration building. I explained to the woman behind the desk my inquiry and she was nice enough to tell me Professor Smith's building and office number. She made no promise that she'd be available or willing to speak to me though.

I navigated the campus with the help of a handy campus map and made it to the College of Liberal Arts and Social Sciences Department building and then climbed the stairs to the third floor where offices were located. I passed a few professor-looking type people as I looked for room numbers. They all smiled and said hello. It seemed like a friendly enough campus.

When I arrived at her office, I was disappointed to see that the door was locked and the lights were off.

"Professor Smith should be back in about twenty minutes," a voice said from down the hall. "She's wrapping up a class right now."

I turned in the direction of the voice as a man with a stack of books under his arm locked his office door. "I appreciate that. I guess I'll wait then."

He nodded and walked off down the hall while I took a seat on the floor outside of her door. If she was coming back soon, there was no reason to leave and miss the chance to speak to her. I leaned my head against the wall and took a deep breath and let it out slowly, along with the stress that had crept into my neck and shoulders. I wanted to solve the case, if not for the victims and their families, then for Luke who had taken it so personally.

While I waited there, I considered the cases individually and as a whole. Early on we had determined that they must be connected given the timeframe they all went missing and the similar circumstances. They weren't as similar as we had initially believed though. Laurie didn't go missing from the bar. She had made it back to the hotel. Daphne hadn't gone missing at all. She went to live with Andy before taking off one night and ending up strangled and dumped in the ocean.

Two of the other women were casually involved with men on the island. While several of them did connect back to Dylan and Ollie, we had no direct evidence that they did anything to the women. As I sat there waiting for Professor Smith, I grew stronger in my conviction that we weren't looking at human trafficking but rather either a series of murders that happened coincidentally or a serial killer operating on St. Thomas.

I checked my phone as a woman called out to me from down the hall. She had a mid-western accent. "So sorry, I'm late. My class went over. I heard you were here to speak to me."

Professor Smith was tall and willowy and had a long mane of blonde hair. She looked more like a student to me than a professor. Her bio said that she was in her late forties. Had I met her before reading the bio, I might have only guessed in her mid-thirties.

I stood and introduced myself. "I left a message earlier today. I just need a few minutes of your time."

She turned to me as she unlocked the door. "Oh, you're not a student? Someone said I had a student waiting."

"I haven't seen any students." I stepped into her office with her and closed the door behind me. She dropped her bag on her desk and tucked strands of hair behind her ears. "I'm looking for some information on sex trafficking in St. Thomas. It might be connected to the cases of missing young women on the island."

Professor Smith frowned and her features grew tight. "I've been following the news. I hate to say it but until this most recent case – Laurie Presley – I had no idea young women were missing. Our news hadn't covered it." She sat down behind her desk and gestured for me to take a seat in one of the two chairs across from her.

I sat and crossed my legs, resting my hands in my lap. "Det. Hanley, who is the lead detective on the cases, decided that the young women had run away. We found that was true in one of the cases, but oddly, it was her body that washed up on the beach."

"How are you involved with this?"

I explained to her my background as well as that of Luke, Cooper, and Adele. I detailed for her our meeting with the Presleys and then being on the beach when Daphne's body was found. "We had no intention of getting involved, but once it was clear that law enforcement wasn't doing anything, Luke felt pulled into it. He struck up a conversation with a reporter from San Francisco who gave him some background information on all the cases. Once Luke is drawn into something, it's hard for him to let it go." I smiled. "To be fair, I'm the same way."

"I understand that." Professor Smith sat back in her chair and appraised me. "You said that you wanted to know about sex trafficking. I'm certainly the right person to come to, but I can already see that these cases don't have the hallmarks of that."

I'd had a feeling she was going to say that. "We had initially ruled it out, but then thought we might be better off speaking to an expert. Anything we can rule in or out at this point would be helpful. When you say these cases don't have the hallmarks, what do you mean?"

"I've been doing this a long time," Professor Smith started, her voice taking on the command of an expert in the field. "There weren't a lot of people willing to dive headfirst into this line of work. I thought it was essential. My background is in human rights and it was a natural fit. I've been to conferences and lectures around the globe. Most of the young women in developing countries who are involved in sex trafficking are runaways. Some had already been working on the street as prostitutes. They have other risk factors that make them susceptible like drug addiction or challenging family lives including other abuse."

"So, the idea of pretty young women being abducted off the street and kidnapped into sex trafficking is false?"

"Incredibly." Professor Smith relaxed as if she was glad that she didn't have to argue it. "I know that's the narrative. I'm not saying it never happens, but it's rare. The majority of children who are reported kidnapped are returned. For nearly ninety-eight percent, it's within the family – parents or other relatives. Even a good portion of the stats on those who runaway return home. Unfortunately, the cases we hear about the most, the ones blasted all over the news, are the rarest cases, which makes them seem more commonplace than they are. Social media also doesn't help with setting an accurate narrative on the facts."

She leaned on her arms. "What risk factors did these young women have? Were any involved in drugs or prostitution or runaways?"

I held up one finger. "We only know of one young woman, Daphne Powers, who definitely stayed on the island. She slipped away from her friends at some point and stayed with a man she had been talking to online for months. She came to St. Thomas to meet him without telling her friends ahead of time about her plan. I spoke to Andy Barber, the man she stayed with and he seemed genuinely conflicted by the plan that Daphne had."

Professor Smith raised her perfectly arched eyebrows. "Andy Barber, the scuba guy?"

"That's him," I said, a slight tone of worry in my voice. "We haven't made that public yet so if you don't mind not telling anyone. Her father hasn't even been notified yet."

"I won't tell anyone. I'm just surprised to hear his name connected with something like this. I've gone to a few of his scuba classes and when I have people visit, I always recommend Andy."

"I don't know that Andy is involved with anyone but Daphne. I have no reason to believe he's connected to the other missing young women."

She nodded. I hoped the subject was dropped but she leaned farther into her desk. A look of uncertainty on her face. "Do you think that Andy killed this young woman?"

I held up my hand to stop her. "We have no information to indicate that right now. We heard from Daphne's friends that she was involved with him, and that's the only reason we went to speak to him. We were shocked when we found out she had been living with him after she supposedly disappeared. I don't believe that anyone, including law enforcement, has evidence that he killed her."

Professor Smith appeared slightly less worried. "We were talking about sex trafficking. As I said, there's nothing I've read in recent reports that would indicate that's the case here."

"Has there been sex trafficking on St. Thomas?"

She frowned. "There's prostitution everywhere, so yes, there is sex trafficking. It's local women typically or from other Caribbean islands."

I believed her but wanted more information to bring back. "I'm not generally into speculating but I want to in this case. Let's say for instance that these young women were kidnapped into sex trafficking – what would be the process?"

"Well," Professor Smith said, giving it some consideration. "If they were kidnapped here on the island and people were looking for them, then they'd be moved off the island almost immediately. They'd be brought to one of the other islands. The problem is these are young women with resources. As soon as they were sent off with a client, they'd seek help. Even if they were too scared to do that, the sex traffickers would fear that's what they'd do. I assume these are somewhat savvy young women and all college-educated?"

"Yes, and some of them come from money. Does that matter?"

"Only in so much as the resources at their disposals. They have families to call and rescue them. The majority of young women caught up in sex trafficking have no other lifelines. I just can't see that's the case here." When I didn't debate back with her or have any other questions, she sat back. "Are you sure about Andy Barber?"

I cocked my head to the side. I didn't answer her question but asked one of my own. "Is there a reason you're concerned? It sounds like it's more than someone whose services you recommended."

"It is," she admitted but paused and didn't say anything more for a few moments. Finally, she pulled out her phone and showed me a photo of Andy with a woman I didn't recognize. "This is my friend. She dated Andy a while back. They still talk occasionally and I'm worried for her now."

"How long ago did they date?"

"Last year. They were only together a few months and they remained friends."

"As I said, I don't have any solid evidence that he's done anything wrong. Daphne was of legal age to do whatever she wanted to do. She certainly caused a lot of stress and concern with her friends and family but no one was even looking for her." I hadn't ruled Andy out of anything so while I was there, I might as well get more information. "Do you know why they broke up?"

Professor Smith stared down at her phone and then placed it on her desk, turning her attention back to me. "My friend said that Andy was a bit unreliable. He'd show up to dates late, he wasn't always where he said he was going to be, and he worked too much. All in all, it wasn't what she was looking for but thought he was a nice enough guy. She didn't see him as serious relationship potential."

"No red flags of abuse or anything like that?"

Professor Smith shook her head. "Not that I know of and I'm sure she would have told me. They weren't as compatible as she had hoped."

She hadn't offered up her friend's name and I didn't want to push. "How often does she speak to him?"

"I don't think often now. We see him out every once in a while for dinner and drinks." She paused. "When did Daphne go missing?"

"Around this past Christmas. Her body was found earlier this week. Are you remembering something?"

"Not really. It occurred to me that I hadn't seen Andy out much since late last fall right before the holidays. My friend had said the same. We joked one night that he must have gotten a girlfriend." Sorrow came over her face. "I feel bad now. If he loved Daphne and he didn't have anything to do with her death, he must be grieving. Have you spoken to him?"

I was almost wishing I hadn't brought up the subject. "I spoke to him briefly. He seemed to be doing okay given the situation." I stood to indicate I needed to go. "I appreciate your time today."

Professor Smith stood as well. "Please let me know if you need anything else. It's so scary to think that a psycho is running around on the island hurting young women. It's terrible what women face. We can't even go on vacation and let our guard down."

I agreed with her on all counts. When I got outside to call a cab, I saw a flurry of texts back and forth between Luke and Cooper. There had been a break in the case.

CHAPTER 26

I made it back to the hotel and was headed for the conference room where I assumed Luke would be when Vic approached and told me that they weren't there. He walked me back outside and around the side of the hotel. I had never gone down the small alleyway that ran down the other side of the hotel. I had passed the area but had never ventured in that direction. There had been no reason to.

I asked Vic questions as we walked, but he assured me that Luke would explain everything. I had no idea where we were going. Farther down the alleyway, Vic turned left and walked through a fenced-off area.

Luke stood off to the side with a woman and dog. There were also three police vehicles, one marked as a crime scene unit. "What's going on?" I asked.

Luke introduced me to Margaret. We said a brief hello and then Luke got down to business. He explained that Gus had followed Laurie's scent down the alleyway and into the hotel. He described the hotel's interior and the staff quarters. "We called Det. Hanley immediately. He came out but he didn't seem quite as excited as we were with the find."

Margaret interrupted. "That's putting it nicely. He didn't think we had stumbled onto anything at all, so I offered to go back and get one of my cadaver dogs." She looked down at the dog lying at her feet. "He picked up the scent in the room and then followed it back to this area and then to the water. He marked several spots in that room though so I'm thinking there was more than one person who had been killed there."

"I assume Det. Hanley took it seriously after that?"

Luke shook his head. "No. I had to call Captain Meadows back home and I got the number of the best FBI office to call. Before I could place the call, Det. Hanley finally relented and let the crime scene unit get to work."

I know Luke had explained what had happened, but I had a hard time understanding it in the context of the young women. "What do you think happened? Someone brought the victims into a room and killed them? Not all of the victims were staying at this hotel. What about video surveillance?"

"No cameras," Luke explained, his voice tight. "This outside door should always be locked but often isn't. The rooms are also locked. Vic explained most hotel staff who work back here in administration and the kitchen have a key. There is a log they keep of who is using the rooms and when they are cleaned. I had him check and there was no one staying in the rooms in question or any of the rooms the nights the victims went missing. Other people have stayed in the room since and they have been cleaned several times and the bedding changed. I don't know what, if any, evidence is left behind."

There probably wouldn't be much evidence at all. "Daphne was manually strangled. That doesn't leave a lot of trace evidence. Couple that with putting the body in water and the forensics on the case is seriously lacking."

While we waited, I told Luke about the meeting with Professor Smith. "It was good I met with her, but overall, I can't see that this is sex trafficking. Her friend had dated Andy Barber, so there is another open avenue if we want to explore more about him." Luke thanked me for speaking to her. I looked around the open parking lot as I stood there waiting. "What is this area?"

"It's where trucks come in with deliveries," Luke said and then pointed away from the hotel. "There's a main road that runs on the other side of the cove and parallel to the beach. Not even five minutes down the road there is a marina with boats. It would be easy enough for someone to move a body out of here, put the body in a boat, and slip into the water nearly undetected."

Margaret said, "You got lucky that Daphne washed up at all. If someone dumped a body far enough out, sea life would get to it almost immediately. At least you know you're looking for someone with access to a boat, to this hotel, and the young women. That has to narrow it down some."

Luke's eyes looked weary and tired. "It's more than we had."

I asked, "How have you kept the media at bay?"

"I haven't," Luke said, leaning against the nearby fence. "I promised them an update once we know more. Det. Hanley breezed in here and said that he was sure that we hadn't found anything. While that isn't helpful, with my promise to fill them in later, they have given us some space."

"What about the Presleys?" I hated to think that Luke had to give the death notification alone.

Luke ran a hand over his head, letting it linger on the back of his neck. It looked like it pained him to talk. His voice filled with regret, he said, "Bill was here with us when we discovered the room. He insisted on staying while the cadaver dog went to work. It hit him harder than he expected. He didn't want to talk. I offered to go with him to tell Ava, but he declined. He wants to be alone, which I understand."

I touched his arm. "This isn't your fault, you know. If Laurie is dead, she was dead long before we ever got involved. There was nothing we could have done."

"I know that rationally," he said, basically admitting that his irrational mind was running away with him, which it was prone to do in certain cases. "We need to regroup as soon as I talk to Det. Hanley. Have you heard from Cooper and Adele?"

I shook my head. "I can text him and see what they found out this morning with Lyle Blaylock." I had forgotten Margaret was next to us overhearing our whole conversation. She gasped at the man's name.

"Sorry, I didn't mean to be so unprofessional." She looked between us. "You think Lyle Blaylock might have something to do with this?"

Luke stepped toward her, dropping his voice. "He was connected with two of the victims. We don't know any more than that. I don't want to tie this to anyone until we know more." He turned around and gestured toward the hotel. "I can't imagine why Blaylock would come to this hotel and murder young women or how he'd even have access."

"That's a good point."

I turned to Margaret. "Do you know much about him?"

"Just what I've read in the newspapers. He has a reputation as a playboy. He's a bit of an enigma on the island. People know he's here and he's always seen out and about, but people don't seem to know much about him. I've heard that he's not what people expect."

"We'll know soon enough." I held up my phone. "I texted Cooper and he said he'd be back to the hotel within an hour. He didn't elaborate on his meeting."

"I need to speak to you now," Det. Hanley said from the door of the hotel, drawing all of our attention. He closed the distance between us and stared up at Luke. "I don't like my time being wasted. There's nothing in that room. It's been thoroughly cleaned."

"Of course it's been cleaned, probably several times now," Luke countered. "What do you expect this far out? You still have to have the crime scene techs go through it. Daphne died of manual strangulation which doesn't leave a lot of evidence. It's more than we had though."

"It's a waste of time."

Luke locked eyes with me and his breathing became uneven. I knew that he was struggling to keep his temper in check. "What's your plan now?" he asked through gritted teeth.

"No plan. This doesn't tell me anything." Det. Hanley dismissively gestured toward the dog. "If he's even reliable, okay maybe someone died in that room. For all I know, it could have been a staff person years ago."

Margaret tightened her hand on the leash. "Det. Hanley, as you know, I was here with my dog, Gus, who picked up Laurie's scent and brought us to the room. Then we brought in a cadaver dog and he picked up the scent of death. His response told me it was fairly recent and that there was probably more than one person deceased in that room. This isn't some staff person who died a while ago. I assure you of that."

He clicked his tongue. "If it's accurate."

"I'm internationally certified to do this work," she barked back at him. "Don't believe the evidence right in front of you if you want, but don't insult my credentials." Her tone and body language told me she wasn't someone to take a lot of guff. Even her dog sat more rigidly during the exchange.

I stepped toward Det. Hanley. "As Luke asked, we'd like to know your plan. We've been working and interviewing people. Isn't it much better to work together on this?"

He swept his hand to the side. "On what? A few girls ran away. You and the media are making a much bigger deal about this than it is. I told you the girls ran away and you even found that Daphne Powers did exactly as I said. She stayed in St. Thomas with a guy she met."

Luke expelled a loud breath, almost a groan. "And now she's dead." He looked at me and explained he had told Det. Hanley about Andy

Barber when he arrived at the hotel earlier.

"Are you going to interview him?"

Det. Hanley shifted his eyes to me. "For what? They are both grown people and can do as they please. I told you she drowned in the ocean. She ran away once. She could have done it twice."

Luke balled his hands into fists. "Are you going to call Daphne's family?"

Det. Hanley dismissed it. "No need. Daphne was an adult who could make her own decisions. Besides, as I just said, it was an accident. She drowned. That, unfortunately, happens with tourists who aren't used to being surrounded by water…"

Luke cursed loudly. "She didn't drown, you idiot. I read the medical examiner's report. It was manual strangulation before she was dumped in the ocean." Luke stepped toward Det. Hanley and for a moment, I worried he might punch him. Instead, he jabbed his finger into the detective's chest. "I'm starting to wonder who you're trying to protect. Is it Dylan and Ollie Carter? Is that who it is? You're friends with his father so you'll overlook the drug dealing, domestic abuse, and kidnapping and murder. What're a few dead tourists between friends, right?"

Det. Hanley stepped back and his hand went to the gun on his hip. He stared Luke down who seemed oblivious to the fact that the detective was ready to pull his gun. I pulled Luke back and stepped in between them.

"Go then, Det. Hanley. Let us sort it out. It's clear you have no interest in finding out the truth or allowing these families to have any justice." I stepped back, forcing Luke to step back too. He rested his hands on my shoulders. "We've got it from here."

"I want you off this island now." He pointed at Luke. "I'm not going to tell you again. You need to leave and take all this nonsense with you. Let us get back to our peaceful island living."

I didn't respond to the detective. I turned my back to him and nudged Luke back. "He is not worth it, Luke. Call the FBI if you have to, but he's not worth the hassle."

Even Margaret could sense that Luke had had enough. While I nudged his chest, she reached out and tugged his arm. Luke's dark eyes grew even darker, they burned with hatred for the man. They stared each other down before Luke simply said, "I think it is time we called in the FBI." Then he turned and stalked off across the parking lot. I let him go, knowing he needed to cool down.

Det. Hanley and his team left too. None of the crime scene techs met my eyes as they left the building and walked past me to their waiting cars. When they were gone, Margaret looked over at me. "Can you really call in the FBI?"

"Most definitely. I'm surprised they haven't been called in already. It's possible the Special Agent who has oversight of Puerto Rico and the Virgin Islands already offered support after the news reports. I assume Det. Hanley assured them they weren't needed."

"Doesn't he have a supervisor or anyone you can call?"

I sighed. "His father is the chief of police. I don't think we'll get very far."

Margaret commiserated with me. Even her dog slumped down on the ground and rested his head on his paws as if to agree that the whole thing seemed hopeless.

CHAPTER 27

After leaving Riley and Margaret standing by the side of the hotel, Luke walked off his frustration. He went straight to the beach and walked in the surf, letting the sun beat down on his bald head. In all his time in law enforcement, he didn't think he'd met a detective more incompetent than Det. Hanley, except for maybe Hanley's father, the chief of police who allowed his son to get away with such reckless and incompetent behavior.

Luke had little recourse outside of calling the FBI. If the local police force didn't request assistance and no federal crime had been committed giving them jurisdiction, the FBI would hesitate to get involved. Luke worried that even if he offered up the killer on a platter, Det. Hanley wouldn't finish the job with an arrest. The only workaround Luke could come up with was speaking to the local state attorney who'd be responsible for prosecuting the case. He didn't want to go it alone though. He'd ask Adele if she'd go with him. She spoke the same legal language and might have more pull in the situation.

With a plan to deal with Det. Hanley in place, Luke could turn his attention to the case. Even if the locals didn't think there was a connection to the hotel, Luke saw firsthand where Gus tracked Laurie's scent, and then the cadaver dog indicated the spots in that room where a dead body had been. Luke had no doubt they were finally headed in the right direction.

If not narrowing down the suspect list, the find gave Luke a direction to point his resources. It was either staff of the hotel or someone staying there or a connection to either. And there was only one person Luke wanted to speak to now.

Luke made it back to the hotel, didn't see Riley so he texted her that he was heading to speak to Vic and that he wanted to take her to a nice dinner later. He felt a surge of renewed energy for the case he hadn't had earlier. He also wanted to spend some downtime with Riley – which always made him feel better.

Luke approached the front desk and asked for Vic. The young woman indicated that he was in his office, not the one behind the desk but in the staff quarters where they had been earlier. She gave Luke the room number and he set off to find him. As he made his way through the lobby, he cut down a short hall to the conference room to see if Bill and Ava were there. He popped his head into the conference room, didn't see the Presleys, and asked the five volunteers sitting in front of telephones if they had any tips from recent calls, but they had nothing for him.

Luke set off back to the staff quarters. It was the first time he did so from inside the hotel and was surprised by how far it was from the rest of the hotel. It wasn't surprising that he hadn't thought about it sooner. The hotel did a good job of making sure that the guests never saw any of the behind-the-scenes actions. Luke assumed most resort-style hotels tried to do the same for their guests.

Luke navigated one corridor and then another until he came upon Vic's office. He knocked once, the young man yelled for him to enter, and Luke found him hunched over his laptop, looking more distressed than he'd been earlier in the day.

"You got a few minutes?" Luke asked as he entered the room.

Vic waved him in. "More than a few. Sit, please. What can I help you with?"

Luke took a seat and pulled it closer to Vic's desk. "There are a few things, but most importantly, I want to see if you're okay. I deal with homicide cases every day and I know that it's not easy. I want to see how you're doing. Don't just tell me fine either. I mean it, for real."

All the air seemed to let out of Vic at once. He sat back in his chair and shook his head. "This is too much. It was bad enough when Laurie Presley disappeared, then you found out she had come back to the hotel. Now, you find that she might have been assaulted and murdered here. The other young women, too. I feel horrible, like I should have been able to do something. I let down these families. I've let down myself."

"Stop," Luke said with conviction in his voice. "That's not a trail of thinking you want to go down. Trust me on that. There's nothing more you could have done. You're not responsible for what a sick mind might do. You've been doing everything you can to help us, to help these families. It hasn't escaped my attention that you are one of these families. I've been meaning to speak to you about your cousin, Amani. I should have done that already."

"You've had so much going on. Don't worry about that." Vic looked toward the door. "I'll be okay. I'll feel better once we catch the person. Then I'll make peace with what I'm feeling."

"Sounds like a good healthy outlook."

Vic moved his laptop to the side and rested his arms on the desk. "I'll tell you about Amani but let's focus on what you need from me first. It's a bit emotional for me to talk about Amani."

"Understood," Luke said with concern. He didn't like having to talk about his sister either, especially in the years following her murder. Every time someone asked him about it, he'd become emotional and not able to control the anger that masked the deep hurt and guilt he had felt.

"You said that there is a log for who stays in those rooms."

Vic nodded. "I've already checked and none of those rooms were taken the night of the murders."

"Right, but did you check the keycards? The killer wouldn't jot down in the log that he used the room."

Vic touched a hand to his head as if he couldn't believe he hadn't thought of that. "Forgive me. I was so focused on the normal protocol that it didn't even occur to me that of course the person sneaking into the room wouldn't alert us." He pulled his laptop back in front of him and connected with the security site that allowed him to track when keycards opened rooms. Luke rattled off dates and Vic checked the room in question for each date and found that a keycard had opened the door. All of the times matched when the victims had gone missing.

"That's only four. What about the fifth?" Vic asked, looking at Luke with confusion on his face.

"That's Daphne Powers and we don't know exactly when she went missing. I have an approximate time and then we know when her body washed up." Luke gave him the date range and Vic checked it.

Vic turned his screen around so Luke could see it. "Nothing that week after the night Laurie disappeared."

"That's okay," Luke said, thinking about the dynamics of that particular case. "Given she stayed on the island with her boyfriend and took off from his house, it's not the same as the others. It might be that there is a different killer or the killer met up with her differently than the others."

"Or Andy Barber killed her?" Vic asked, his eyebrows raised in a question.

"Yes. It's possible Andy Barber killed her. We don't know and we won't know since Det. Hanley can't be bothered to question him." Luke didn't even try to hide his frustration and disappointment. "It is what it is at this point, as they say."

Vic tapped on the screen. "Let's work with what we have then. That back door is rarely locked. It's supposed to be but staff are in and out of there so frequently that they forget to lock it."

"When is it supposed to be locked?"

"All the time, but it gets hot and stuffy down there in the kitchen even with the air conditioning so they leave it open during the day sometimes. Plus, there are shipments every day. At night, the door should be locked. It doesn't always happen."

"Is it hit or miss that it's left unlocked or something that happens frequently?" Luke hoped they could start narrowing down the potential suspect list.

Vic frowned. "I'd like to say it's hit or miss, but it happens more nights than not. In our defense, we've never had an issue. There is only a window of about four to five hours where the area is unattended between the night staff leaving and morning staff coming in."

"I know you said there are no security cameras down there, but is the area patrolled by security?"

Vic looked away and shook his head. "I admit it's a huge security gap that wasn't an issue until now."

"I'm not judging," Luke said, not wanting Vic to feel any worse than he probably already felt. "It's an easy place for there to be lax security, especially if it's been going on without any problems. I need to narrow down who had access and who knew about it. The killer is one of the two."

Vic raised his eyes to the ceiling and sucked in a breath. "Do you think the killer is someone on staff?"

"Possibly. I'm not going to know that until I start interviewing people. To do that, I need to know the ins and outs of the hotel. I need to go in like I know what I'm talking about." Luke had a feeling that Vic was holding something back from him. He locked eyes with Vic. "I know every place of employment has secrets – things only the employees know, rules that are commonly broken. Even in my police station back home, we have workarounds for things – silly things like the fact that the unit secretary sometimes steals my lunch so I bring two sandwiches or the person who is supposed to refill the copy paper never does. The evidence room is supposed to be locked at all times, but sometimes during the day when we are in and out of there, it's not locked. As I said, I'm not here to judge. I want to know the truth."

"The back door is left unlocked because sometimes our employees use those rooms to hook up with their dates," Vic admitted quietly. "Many of our staff are young and have roommates. Some are far from home, too. On occasion, people use those rooms when they are not supposed to and don't always log in. It's common knowledge it happens among the staff. When you interview the staff, you're going to need to let them know you know that and don't care about that or you won't get anywhere. They will be worried they will get in trouble."

Luke said he'd be gentle with them. "I need a list then of everyone who worked down there including the administration staff and housekeeping."

Vic pulled open a drawer and slid several pieces of paper across the desk. "I printed them out earlier. I knew you'd ask. There are names, addresses, phone numbers, and schedules for this week."

Luke took the pages and shook them in his hand. "I appreciate this." He folded them and kept them in his lap. "Tell me about Amani."

Vic took a breath and let it out slowly. "She was like a little sister to me. We grew up together and spent a good deal of time together when we were younger. Even as we got older and went to high school and college, she was always around. She had her group of friends and I had mine, but we spent time together when we could. I always assumed someone had been watching her because of how she disappeared."

Luke tried to recall the story he had heard earlier from Grady, the reporter. "She was out with her friends, right?"

"Yeah, and they all walked home together. Amani got to the road she lived on and turned down it by herself, leaving her friends to walk to their houses. She lived a few houses in on the street, but she never made it home and was never seen or heard from again."

"Was Det. Hanley investigating?"

Vic scoffed. "If you can call it that. It was like the missing women now. He said Amani must have run away or had a secret boyfriend the family didn't know anything about. She had a boyfriend at the time but he was out of town. I'm sure he wasn't involved. No," he said, shaking his head in anger, "it was someone watching her and then they struck at a moment of weakness when she was alone."

Luke tended to agree with him. "Was there ever any leads or information to go on?"

"Someone had said there was a bartender at the Sunshine Bar who had hit on her, and when Amani rebuffed him, he grew angry and called her names. He told her she'd pay for turning him down. I spoke to him though and he had an alibi. He was working that night and other people saw him there. I ruled him out quickly."

Luke never liked to lead a witness, but this was as cold as a case got. "We have been talking to several people connected with victims. I've mentioned some of those names to you – Dylan and Ollie Carter, Samuel Fletcher, and Andy Barber. Any of them know Amani?"

"Amani went to school with Dylan and Ollie. They had both been in her class since elementary school. Samuel Fletcher was here at the hotel on and off. He was still in his diplomatic role at the time. And everyone on the island knows Andy Barber. Amani had taken scuba lessons with him. Everyone did though. He runs a highly successful local business. You'd be hard-pressed to find any local who doesn't know him."

That's what Luke had been afraid of. His suspects were known to nearly everyone and therefore hard to rule in or out. "Is there anything else you can tell me about her disappearance that you think would help?"

"Not that I can think of right now. I'm left with one question for all of it. Why is Det. Hanley so dead set against stopping a killer – even one that may have killed his niece?"

If Vic, who was family to the man, couldn't figure him out, Luke didn't stand much of a chance.

CHAPTER 28

Before Cooper had a chance to make it back to the hotel, Riley asked him if he could stop by Andy Barber's scuba business and interview him again. Since Det. Hanley wasn't going to bother, someone should speak to him again. Riley didn't have any evidence that Andy was guilty of anything, but his name had come up a few times during the investigation. According to Luke, he was well-known in St. Thomas.

Riley had updated him about what Luke discovered at the hotel and how he was going to proceed. They were in the middle of interviewing some of the hotel staff right now. Cooper had offered to come back and help them, but Riley said they had it under control and wanted him to have a chat with Andy.

Adele was tired from their day out, so he told her to head back to the hotel to nap before dinner. After interviewing Lyle Blaylock, they had a lovely lunch overlooking the ocean and then visited Blackbeard's Castle. Then they stopped by a few shops. All in all, it had been a lovely day together.

After taking a quick look at a map to find Andy's business, he was surprised to find that it was right in Harbor Cove. He took a cab back to the hotel with Adele and then walked the beach until he found the small ocean-side building that housed Andy's business. The square white building had an open window and a young man sitting on a stool in front of an array of snorkeling gear. There was a cash register and a sign-in sheet. Not far from the building was a pier jutting out into the water with one empty boat slip. Cooper assumed it was for the scuba boat that Andy used during excursions.

Cooper didn't see Andy though. He walked to the counter. "Is Andy Barber around?"

The kid looked up at the clock on the wall. "He went out with the last tour of the day. He should be back in about ten minutes if you want to wait." He nudged a clipboard toward Cooper. "If you want to sign up for a tour, we have some available tomorrow."

Cooper politely declined. "Have you worked here long?"

"About a year," the kid said. "It's a good job and Andy pays well. I'm here after school and on the weekends when he's the busiest."

Cooper looked down toward the water and back at the kid. "Does Andy have anyone else that takes people on the tours or is it just him?"

"It's off-season right now, but soon he'll have a few more people working for him. It's a seasonal thing. He does a good business year-round though. I don't think I know anyone who knows the waters around St. Thomas the way Andy does."

Cooper made a mental note to tuck that away for later. He pulled out his phone and showed the kid a photo of Laurie Presley. "Do you recognize this girl?"

The kid studied the photo. "That's the missing woman, right?" When Cooper confirmed, he shook his head. "I see too many people to remember anyone. I've seen her on the news recently. Not sure if I ever saw her here. If you want to know if she took a tour, you need to ask Andy for the waivers. Everyone who gets snorkeling equipment or goes out on his boat has to sign a waiver."

"Where does Andy keep those?"

The kid hitched his thumb over his shoulder. "Andy's got a desk in the back here and a filing cabinet full of signed waivers. I think he said he has to keep each waiver for three years for legal reasons."

Cooper couldn't believe the kid was giving him so much information. He didn't want to press his luck in case he needed to come back. He thanked him and walked off down the beach. Cooper walked far enough that he could drop down in the sand and watch the pier to wait for Andy's boat to return. In the meantime, he'd soak up the last bit of sunlight for the day.

Adele texted him a few minutes later about reservations for a restaurant later that evening. She told him that Luke and Riley wanted to splurge on a nice dinner out and had invited them to come along. She assured Cooper she had looked at the menu and there was food he liked.

He smiled reading her text. He'd never had a relationship with a woman who had taken care of him like that or even cared what he liked or didn't. He texted Adele back, thanked her, and assured her that whatever they agreed on would work for him. He didn't care where they wanted to go. He was all in and up for a relaxing night. As he hit send, Andy's boat pulled into the boat slip.

A handful of people in bathing suits climbed up on the dock and walked back toward the building. Andy waved them off and remained on the boat. Cooper assumed he had cleaning up to do after his guests' departure. He pushed himself off the sand, brushed the sand from his backside, and walked the distance back.

Cooper waved to the kid and then walked out onto the short pier to the boat. When he reached it, he took a moment to look around. When he was satisfied that nothing seemed amiss, he yelled for Andy who wasn't anywhere in sight. Cooper figured he was in the small cabin that sat in the middle of the boat. "Andy, it's Cooper. We met the other day."

A moment later, Andy stepped out of the cabin and turned his head to the side to face Cooper. "I remember. Can I help you with something?"

Cooper pointed to the boat. "Mind if I step aboard?"

Andy waved him on. "I'm getting back from a tour and finishing up for the day." He squinted at him. "I got a message from Det. Hanley who said he knew about Daphne and not to worry about it. He didn't even want to speak to me."

"I heard," Cooper said. "I had a few follow-up questions from the other day. As you know, the cops still haven't figured out who killed Daphne."

"Det. Hanley said in his message that she drowned and that it was an accident."

Cooper hated that they weren't all on the same page. He leaned against the railing of the boat. "I know he's been saying that. It's not true. As we said the other day, we've seen the medical examiner's report. It was strangulation."

Andy shrugged. "If you say so. I don't understand why the cops would say something different. I'd much rather think it was an accident than someone killed her. I'm sure she was scared and I don't like to think of her that way." He bit his lower lip as he looked over at Cooper. "What else did you need to know?"

"You told us that once Daphne committed to staying in St. Thomas with you that she rarely left your house for fear of being seen. What did she do during that time?"

"She read books and watched television." Andy ran a hand over his head. "That was the issue. Daphne was bored. She had been going to school and was with her friends. She committed to something that she hadn't thought through. I told you I tried to get her to tell her family. Even if she argued with them, she'd be comfortable to resume life. She kind of shut off for a few months and it hurt her and our relationship."

Cooper pointed to the cabin and then back to shore. "If you're on this boat most days and running your business – which I hear is quite successful – how do you know that Daphne was staying in the house all day? Isn't it possible she left and you didn't know?"

His expression told Cooper this might be the first time Andy had considered that. "I guess I wouldn't know. Her behavior and complaints as the days and weeks wore on told me that she wasn't leaving. If she was going out and doing things, I don't think she'd be complaining as much."

"Fair enough." Earlier, after Riley had asked him to interview Andy, Cooper had done a little research. He knew Andy wasn't going to be happy with what he had to say. "You told us the night Daphne left she called a cab. The local cab company has no record of her taking a cab that night. There was no fare picked up at your house or anywhere on your street. I'm interested in finding out who picked her up from your house. Finding that person might be the missing piece in finding her killer."

Andy looked away. "I don't know what to tell you. I can't tell you what I don't know. As far as I knew Daphne didn't know anyone else here."

Cooper pushed himself up off the railing and stood to his full height. "What if I told you I think Daphne was seeing someone else behind your back? How would you feel about that?"

Andy's eyes shifted back and forth. "I'd say that you don't have any proof of that. Why would Daphne stay with me and go through all that trouble of disappearing to then cheat on me?"

"You said it yourself, Andy. She was bored with her life here," Cooper said evenly, making his point. "She's at home bored while you're at work. She had nothing to do. I imagine Daphne had a pretty exciting life back in London. Her family had money and she went to the best schools. She was adventurous enough to chat up some guy on the internet and then fly all the way here to meet you."

Andy watched him for a moment. "If she was cheating on me, then I never knew."

Cooper didn't have any information to confirm that Daphne had cheated on him. "Someone killed her, Andy. Either Daphne knew more people in St. Thomas and trusted someone enough to pick her up at your house or you killed her. Those look like the only two possibilities to me. We only have your word that she left your house that night. She left her clothes at your place and her phone. I don't know too many women who'd leave a relationship and leave everything behind."

Andy wasn't taking the bait. He had balled his hands into fists but the rest of his body remained relaxed. He appeared unbothered by what Cooper was saying. "The cops cleared me."

"The cops didn't investigate." Cooper took another step toward him. "The cops also keep saying Daphne drowned when we know she didn't."

Andy shrugged again. "As I've said a few times now, I don't know what I don't know." He gestured toward the cabin. "Anything else? I need to finish up for the night."

Cooper pulled his phone from his pocket and showed Andy the screen. He scrolled through photo after photo of the missing young women. "Did any of these women take a tour with you?"

Andy only glanced at the photos. "I get so many people in and out of here I don't remember. They could but they didn't stand out to me if they did."

Cooper put his phone away. "Any way you could double-check that for me? I'm sure you must keep some records."

"No. I don't run that kind of business. I might have some email addresses for my email marketing but they don't have any names attached." Cooper asked about the waivers, but Andy ignored the question and stepped back inside the cabin. Before he closed the door, he said, "Sorry I couldn't be more help."

"I'm sure you are," Cooper muttered and stepped off the boat back onto the pier. He took one last look at Andy through the glass door that went into the cabin and then walked back down the pier. He saluted the kid working and then headed back to the hotel.

Hours later he had on nice dress pants and a shirt, sans tie, gratefully. Cooper sat with Adele, Riley, and Luke at a round table near the window overlooking the ocean and nearby marina that was home to yachts none of them could afford. They had splurged on expensive wine and appetizers. By the time their dinners were placed in front of them, everyone looked at their plates like they couldn't eat another bite, but then dug in because the food looked far too delicious to not eat if freshly cooked and hot.

They spent the night chatting, getting to know more about Adele. Cooper wasn't sure why she had become the topic of conversation, but he was glad she could spend time telling Riley and Luke stories about her childhood and about her sister who had been murdered. Cooper had heard all the stories before and loved the way Adele's face lit up when she remembered her younger sister. She had tons of stories that were mostly happy.

By the time dinner was winding down and they had all passed on dessert, Cooper had been lulled into a food coma and sat at the table thinking about how much he loved his created family. That's what they all were – family. He had never had a brother but Luke certainly was close enough to him to be one. Riley was more than a business partner and wife of his best friend – she was the rock he never knew he needed in his life until she filled the role. Then Adele, his wife – she was, well, Cooper had no words for it. She was his everything.

"Are you tearing up?" Riley asked, pulling Cooper out of his train of thought.

Caught off guard, he chuckled and patted his stomach. "I was thinking about how much I want dessert but can't eat another bite." He didn't hear Riley's response because as he looked across the restaurant, he saw Andy Barber and a young woman being seated at a table. Cooper watched the intimate way Andy caressed the young woman's hand.

Cooper looked to Luke. "Do you mind escorting Adele back to the hotel? There's something I need to do right now." He reached for his wallet to give Luke money but Luke refused. Cooper pulled twenties out of his wallet anyway and put them in a neat pile on the table.

"What is it?" Adele asked, reaching for him.

"I can't tell you all. You're going to have to trust me."

"I trust you," Luke said, assuring him that they were fine if he wanted to go. "Do you want one of us to go with you?"

"No." Cooper rose from the table and headed out of the restaurant without looking back.

CHAPTER 29

I let Cooper get about twenty feet ahead of me but trailed him the whole way back from the restaurant to the beach on the other side of Harbor Cove. He cut down onto the sand and that's when I called his name.

He turned sharply to yell at me. "What are you doing, Riley? I said I need to handle something alone."

I caught up to him. "We – meaning the four of us – don't let each other go off alone in the middle of murder investigations. I saw the way you looked at Andy Barber across the restaurant. What's the plan?"

"You saw him too?"

"I don't miss much." I poked him in the side. "Come on, what are *we* doing out here?"

He leaned down closer to me. "Are you sure you want to?"

"I'm in, Cooper. Tell me what we're doing so we can get on with it. It's kind of creepy on this beach at night."

Cooper explained that Andy Barber had lied to him about his record-keeping practices. "He denied having any records, Riley. The kid who works for him told me there'd be a record of everyone who rented snorkeling equipment or went on a scuba tour. He told me that before I spoke to Andy, so I knew he was lying at the time. I didn't call him on it because I want to see those records for myself. I'm breaking into his building."

The sun had set hours ago and the only light was from bars down the beach and the moon and stars overhead. I turned toward the building, which looked like little more than a small square shack on the beach to me. "How are you breaking in?"

"Just trust me," he said and headed down the beach toward it. We walked right up to the small square building that housed Andy's business. The front, facing the pier and water, had an open window covered by a flimsy piece of plywood that Cooper explained worked on a hinge to open and close.

As he wiggled the plywood, I said, "I'm surprised more people haven't broken in. There is nothing secure about this place."

Cooper pounded his fist on one side of it and then did the same on the other and the plywood gave way, unlocking. Just as Cooper placed his hands on the counter to hoist himself over, voices echoed in the distance. He glanced back at me. "Should I wait?"

I couldn't tell where the voices were coming from because it was so dark. I squinted and looked down the beach. I could barely make out a shadow of people moving toward us. It took them getting closer before I realized it was a group of five people.

"People are coming. Give it a minute." I moved in closer to Cooper and reached for his hand to pull him close to me as if embracing. He got the idea quick enough and leaned his head down toward mine and put his hands on my hips. We both tried not to laugh at our awkward intimate embrace. I had never been this physically close to Cooper before and it felt all wrong. We were all odd angles and elbows. The look on his face told me he felt the same.

As the group walked right past us, one of them giggled and another shouted, "Get a room!"

We couldn't hold back laughter and stepped away from each other. I waved to them and we all had a good laugh. When they disappeared down the beach and were out of sight, Cooper got back to work while I remained the lookout.

He got over the counter in one swift movement and lowered the plywood as he turned on the flashlight on his phone. Once the plywood was closed, I could no longer see what he was doing. I walked around the building to see if anyone up the beach could see the light from Cooper's phone, but thankfully, it didn't penetrate through the building. If anyone passed by, if they were able to see anything in the darkness, I'd look like a lone shadow on the beach.

I walked back around to the side Cooper had entered and let the minutes tick by. "You need to move it along," I said in a hushed tone, growing impatient but not sure why. There was no one else out there with us and Andy would still be at dinner.

There were a few flashes of his camera, the drawers of a filing cabinet opening and closing, a few more flashes, and then Cooper hopped back over the counter. He messed around with the plywood, but I couldn't see what he was doing. "That will be enough to hold it. Maybe he'll think the wind knocked it open. It wasn't very secure to begin with."

"Hardly anyone is around. I'm sure no one is breaking in to steal snorkeling gear in the dark."

"There's no cash drawer or anything in there, just equipment, a desk in the back, and the filing cabinet." Cooper wiggled his phone in front of my face. "With the dates of when the girls were here and Andy's neat tracking system by month and year, I was able to find that all of the young women rented snorkeling equipment from him and two of them went out on his boat for a scuba tour."

"All of them?"

"All of them," he said with emphasis. "The hotels the victims stayed in are all right here in this area around the cove. I'm sure this was the closest place to go snorkeling or scuba diving – which is a popular thing for tourists to do. Adele and I talked about doing it before we arrived. I'm sure if we had done it as planned, we would have used Andy's business, too."

"Maybe we should."

"What do you mean?" Cooper asked as we started to walk back toward the hotel.

"You and Luke are scuba certified already, right?"

"It's been a while since I've gone, but I've renewed my certification. I'm sure Luke did the same. You think we should take a tour with Andy out on the boat?"

That's what I was thinking, but I couldn't put the pieces together to have it make sense. I explained to Cooper what I was thinking. "Daphne's body was dumped in the water here, seeming right where Andy takes his boat out. I think we can call in the morning and ask where the scuba tour goes and then you and Luke can rent a boat and the equipment with someone else and go take a look at what's out there. If you go with Andy, it might be too obvious what you're doing."

Cooper scrunched up his nose like he wasn't sure it was a good plan at all. "Just because Daphne was found here doesn't mean all the young women were dumped in the ocean. Not to be morbid but if they were, marine life would have gotten to them by now and there'd be nothing left."

"Laurie Presley was recent." I knew what Cooper was saying and I didn't disagree with him. We were running out of options and we'd have to be heading home soon. "It's worth a try. Worse comes to worst, you and Luke have some fun scuba diving. Adele and I can rent some snorkeling gear from Andy and see if we can chat with him some more."

"I don't know if I want you both talking to him alone."

I stopped and put my hands on my hips. "So, you do suspect him?"

Cooper turned back to me. "I don't *not* suspect him. I don't know what I suspect him of though. He might not have wanted to implicate himself further in this mess so he lied about his record-keeping. He was already tied to Daphne and he might have not wanted me to go through his files digging around for evidence. I'm not law enforcement. He's been cleared by Det. Hanley. He doesn't have to play ball with us. He might not be hiding anything at all. But we also don't know who is involved, so I don't think you both need to put yourself in harm's way unnecessarily."

"Oh, us little women might put ourselves in danger, whatever will we do," I said, mimicking a terrible southern drawl and adding a curtsy for effect. "Give it a rest. We are renting snorkeling equipment not going out on his boat alone with him. If we were home, you wouldn't second guess this. Besides, we were at dinner with Dylan and followed him back to Ollie's place. Don't do that thing to Adele that Luke did after we got married and suddenly get all protective and not want her to do her job. She's a criminal defense attorney. She's going to be working with hardened criminals every day."

Cooper chuckled and ran his hand down his face, scratching his scruff. "I am doing that, aren't I? To be fair, Luke wanted you to stop investigating before you got married. I'll run it by Luke when we get back." He started to head back up the beach, but I wasn't ready to go yet.

I sat down in the sand and called him back over to sit with me. "They aren't going to want to leave if we don't find anything." I finally expressed my biggest concern aloud.

"I know," Cooper said, sitting down next to me. He stretched his legs in front of himself and leaned back on his hands in the sand. "I've been worried about the same thing. Adele wouldn't be happy that I'm telling you this, but she had a nightmare last night about her sister. She saw her drowning and as she tried to reach for her, she slipped out into the water and kept floating away from her. As Adele went into the water, her sister slipped under and she wasn't able to save her. She woke up screaming and flailing her hands around. Does Luke ever have nightmares like that?"

"He hasn't for a long time, not since he solved the case and his sister's killer went to prison." I tried to remember the last time he had woken up from a nightmare and it had been a long time. I wanted to remind him that Adele didn't need to help with the case. I knew that was as likely as telling Luke he didn't have to. "We need to keep reminding ourselves that this is more personal for them. It's going to be hard to get them to go home if it's not solved. I don't see either of them walking away from the case that easily."

Cooper turned to me. "What do we do then?"

"The easy answer is we solve the case in the time we have left. If not, then we need to remind them that this isn't their fight. They did the hard part already – they solved their sisters' murders. Someone else will have to take up where we left off. Sometimes justice isn't that easy to find in cases like this."

"No real answer then." Cooper looked up at the sky.

"No real answer," I said, softly echoing his words. We sat there for a while talking about the cases and what more we could be doing – which wasn't much. After about thirty minutes, Cooper stood and reached for my hand, pulling me up with him.

"I wanted to go back with definitive proof of something," he said as he brushed the sand from his pants. I thought we'd start walking back to the hotel but we stood there talking more.

"We are," I reminded him. "You found that Andy Barber had a connection with all of the victims. You have proof on your phone. Even tiny steps are a step forward." I gestured up the beach toward the hotel. "He has a boat. He could have easily gotten the victims out of the hotel and onto his boat and dumped their bodies."

"How would he have access to the hotel?"

"I don't know." I hadn't considered that. I was merely throwing out ideas that came to me at the moment. "You know what we need?"

"Beer?" Cooper asked, smiling down at me.

"Besides beer," I said and he shrugged. "We need to go over all the evidence we have collected and consider who has the most access based on what we can confirm."

"Did you and Luke find out much when you interviewed the hotel staff?"

We didn't talk about the case at dinner, so we hadn't updated Cooper or Adele about what we found, which wasn't much. "Nothing promising. Most everyone has an alibi for the nights in question. Some of the staff didn't even work there for all of the disappearances. No one saw anyone going into that room or had any evidence that pointed in any direction. It's been confirmed that the door is frequently unlocked. We also heard a few employees say that sometimes the doors to the rooms aren't closed all the way either."

"That means someone from the street could walk in through that door and use a room and no one would be the wiser." Cooper shook his head in disbelief.

"Technically that's true. But it would have to be someone with prior knowledge. No one about to assault a woman is randomly going to be trying doors. This killer is organized and has a plan ahead of time. He has to or he would have been caught by now."

"You don't think it's any of the staff?"

I shook my head. "Not anyone that I interviewed. Luke asked me a weird question before we met up with you for dinner. He asked if I thought it could be Vic."

Cooper pulled back in surprise. "The guy he's been relying on for help this whole time?"

"The very one. Luke reminded me killers will often insert themselves into investigations to be helpful. He said that Vic has the most access to the rooms and the ocean is right outside. Vic grew up in St. Thomas so Luke was sure he'd have access to a boat too. He also reminded me that killers can sometimes kill someone they know before branching out to strangers."

"Vic's cousin is still missing," Cooper said quietly, more to remind himself.

"Right." I couldn't see it though and told Cooper that. "Vic doesn't vibe me as someone hostile toward women, and he's done everything he can to help not just us but Laurie's parents. He's pulled records for Luke and gone out of his way. I can't see it."

Cooper couldn't either, but I didn't want to clear him from my list that easily.

CHAPTER 30

The next morning at ten, Luke and Adele made their way over to the state attorney's office. Luke had called that morning and asked for a meeting. They wouldn't be meeting with the elected state attorney but rather Dale Bishop, one of the assistant state attorneys responsible for prosecuting serious cases like homicide. That was exactly who Luke had hoped to be speaking with. He didn't want to deal with the bureaucracy of the cases. He wanted someone who'd get down in the weeds with him and help sort out the best plan of action.

Luke had also asked Dr. Gloria Wheatly, the medical examiner, to call the office ahead of time to let Dale know her thoughts on the Daphne Powers homicide and Det. Hanley's inaction to date. Luke hoped it might grease the wheels a little before he and Adele arrived.

The three-story building had a wall of windows at the front and a large sign indicating that it was the state attorney's office as well as the local criminal and family court. The building housed all three, which wasn't uncommon in some jurisdictions. Luke and Adele entered the building and were greeted at the front desk. They followed the check-in procedures including walking through a metal detector.

Once they were admitted, they took the stairs to the second floor and were met by Dale Bishop in the hallway. The tall dark-complected man with a firm handshake introduced himself to them and then guided them to his office. He sat at a table and gestured toward the chairs.

"I appreciate you meeting with us," Luke said as he sat. He explained his background and then looked to Adele so she could do the same. When she was done, he added, "We don't normally get involved in criminal matters outside of our jurisdiction. We are staying at the same hotel as the Presleys, who are quite distraught about their daughter. Then we were on the beach when Daphne Powers's body washed ashore. The case kind of fell in our laps so to speak."

"I saw you on the news and read about it in the newspaper." Dale gestured toward his laptop on his desk. "It's made international news. I can't say I love how the media is talking about St. Thomas, but given the circumstances, I can't complain about the media attention. How can I be of help?" Dale sat back and crossed his legs. He seemed eager to hear what they had to say, which Luke took as a good sign.

"We've not had much luck with Det. Hanley, which is the only reason we've become so involved," Luke said, looking to Adele to see if she wanted to add anything.

Adele smiled and folded her hands on the table. "What Luke is trying to say so nicely is that Det. Hanley should be removed from the case and a new detective assigned. To say that he's been derelict in his duties would be an understatement."

Dale sat stone-faced and gave nothing away. "Have you spoken to the chief?"

"His father?" Luke asked, locking his gaze with Dale who nodded his head once. "We have not connected with the chief of police because we figured it would be a waste of time. Is he going to reprimand his son? There is already enough evidence for him to do that if he was willing."

"How so?"

Luke kept eye contact with the attorney and didn't waver. "As I'm sure you know, Det. Hanley stated to the media that Daphne Powers fell into the ocean and drowned. Dr. Wheatly's report indicates that it was not an accident at all but rather Daphne was manually strangled and then her body dumped into the ocean. She told that to Det. Hanley and he is still insisting that it was accidental. Even going so far as to clear the man who Daphne was staying with and the last person to see her alive without even so much as an interview or a search warrant at the man's home."

Dale sat a little straighter. "I don't understand what you're saying. Daphne was staying here in St. Thomas with someone? She didn't go missing?"

Luke explained the case from start to finish including everything that Riley and Cooper had initially discovered and then Cooper's discovery the night before connecting Andy to all of the victims.

Luke tried to keep his tone even and calm. "I know that Andy's business is important to this community. He's well-liked. I'm certainly not saying that he killed Daphne or had anything to do with the other disappearances, but we don't know what we don't know. The situation warranted much more investigation. Det. Hanley is simply not doing his job. That situation, unfortunately, played right into his narrative that these young women ran away with men. Yes, that happened in this instance, but Daphne still ended up deceased and not by drowning. Someone killed her."

Dale started to ask another question, but Adele politely interrupted him. She pointed to Luke. "Without Luke's involvement with this case, we would all still be thinking that the last place Laurie Presley was seen alive was the Sunshine Bar. It was Luke who found the video showing her being approached by Samuel Fletcher at the side door." Adele explained the use of the search and cadaver dogs and how Det. Hanley dismissed the whole thing.

Dale adjusted in his seat again, this time uncertainty on his face.

"You think Samuel Fletcher, the British diplomat, is somehow involved in this?"

"Again, we don't know what we don't know," Luke said, frustration edging into his voice. The last thing he wanted to appear was irrational or too speculative. "I'm sure you saw on the news that Laurie was approached by a man that night at the side door to the hotel."

"I saw that, yes. I didn't hear any follow-up report that the man had been identified as Samuel Fletcher. That brings a different dynamic to this case – a political one and we must be careful."

"That's exactly why I've not released his name to the media yet." Luke leaned into the table and tried to convey the seriousness as best he could. "Dale, in a few days, we uncovered that Fletcher is buying drugs from a local drug dealer, Dylan Carter, who was also seen with a few of the victims. Fletcher tells me that he was with a local prostitute during the nights of the disappearances. I spoke to her and believe she's lying. I think she's covering for him."

Dale pushed himself from the chair and began pacing the room. "Drugs. Prostitution. All of this going on under our noses and no one is the wiser. One young woman is dead and others still missing. What is happening here in St. Thomas?"

"That's why we're here."

"It's nice of you to help, but it doesn't make sense to me why you would." Dale stared down at the both of them expecting an answer.

Luke hadn't planned to go into his personal story about his sister's murder, but he felt it necessary to give the state attorney some background as to why he felt so compelled to right some wrongs. Luke started with Lily's disappearance in college and then brought the man to the present day with the investigation, including connecting with Adele on her sister's case and the resolution to it all.

Luke turned his body so he was facing Dale. "I can tell you from my experience, there is nothing like the feeling of bringing a family some answers and allowing them to have some justice. It will never bring back the person they lost, and it won't ever ease the pain of grief, but it does bring some solace to the situation. My mother is finally able to sleep at night. I'm not walking around with guilt weighing me down. All I'm trying to do is help these families – even if it means sacrificing one vacation."

Dale had stood there stone-faced while Luke told him his story. "I don't know what to say. I had assumed you were…" He didn't finish his thought.

Adele didn't let the uncomfortable silence sit. "These young women are close in age to our sisters. It was my wedding and honeymoon. I can assure you that if the local cops were doing their job, the only thing I'd be focused on is the sun, beach, and drinking fruity drinks. The last thing I wanted to do this week was work. Someone has to care about these young women. Their families are hurting and need answers."

Dale ran a hand down his face and expelled a breath. "I appreciate you bringing this to my attention."

"That's only part of the story," Luke said. "Let me tell you the rest and get you completely up to speed." Over the next twenty minutes, Luke laid out all of the information they had uncovered about each of the victims and their disappearances and the connections across the cases. When he was done, he said, "We've made significant progress within a few days. We are going home soon, and if this isn't solved, then someone needs to carry on our work and it's not going to be Det. Hanley. In addition, even if we find out who killed Daphne or uncover a suspect in the disappearances, what are we supposed to do? We have dropped evidence in Det. Hanley's lap and he's done nothing. I have no arrest power in St. Thomas. We are here meeting with you today because we need an ally with the power to do something."

Dale nodded. "I wish you had come to me sooner. I'm willing to do whatever I can to help." He sat back down at the table. "What do you think is the best course of action?"

"Det. Hanley needs to be held accountable," Luke said with conviction in his voice. "His incompetence can't continue, but I don't think this is the time. I suggest we make more headway in the case and when we leave, we hand everything over to your office. At that point, you can determine how to handle Det. Hanley."

"I agree with that. I'd rather not get into it with the chief right now, not while the case is still pending."

"How much power over the cases do you have?" Adele asked.

"The elected state attorney has a great deal of sway with the chief. I don't want to expend that political capital unless we need it." He considered the options, asking Luke a few questions and then thinking through his answers. After a moment he said, "If the case remains unsolved when it's time for you to go, yes, hand over everything you have and I can give it to one of our in-house investigators. From there, I'll take it to my chain of command. For now, keep doing what you're doing."

Luke wasn't sure how that would be helpful to them. "I have no power to arrest anyone here. I don't have a gun with me or even handcuffs. What am I supposed to do if I find the killer?"

Dale nodded and stood. He paused at his chair for a moment and then marched across his office to his desk. Dale opened and closed one drawer and then pulled out another. He remained hunched over going through the contents and then stood upright, dangling a metal pair of handcuffs off one finger. "You can take these with you."

Luke assumed zip ties would have worked just as well, but if Dale wanted him to have official handcuffs that would work. "Should I bring the perp into the police station?"

"Call me first and I'll meet you there. In the meantime, I'll run our meeting by my boss and keep him apprised of everything. I assume, like me, he'll be horrified by what he hears." Dale walked over to the table and handed Luke the cuffs. "This is a rather unusual situation and not something I've ever experienced before. Given the Presley family has asked for your help and you're all highly qualified to do this work, no one in this office will stop you. I can't keep Det. Hanley off your back if he feels like you're stepping on his toes. You'll have to deal with that on your own, so watch your interactions with him."

This didn't surprise Luke, so he wasn't upset by the news. "I can deal with Det. Hanley. He's already threatened to run me out of St. Thomas and arrest me. After this last time, I believe he's figured out he's not going to stop me."

As the meeting wrapped up and they stood to leave, Adele asked one final question as Dale shook her hand. "We know that Amani Hanley has been missing for some time now. She is Det. Hanley's niece. Do you know much about that case?"

Dale tightened his grip and locked eyes with her. "That case has been a thorn in my side since it happened. Our office was involved because it was a high-profile case at the time. The granddaughter of the chief of police goes missing. That's a big thing."

Luke admonished himself for not making the connection sooner. "I hadn't thought of that," he admitted. "I was thinking in terms of Amani being Det. Hanley's niece. I hadn't even considered that she was the granddaughter of the chief. I heard that Det. Hanley insisted that she ran away. Is that true?"

"That is true and why this office got involved. There was some tension between the chief and his son over the direction of the case. To this day, Det. Hanley insists that Amani ran away with her boyfriend but he said he never saw her again. There is nearly no evidence in the case, which has compounded the frustration."

Adele asked, "Who was her boyfriend?"

"Dylan Carter, who you've mentioned in connection to these cases."

Luke shook his head. “I spoke to her cousin, Vic. He said he had spoken to the boyfriend and he was away at the time. He never said it was Dylan.”

Dale ran a hand down his face. “Amani was seeing two people. The family didn’t know about Dylan and it hasn’t been widely released. It wouldn’t surprise me if Vic didn’t know. Dylan’s well-connected father provided him an alibi and refused an interview with his son. Our hands were tied at that point and we couldn’t make his name public.”

Luke should have been shocked but he wasn’t. “I’ve not removed him from my suspect list.”

“Nor should you,” Dale said. “He’s well-protected and I have no idea how you’d ever prove it if he was involved.”

That’s exactly what Luke had been afraid of and what he was considering facing head-on.

CHAPTER 31

Mark Twain once said that if the first thing you do in the morning is eat the frog, you can go through the rest of the day knowing the worst is behind you. I try to live by that philosophy on productivity. I tackle the worst task first and get it out of the way. It's why I exercise first thing in the morning. If I don't, I can spend all day talking myself out of it.

That's why right after Luke left with Adele, I called Daphne Powers' father. I barely got out an introduction when he asked to video chat with me. I readily agreed because there was nothing better than interviewing someone face-to-face even over video chat.

Daphne's father, Edward Powers, was not what I had expected. I had pictured an older, gray-haired, stern man who might be dismissive and uncaring that his daughter had been alive and well during a time he might have assumed her deceased.

The man on the screen of my laptop was, at least in looks, directly opposite the image in my head. Edward was in his late forties, had a full head of dark hair, an easy smile, and was quite handsome with a strong jaw and bright blue eyes. Even while wearing a business suit, it was clear that he kept himself in shape. He also seemed genuinely eager to hear what I had to say about his daughter.

I delivered the news as gently as I could and waited while Edward choked up at the news. I went on to explain that we had been on the beach when her body washed ashore and that it had been one of the factors that led us to become involved.

I explained, "We received information from Daphne's friends that she had been involved with Andy Barber for some time, and it was when we went to his house that I discovered some items that belonged to a woman. When we confronted him, Andy admitted that she had been living there. He told us that Daphne planned her disappearance."

Edward sat back in his chair and stared off to the left. When he turned back to me, he asked only one question. "Was she happy there?"

It wasn't a question I had assumed he or any father in the same situation might ask. I didn't feel comfortable answering it because I didn't know. "I can't speak for your daughter, Edward. All I can tell you is what Andy told me and you can take that for what it's worth. He said that she wanted to stay with him, but that the act of faking her disappearance and all the limitations that brought made it challenging for her. They argued a lot. Andy said that he asked her to call you or the cops and explain what she had done. That way they could be together properly. Andy said that Daphne refused and that you'd never accept their relationship. Is that true?"

Edward's eyes shifted away from the screen and then back. He slowly nodded his head. "My daughter didn't seem to know what she wanted in life and that was okay. She was young and there was time for her to figure it out. Daphne was impulsive and didn't make the best decisions."

"Did you know about Andy?"

"I didn't know his name before she left, but I suspected she knew someone there. That was one of the reasons I didn't want her to go on this trip. I had come to learn about her online 'relationship' with someone and I was worried for her. She seemed to be far too attached to a stranger she had never met in person." Edward took a sip of water. "When I tried to speak to her about it, she shut me down."

"I can understand your concern. I don't know that I would have let my daughter even go on the trip."

"I couldn't stop her. I tried. We argued about it non-stop in the weeks leading up to it, but Daphne was an adult and had to make her own decisions."

I checked the notes next to my desk for questions that I had wanted to ask. I refocused my attention on Edward. "Did you have any contact with Daphne when she was in St. Thomas?"

"We had one short phone call two days before she went missing." Edward turned his attention to something next to him and then tapped down on his desk. "I wrote it down when I learned she had disappeared. We spoke for eight minutes. I tried to get the name of the person she knew there and she insisted there was no one. Later, when her friends came back without her, I got his name. That's when I learned about his temper."

I wanted to know everything he knew about Andy Barber. "If you don't mind me asking, what had you found out about him?"

Edward held up several pieces of paper that I couldn't read because they were too far away. "Andy had several assault charges on his record – five to be exact. Only one was in St. Thomas. There were others in Aruba and St. Croix. In one case, he had seriously injured a man. He seemed to have a hot temper and I wouldn't want someone like that with my daughter – let alone across the globe from where I could protect her."

We had heard that Andy had a temper. It wasn't something I had witnessed firsthand though. Cooper had said that he seemed like he might snap and was trying hard to keep it under control while he had spoken to him. "Did you call the police about your concerns when Daphne was missing?"

"Of course. We were told they had cleared Andy. I'm guessing now that they never even checked with him. I should have come there myself. I trusted the police."

"Will you be here in St. Thomas soon?"

Edward shook his head "I wanted to come and get Daphne's belongings and be there to transport her body back home for burial. It was too much for me and my brother said he'd go in my place." He took a breath and then cautiously asked, "Det. Hanley insisted that Daphne must have been drinking and fell into the ocean one night. I heard from the medical examiner that Daphne was strangled and that her death is considered a homicide. I don't mean to seem cold, but dead is dead to me. If my daughter was murdered, who was responsible? Andy?"

"That's what we are trying to figure out now." I glanced at my notes again and skimmed through the questions, most of them Edward had answered. There was one last question that I felt was a long shot. "Do you know of anyone in Daphne's life that might have known she stayed here and faked her disappearance? None of the women on the trip with her offered any information about the fact. Right now, all we can go on is Andy's word and he has every reason to lie if he was involved with her death."

"Kendra," Edward said, not even hesitating. "If anyone knew what Daphne was up to it was her best friend, Kendra. She didn't go on the trip to St. Thomas because she graduated college last year and is already working as a nurse. She wasn't able to get the time off to go to St. Thomas, so I imagine that's not a name you've had until now."

Edward provided her phone number and her screen name, encouraging me to try to connect with her via video chat because she was on frequently. He said that Kendra had been chatting with them frequently as they all worked through their grief. I promised I'd try as soon as we hung up. He told me that he'd text her and provide my screen name so she wouldn't be caught off guard. All in all, the conversation with Edward didn't go as poorly as I had anticipated and

I walked away with another source of information.

About twenty minutes later, after going through some logistical challenges to get us both online at the same time, I was sitting face-to-face with Kendra. She had short blond hair cut to a blunt bob and a pair of dangling purple earrings. I got a sense of calm and warmth from her and liked her immediately.

"I hope you don't mind speaking to me on such short notice." I gave her some background about how we were involved and she seemed to understand and had no questions about it. I repositioned myself on the desk chair and crossed my legs under it. "I'm going to get straight to the point. We know that Daphne remained in St. Thomas with Andy and didn't disappear when she first seemed to go missing. I just need to know if you knew that or had any contact with her while she was in St. Thomas."

Kendra deflated in her chair and a tear ran down her cheek. "I feel like a horrible person. I knew at the end that Daphne was in St. Thomas. We had spoken the day she went missing for real. She said she was leaving and couldn't stand being around Andy for another second. She seemed a bit afraid of him, too. She also thought he was cheating on her."

Her words came out in such a rush that it was hard for me to understand what she was saying. "Let's slow down and take it a step at a time. I assume Daphne called you at some point."

Kendra nodded. "She called me the morning she went missing – morning her time, mid-afternoon for me. I was shocked and immediately wanted to call her parents, but she said no, that she was on her way back to London and she'd explain everything then. She wasn't sure what she was going to tell them but assumed her family would be so happy to see her that it might negate any anger they felt."

"Did she already have a ticket for a flight home?"

"I didn't see it or anything but I assume so. She was packing up her things and heading for the airport. She was calling to see if I'd pick her up that night from the airport. When she wasn't on her flight, I assumed she changed her mind. Daphne did things spontaneously. I figured they got into an argument and she'd call me in a day or two and explain. She never called and her father told me her body had been found – that she accidentally drowned."

Setting the murder aspect aside, for now, I asked, "Is there a reason you didn't tell her father what you knew?"

Kendra rubbed her right eye. "I knew I should have, but I didn't want to cause them more pain. It seemed like too much. I would have told them. I wanted them to get through the initial grief first."

I could understand that. I hadn't wanted to deliver the news to Edward earlier that morning and we had no personal connection. "Can you share with me Daphne's concerns about Andy?"

"Daphne said he was controlling and that when he wasn't at work, she assumed he'd be home with her. He spent nights at bars and came home smelling like beer and cheap perfume. She assumed he had been cheating on her. There were nights he didn't come home at all. He said he had stayed on his boat, but Daphne wasn't sure she believed him. A couple of nights before she left, Andy had come home looking disheveled and they argued well into the early hours of the morning. She decided then and there to leave him."

I perked up at that information. It had only been a few nights prior that Laurie Presley had disappeared. "Do you know what night that had been exactly?"

"Hold on and I'll check my phone." Kendra got up from her desk and disappeared from camera view. She returned holding her cellphone. She sat back down and scrolled through her texts. Kendra didn't look up at me but kept reading from her phone. "It was the previous Saturday night. Daphne said that he came home at three in the morning and that his shirt was ripped and he had scratches on his chest. She assumed he had wild sex with a woman and she was done with it."

My mouth was dry as I put the pieces together. Andy had come home at three in the morning the night Laurie Presley disappeared. The timing certainly allowed him to be involved with her disappearance. His boat was right there in the cove. Cooper said each of the victims had used his business. That didn't mean he had met them though. *Could it be him?*

I kept my expression neutral as I delivered devastating news. "Kendra, I hate to be the one to tell you this, but Daphne was murdered. There is a detective who has made a statement that she drowned accidentally. The medical examiner doesn't believe that's the case. Daphne was strangled before her body was dumped into the ocean."

Kendra's hand flew to her mouth and her eyes bulged. "Oh my god. It's Andy."

"Why do you say that?"

Kendra shook her phone furiously at me. "In one of the last texts she sent me, Daphne complained that even sex with Andy was weird and that he liked to choke her. She kept trying to get him to stop and he wouldn't."

I tried to hide my shock but it wasn't easy. "Send me a copy of those texts." Andy now had no alibi and too many other connections to dismiss. He was suspect number one as far as I was concerned.

CHAPTER 32

That afternoon, Luke, Cooper, and I sat in front of the case board in our hotel room. Adele wanted some downtime and we couldn't have been happier to encourage her to go shopping or whatever else she had planned. She deserved it more than any of us. She was the bride after all and her honeymoon hadn't turned out anything like she had planned.

"I need to wrap my head around these cases. There are too many moving parts. I need some grounding," Cooper said, kicking back in the chair. He had one leg on the ottoman and a coffee in his hand. He had a casual vibe but an intense stare fixed on the board.

Luke stood near the board and had already written a few more notes on it since the last time I had taken a look at it. His first order of business was to update us on his meeting with the assistant state attorney. I was happy they had taken Luke's concerns seriously and had given us the go-ahead to keep pursuing the cases and had a plan for after we left. That had tempered my fear about Luke and me going back home with the cases unsolved.

Luke clicked the top on and off a marker. "While I don't normally like to speculate on a motive for cases, I think we can safely say this is a sexual homicide. We are probably looking at a serial killer."

That wasn't news to me. I had assumed so when I saw the body count. The average murderer didn't kill with such regularity and in such a pattern. "Do you think it's Dylan and Ollie? There have been times when two people were working in tandem. The Hillside Stranglers in California in the late 1970s come to mind. The killers, Kenneth Bianchi and Angelo Buono Jr., were cousins like Dylan and Ollie and their preferred method was strangulation. They targeted sex workers though and not college-aged girls on vacation."

"Still easy prey," Cooper said quietly almost to himself. He looked over at me sitting on the couch. "Both the Hillside Stranglers and this killer are choosing vulnerable young women. The victims here were far away from home, in an unfamiliar environment fueled with alcohol, and I'm sure their guard was down. The killer is practiced at this, controlled and methodical."

"I agree with that," Luke said. "That's why I don't think the killer is Dylan or Ollie. I know all the connections are there but they are the most obvious choice. They are in the same age range as the victims and have had contact with most of them. We also know that Ollie has been violent with women before. They are sloppy though. I can't see them committing this crime and being so methodical they haven't gotten caught or left evidence behind."

"I can't rule them out yet," I said stubbornly. "Even though I'm fairly certain it's Andy Barber, I'm not ready to rule out Dylan and Ollie."

"They are detestable," Cooper said as he took a sip of his coffee. "I'd love to arrest or shoot either of them. Truly, they are terrible. I've always hated guys like that – rich, smug, and protected. I have to agree with Luke though. The evidence isn't there for me. I think what clinched it for me is that we know Dylan sold Samuel Fletcher drugs the night Laurie Presley disappeared. We know it was Fletcher who walked her to the hotel door. By that time, Dylan was already back at the bar and was seen for the rest of the night. He can't be in two places at once."

"Ollie is unaccounted for that night," I reminded them. "Who is to say he's not involved in this without Dylan."

Luke clicked his tongue. "Possible but not probable and we have no evidence to connect Ollie to any of these. The evidence on Dylan is stronger and that's not getting us anywhere. Let's move on. Tell me your thoughts on Andy Barber."

I went over the calls I had with Edward and Kendra leaving nothing out including Andy's interest in choking women during sex. I started counting things off on my fingers. "Andy knows the island. He has a boat that's parked close to the hotel, and to where Daphne's body washed up. We have evidence that he could have been in contact with each of the victims. We know that he had a volatile relationship with Daphne and that he now has no alibi for the night Laurie Presley disappeared."

"All circumstantial," Luke said, much to my annoyance.

I raised my voice. "It's all going to be circumstantial. We have no solid evidence of anything. No bodies. No evidence. No crime. Daphne's body was in the water so long there is no evidence. We also have no eyewitness testimony. We have nothing but circumstantial evidence." I looked over at Cooper. "What do you think? You've had a one-on-one with him."

"You're both right. Andy is at the top of my list and it's all circumstantial." He shot Luke a look of apology. "Riley is right that we have no evidence. The likelihood is that unless we get someone to confess or catch them in the act, we have nothing. And since we've been here and have started digging around, I'd suspect that the killer is going to lay low so the chance of catching him in the act is almost nothing."

Luke didn't respond but turned to the board and wrote down some notes under Andy Barber's name. He'd had the least amount of interaction with him, so I wasn't surprised that he wasn't at the top of Luke's list. With his back still turned, he asked, "Are you sure you want to rule out Lyle Blaylock?"

Cooper sat up straighter in the chair. "There's nothing there, Luke. He was open and honest with us. He was charming but not too charming. He admitted that he had a fling with Freya Reid and with Ruby Wallis. Blaylock even admitted that Ruby was more of a sex thing and he had far more in common with Freya. He seemed to genuinely like Freya. He's clear across the island, and other than those two short flings, nothing connects him to these cases. We can't even connect him to the other victims. He let Ruby's father stay with him. That's hardly the act of a guilty man."

Luke turned and raised his eyebrows. "Do you have any reason to suspect him? Anything at all even if it doesn't seem significant?"

Cooper shook his head. "Nothing. I'm not saying this because I was starstruck, which I was a little. He has a secluded home and his own private beach. If he was going to kill someone, he wouldn't be doing it in the staff quarters of a hotel. Even if he didn't want to bring the victims to his home, even though both Freya and Ruby were there, he's got enough resources to choose a more private place to kill them. I don't think he'd risk being recognized like that."

"Fair enough." Luke went to the board and moved the photo of Lyle Blaylock out of the suspect list but still kept him on the board. "What should we be focused on at this point?"

I knew what Luke was avoiding. He didn't want to talk about Vic as a potential suspect. We needed to hash it out. "What about Vic?"

Luke shook his head. "I know that I'm the one who brought that up earlier, but no, I've changed my mind. It can't be him."

"He has access to the hotel and the rooms anytime he wants," Cooper countered. "Laurie Presley was staying here as well as Freya Reid. The other victims were in hotels close by. He certainly had the means to do this more so than anyone on that suspect list."

Luke held firm. "I've never in all the homicide cases I've worked had someone so helpful." He held up his hand to stop us from arguing. "I know what you're going to say – that a killer will often try to help with the investigation. That's what made me question it too, but Vic isn't like that. I've had more contact with him than either of you and there is no way I can imagine him doing it. There isn't a psychopathic bone in that man's body." He put his hands on his hips and glared down at us like he was annoyed we would have broached the subject.

Cooper and I shared a look and let it drop. "That leaves us with Samuel Fletcher. He has access to the hotel and he was in close contact with Laurie Presley on the night she disappeared. There's nothing to say he didn't continue walking her around the hotel and right into the side door to one of the rooms. It makes sense he wouldn't risk bringing the victims up to his room because of surveillance but he'd have heard about the side door being open and the staff area."

Cooper added, "He has been in this hotel on and off for years and now practically lives here. He's comfortable here and even if people saw him, they might not question what he's doing. Fletcher also has a background of harassment of women."

Luke ran a hand over his head. "I agree with all of it. There's just one problem – he has an alibi for every night there was a disappearance."

"You said you thought it was bogus," Cooper said.

"It could be but I can't prove it. The only way that happens is if Charmaine decides she wants to stop protecting him and comes forward with the information. Then it's a wide-open playing field for us. Right now, there's not much to go on. We have him connected to Laurie Presley and sharing a cab with Gia Tibbitts but that's it."

I remembered something from earlier in our investigation. "Did you ever find out who left you the note pointing us to Samuel Fletcher?"

"No. Vic said he was going to look through some surveillance video and talk to the person who was at the front desk at the time and see if he could find anything. With bringing in the dogs and all, I haven't followed up. It got pushed down the priority list."

I had an idea, but I wasn't sure that Luke was going to go for it. "Hear me out before you say no."

Luke cocked his head to the side. He knew whatever I was about to say was going to either be completely outrageous or annoy him. He'd had the same look many times during our relationship. "Go ahead," he said stiffly.

"Let me interview Vic. Let me rule him out." I stood and went to him, resting my hand on his chest. "I don't doubt that Vic is innocent in all of this. I'd feel better if you let me speak to him and rule him out though. That's all I'm asking. I have a different interview style and he might remember something that he hasn't told you. I can ask him about the note as well."

"I think it's a good idea, Luke. You initially brought it up for a reason. Let Riley explore it and we can let it drop," Cooper echoed. "I'd like a crack at speaking to Samuel Fletcher. I have a way of getting under people's skin. I know he's a British diplomat and there are potential political implications. I can walk a fine line."

We had boxed him in and if he said no, then he wasn't objective in the case. If he said yes, Luke would worry the entire time that we were seeing something he missed.

He threw his hands up in defeat. "Run with it. I'm going to take a look at Andy Barber. I might not interview him again. I'd like to start asking around about him. We haven't interviewed the staff at the Sunshine Bar yet, and I'd like to see if Andy is a regular there."

I turned to Cooper. "Did you tell Luke my scuba idea?"

"Not yet." He leaned forward in the chair. "Riley thinks that we should go scuba diving around the cove and see what we can find. She suggested that we find someone other than Andy to take us and we can get an idea of where he's going out in the water and see if we can find anything."

Luke looked skeptical. He presented the same argument that Cooper had about nothing being in the water that long. He talked himself out of it and then into it in a matter of minutes. "I guess it can't hurt and it would give us a day out on the water. I'm sure it won't yield much, but I'm not opposed to it. I'll call around today and see if I can find a company with availability."

Cooper said, "I'm game if you are. I didn't want to waste any time."

"I don't think anything is a waste of time at this point. We have nothing to go on. It's a shot in the dark like everything else we are doing."

With our assignments for the day, we split up and promised to meet back in our room at seven for dinner. Cooper said he'd update Adele on anything she wanted to know, but he was hoping at this point she just enjoyed the last few days of vacation.

CHAPTER 33

Cooper left Luke and Riley's room with the elevator code to reach the penthouse. He'd take a shot at trying to speak to Samuel Fletcher. He got in the elevator, punched in the required code to reach the floor, and waited as the elevator brought him upstairs. The door opened to a mess of towels on the floor right in front of him. He assumed that housekeeping was hard at work cleaning the penthouse. He took it as a sign that Fletcher might not be available.

Cooper approached the door and knocked. He was surprised when Fletcher opened the door and asked him what he wanted. Cooper explained who he was and why he was there.

Fletcher rolled his eyes and shook his head. "You're wasting your time talking to me when the real killer is out there, but come on in. I have nothing to hide." He stepped out of the way and let Cooper in. They went into the living room and sat down.

"Want a whiskey?" Fletcher offered, picking up a glass from the side table. "This conversation calls for more alcohol."

"I'm fine, thanks. I know Luke was up here and spoke to you already. I know what you told him about buying drugs from Dylan and then meeting with Charmaine. Your alibi checks out."

"Okay, then why are you bothering me?"

Cooper leveled a look at him. "Charmaine's not a great liar. Usually, you wait to give an alibi for the time asked, not just volunteer the information like you've been prepped to respond. Even if it was accurate information, it was suspicious. The problem for you is Luke didn't believe her."

"I can't control what he believes," Fletcher said with a shrug. "If you knew Charmaine the way I do, you'd know she doesn't like to waste a lot of time unless it's in the bedroom, and then she'll give you all the time you're paying for." Fletcher knocked back the whiskey in one gulp and then laughed at himself.

Cooper didn't share in the laughter. He didn't think there was anything funny. "That might be true, but as far as I'm concerned, you're still a suspect."

He held his arms open wide. "Pile it on. I don't care. I've lost my job, my reputation, and my home. There's not much more you can take from me."

Cooper offered a sly smile. "Your freedom is at risk."

Fletcher laughed again, hitching his thumb over his shoulder. "You think that stupid Det. Hanley is going to arrest me? I'm not admitting to anything, but even if I committed a crime right in front of him, he's not bright enough to figure it out. I've been living here for months partying all I want. I have committed a crime in the middle of the street and no one has stopped me yet. I'm untouchable." He raised his eyes to Cooper. "Don't you know arresting me might cause an international scandal that the authorities in St. Thomas certainly don't want? I'll continue to have all the freedom I desire. Why do you think I stay here?"

Cooper didn't say anything for a few moments. He didn't think Fletcher was admitting to involvement with the disappearances of the young women. Still, though, he admitted that he could get away with whatever he chose. That kind of thinking mixed with nothing to lose brought out the worst in people. The fact that Fletcher admitted he had lost everything could also be a stressor that led to murder. Cooper had seen it before in cases.

Cooper leaned forward. "Regardless of what Luke thinks, I don't think you've done anything wrong. I'm here because I believe you can help us. I have a few more questions, but do you mind if I use your restroom first?"

"Have at it. It's the first door before the bedroom." Fletcher stood when Cooper did. "I'm calling down for something to eat and more whiskey. You want anything?"

Cooper declined and headed toward the small hallway off the main living area. There was one door, which was the bathroom, and then the door for the bedroom straight back. Cooper paused for a moment to see if Fletcher would follow him, and then when he heard the man on the phone with room service, he moved swiftly to the bedroom door.

He slowly turned the handle, hoping not to make any noise, and pushed open the door. He didn't go inside but scanned the room from the doorway. The bed was crisply made, although one pillow had a head dent like Fletcher had laid down briefly and then got back up again. There was a pair of dress pants slung over the back of a chair, the end tables were free of clutter except for what looked like a phone charger plugged into an outlet, and there were no clothes or shoes visible in the room. Cooper wanted to go in and search more thoroughly but resisted the temptation to do so.

He backed out slowly and as he did, something shiny caught his attention poking out from the closet door that had been left slightly ajar. Cooper crouched down so he'd be level with it. There was one strappy, silver sandal lying sideways with the toe of the shoe in the closet track preventing the door from sliding closed all the way.

From this angle, Cooper could see that where the thin strap crisscrossed there was a tiny flower buckle. He pulled out his phone, zoomed in on the shoe, and snapped a quick photo before closing the door and going into the bathroom. He quietly closed the bathroom door, flushed the toilet, and turned the faucet on the sink. He only had a few moments before needing to be back out to the living room. He opened the medicine cabinet expecting to find pill bottles but there was nothing but a tube of toothpaste, deodorant, and a toothbrush.

Cooper shut off the water, closed the cabinet, and met Fletcher back out in the living room. He was on the phone talking to someone but the conversation seemed more personal than an order for room service. His face was animated and his side of the conversation seemed jovial, laughing and bantering with whoever was on the other end. Cooper sat back down and waited for him to finish.

When Fletcher was done, he tossed the phone on a nearby side table. "So, what else did you want to know?"

Cooper breathed a sigh of relief that Fletcher hadn't been suspicious that he'd been snooping. "Do you know many of the hotel staff here?"

"A few. You spend enough time here and you see the same people over and over again."

Cooper pointed to Fletcher's phone. "You said you were going to call room service. I assume you do that often?"

Fletcher nodded. "Just about every meal. I go out once in a while but eat here the majority of the time. The chef will cater to any request. He's good too, one of the best on the island."

"You must know the kitchen staff fairly well then," Cooper said evenly. He hadn't thought about Fletcher's connection to the kitchen staff before he had mentioned room service.

"It's mostly young kids that bring up my food."

"Do you ever go down to the kitchen area and watch him work his culinary magic?"

Fletcher narrowed his eyes. "Is there a reason you're asking?"

Cooper eased a smile. "No. I like watching chefs cook. I wondered if you were like me in that regard. There's a restaurant back in Little Rock where you can watch the chef prepare your meal. I was curious, given how much you're in the hotel, if you ever went down there and watched him work or in your case maybe oversaw his work since you make special requests."

Fletcher shook his head. "I don't mingle with the staff. They are there to serve."

"So, you've never seen the inner workings of the hotel?"

"Asked and answered counselor," Fletcher said with a laugh. "What's this about?"

Cooper kept his stare locked on Fletcher. "You said you walked Laurie to the front door of the hotel the night she disappeared. A search and rescue dog picked up her scent. Funny thing though, she didn't go into the front door of the hotel. He followed her scent around the side of the building to a staff entrance and then to a room often used by staff who are spending the night at the hotel. Do you know anything about that?"

Fletcher showed no reaction or emotion on his face. "Are you thinking that someone working at the hotel had something to do with her disappearance?"

"It certainly would appear that way." Cooper kicked his legs out and crossed his ankles, trying to make it seem like nothing more than a casual chat. "You've been around here more than any tourist coming in for a week's vacation. I was hoping you could tell me your impressions of the staff. You're a smart guy who has traveled the globe and met more people than I'll meet in a lifetime. You seem like you'd have a good instinct when it comes to these things."

Fletcher puffed out his chest and sat up straighter in the chair. "Are you asking me who I'd consider capable of killing someone?"

It was interesting to Cooper that he went right to that. "If you have someone in mind you think is capable, sure. But I'm starting to doubt that one person could pull off these disappearances."

Fletcher kicked his feet up on the ottoman. "Do you think two people are involved?"

"I think it's more than one person."

"Interesting. Even that dumb Det. Hanley hasn't speculated that." Fletcher stared at Cooper, who remained unmoving and didn't break eye contact. "I'm sure there are many ways to speculate on this case, but that's what you do as an investigator, right? It's all speculation. Throw it all at the wall and see what sticks."

"That's a crude way to describe it, but it's not far off. We certainly look at everything in front of us and then make educated connections using logic, reason, and the available evidence – which in these cases is little to none." Cooper knew that Fletcher probably didn't like cops or investigators given his past. It was an investigative reporter who broke the story of his sexual harassment and a private investigator who had worked to find other victims and convince them to come forward.

Cooper folded his hands in his lap. "I'm not asking you to guess or speculate. I'm asking if you saw anyone from the hotel out front that night or have heard any chatter about these cases. Did anyone slip and say anything you thought odd? For all I know, you have deep friendships with people on the staff and you're sitting there on a gold mine of information. I could understand if you didn't want to get involved any more than you are right now."

Fletcher smirked. "Are you saying that you think if I knew who did this, I'd keep my mouth shut and let them keep killing young women?"

"I'm not saying anything or accusing you of anything," Cooper said evenly, returning the smirk. He knew that Fletcher was trying to play games and he wasn't interested in it. "If you don't know anything that's fine. I just thought it might be useful to speak to someone who was there that night and who seems to have more of a command of the hotel than most guests." Cooper stood to leave. "I won't take up any more of your time."

Surprisingly, Fletcher gestured for him to sit back down. "I might know a few things. I was messing with you. It's not often that I get to banter with someone marginally close to my intellect. You seem like an intelligent man, Cooper."

"I appreciate that." Cooper sat and crossed his legs again, waiting. He wasn't going to ask another question. He'd sit in silence and wait him out.

After a few beats, Fletcher relented. "It was a few of the waiters who connected me with Charmaine and Dylan. Drugs are running through the hotel. One of them sells me coke when Dylan is busy."

That didn't surprise Cooper at all. "You ever heard them talk about the disappearances?"

"No one has said much. As I said, I'm not too friendly with the staff." Fletcher leaned forward and jabbed his finger toward Cooper. "I'd tell you though, I'd take a look at the chef down there. I know I praised his culinary skills, but there's something shady about him."

"You don't have any real proof of his involvement though?"

"No." That didn't stop Fletcher from going on and on about the chef and his potential involvement. It was obvious to Cooper he was a man who liked to hear himself talk, but he wasn't convinced the chef had anything to do with it.

When Fletcher finished, Cooper said, "Is there anything else you think I should know?"

Fletcher shook his head. "I hope it's helpful information."

Cooper nodded once and then stood. He extended his hand to Fletcher before he left the room. "If you hear of anything else, let me know."

As Fletcher walked him over to the door, he continued to make his case. "Take some time and consider the chef. He is the one with keys to the staff door. He is the one who lets in the shipments and oversees all of that. Plus, he controls the schedule so he'd know who was around. If anyone was bringing girls into the hotel that way, he'd be the guy. Nothing happens down there without his knowledge." He patted Cooper on the back as he walked out.

Cooper stepped out of his reach into the hall. He turned back to Fletcher briefly only to say, "For a man who has never been down to the kitchen or mingled with the staff, you sure know how it all works." Cooper smiled and watched as Fletcher's smile faltered. He left without looking back.

CHAPTER 34

I had stopped at the front desk to chat with the woman working. I was looking to see if she happened to have any information about who had left the note for Luke. She had no idea and hadn't been working that day or even the one before. She was nice enough but dismissive so I kept it brief. She told me that Vic was in his office and I could find him there.

On the way to the hallway that led me to the staff area, I popped my head into the conference room doorway and found it nearly empty except for one lone volunteer sitting at the table. She had her head buried in a book and didn't even look up when I opened the door. I stepped back and let it close without disturbing her. Luke had told me that the tip calls had dwindled to one every few hours. Most of the volunteers had stopped coming in and there was only a handful who remained.

After finding out that a cadaver dog had picked up the scent in the same room that Laurie was tracked to, most of the volunteers had realized that she'd not be coming home and there was no point to search anymore. I couldn't blame them but felt the heavy weight of guilt for taking hope away from the Presley family. Luke had reminded me that we weren't doing them any favors by allowing them to have hope about something that wasn't going to happen. I knew he was right but still felt guilt for it.

I had hoped Ava and Bill would be in the conference room, but after a short statement to the press the night before, they had retired to their hotel room and we hadn't seen them since. Luke had called and left a message. I assumed they'd need time to grieve and decide their next plan of action.

It would be hard for any parent to head home without their child – living or deceased. The thing about missing person cases was that if there was no hope to find the person alive, the least investigators wanted to do was provide their loved one's remains so they could have a proper final resting place. I didn't know that we'd get that for Laurie Presley.

I stopped by the coffee stand and poured myself some and then doused it with too much milk and sugar – just the way I liked it – and then headed to see Vic. I followed the hallway maze until I found his office and rapped my knuckles against the closed door and Vic told me to enter.

I stepped into his office. "Vic, I was hoping you'd have a few minutes to speak to me."

"Sure, is everything okay?"

I sat down in the chair across from his desk. "No updates if that's what you mean. Luke, Cooper, and I are speaking to everyone again. Luke is running down some leads and we haven't spoken as much so I thought I'd ask a few questions if you have the time."

Vic sat back in his chair. "I'm not sure what more I can share, but I'd be happy to see what else I can add."

I told him how much I appreciated that. "Were you working the night Laurie Presley disappeared?"

"I was here earlier in the evening but not when she came back. I was home by then. I was on-call though should anyone need anything. No one called. I had no idea until later the next day that anything was wrong."

"Do you live alone?"

Vic's smile faltered. "Am I under suspicion for something?"

I shook my head. "It's the routine questions we asked all the staff here. Luke said he hadn't interviewed you the way he had other staff so to be thorough I figured I'd do that now quickly."

"That makes sense, I guess," he said, his smile not returning. "Yes, I live alone. The staff saw me leave at nine that night. I always stop in and say hello to one of my neighbors and then I went into my house. I didn't leave again until the next morning. That's about all the alibi I have for you. I work close to sixty hours a week. I don't have much of a life outside work right now. I'm saving money for the future."

"I understand that. Before Luke and I got married, I lived alone for a long time." I asked about the dates of the other disappearances and Vic gave the response most people who hadn't done anything wrong would give – he had no idea what he was doing those nights because they didn't stand out in any way.

He rested his arms on his desk. "Other than meeting friends once in a while and doing basic errands, you can find me here or at home. That's it – my whole life for right now. I don't even get much time for family, not that I get along with them much anyway."

I put a pin in the Hanley family for now. I had other things more pressing. "Did you interact with Laurie and her friends while she was here?"

Vic didn't even need time to think. "Not that I'm aware of. Nothing that stands out to me. I speak to so many guests that unless the request is unusual or there is a problem, it doesn't stand out to me. I could have walked by Laurie twenty times or handed her something from the front desk and I'd have forgotten about it five minutes later. There has to be a reason why people stand out to me. You, Luke, and Cooper I'll remember for the rest of my life. A group of twenty-something young ladies that don't trash the hotel or need anything special, I've forgotten moments after seeing them."

We spent the next several minutes going back and forth over a few more questions. All in all, I found Vic to be truthful and a stand-up guy. I had no reason to suspect him and felt comfortable now in agreeing with Luke that Vic wasn't our guy. My cellphone chimed in my pocket and I pulled it out to see a text from Cooper. He was asking if I knew much information about the hotel chef. I'd respond in a moment.

Vic was watching me from across the desk, so I held up my phone. "Cooper. He's asking if we had spoken to the chef here."

Vic pulled back, a look of concern spreading across his face. "Chef Andrew had nothing to do with this. I'm more likely to be the culprit. He is one of the most stand-up men you could ever meet." He rubbed his forehead. "Not to mention that it would ruin us if he did."

A lot was riding on Vic's shoulders and I wanted to reassure him. "That's not why Cooper wants to speak to him. He believes he might have been an unwitting witness. He wants to have a brief conversation to sort it out."

Vic didn't seem convinced, but he wasn't going to argue. "Chef Andrew will be in the kitchen now. If Cooper wants to come down here, I'll get him and you can speak in my office. Chef Andrew won't want to take a lot of time though. He's rushed in the kitchen as it is."

I assured him we wouldn't take any more time than necessary. As Vic left, I texted Cooper to meet me in Vic's office and provided him the directions to get here. Within ten minutes, Cooper was seated next to me and Chef Andrew sat in Vic's spot. He had left us alone with the hotel's chef and closed the door behind him.

Chef Andrew was a large man both in height and width. He wasn't fat but rather muscular and well-conditioned. His biceps strained the fabric of his white chef's coat. He had met us earlier when we initially interviewed the staff.

What Cooper said surprised us both. "I'm only here because I want to rule you out quickly because I don't think there is any evidence to even substantiate me talking to you. It was suggested by a hotel guest that we might want to look at you for being responsible for the disappearances of the young women."

I couldn't believe what I was hearing and assumed Cooper had heard that from Samuel Fletcher as a distraction from his guilt. Chef Andrew didn't like the sound of it either. He crossed his thick arms over his beefy chest and stared down Cooper.

"I said this was ridiculous and I meant it," Cooper assured him. "You do have a key and you do set the schedule. I was told that you know everything that happens in the kitchen."

"In the kitchen, yes, with my staff, but not the entirety of the hotel," Chef Andrew said, his voice a deep baritone. "I'm not the last one to leave at night. There are other staff here doing the final cleanup. I have five daughters at home and my wife. Three of my daughters are around the age of the victims. It makes me sick to think that something happened to them close by where I work every day. I assure you that if I knew the person responsible, you might be sitting here speaking to me for another reason. I don't know that I could control myself around them. They don't deserve to live a life in prison. In my opinion, death would be the only option."

I believed every word he said and did not doubt that he'd have no problem bringing his own sense of justice to the case. I shared a look with Cooper, who didn't seem to have other questions. "Do you know Samuel Fletcher?"

"Yes, everyone here does." His features were tight, and I got the sense that he didn't like the man.

I locked eyes with him. "Have you had any issues with him?"

Chef Andrew shifted his eyes to the side. "We aren't supposed to speak badly of guests here at the hotel."

"I understand that and your impressions of him won't go further than our investigative team." I pulled the chair closer to the desk, scraping the bottom on the floor and drawing his attention. "What you know may help save another young woman from suffering the same fate."

Chef Andrew's head snapped front and center. With his eyebrows raised, he asked, "You think Samuel Fletcher had something to do with these young women?"

"We don't know," Cooper admitted. "That's what we are trying to figure out. I interviewed Fletcher before I came down here. He told me that I should be looking at you as the one harming these young women."

Chef Andrew slammed his closed fist down on the desk. "That's preposterous. I'd never harm a young lady like that. I'd never harm anyone unless they truly deserved it or in the protection of others."

Cooper tried reassuring him. "We are only here because he seems to have a grudge against you and I'm trying to figure out why. Has he ever been down here to this staff area?"

"Too many times. Fletcher has a multitude of demands and none of them ever seem to correspond to our regular menu or the special menu I do each day. I've often found him standing over my staff barking orders at them." He shook his head in disgust. "I've kicked him out of my kitchen more than once. He's a bully and I don't like the feeling I have around him."

"Fletcher has been down here to this staff area?" Cooper asked with confidence in his voice. "I asked him that and he assured me he'd never been down here with the staff. That's also when he pointed the finger at you."

"That's a lie. Ask anyone in my kitchen and they will tell you the same. He walks into that kitchen as if he owns it. He's been down here more times than I could count. We have all spoken to him about it but he does what he wants. Fletcher pays the hotel a good deal of money to live here, so they don't say anything to him."

Cooper was quiet for a moment before asking, "That would mean he'd know the lay of the land and when that back door was unlocked. He said something curious to me when I interviewed him. He said that the door went to the shipping area. I had wondered how he'd know that if he hadn't come down here before. I'm glad there is definitive proof now that he has."

An idea struck me and Chef Andrew was the perfect person to ask. "Are you able to unlock that side door from the inside without a key?"

He nodded. "It's a bolt lock turned from the inside, yes." Chef Andrew seemed uncertain why I'd ask that and then all of a sudden recognition took hold. "Fletcher could have come down here before going out and unlocked the door without anyone knowing. It might not have been staff that left the door unlocked."

That wasn't all. I speculated, "Down here with the staff, Fletcher could have swiped keys or a keycard. If he felt comfortable coming down here and bothering staff while they were working, there's no telling what he was up to when there weren't any staff working back here at all."

I felt like we were finally a step closer to learning the truth. Finding enough evidence was going to be another challenge. I couldn't even think about the potential political fallout.

CHAPTER 35

In the late afternoon, Luke walked to the Sunshine Bar and stepped inside, finding it a little more crowded than he had thought it would be for that time of day. Several journalists that had been staying at the hotel were sitting at tables eating and drinking. It must be a slow news day for them.

Luke took a seat at the bar and ordered a beer. His patience for the case had ground to a screeching halt. He had spoken briefly with Captain Meadows and Det. Tyler, who encouraged him to let it go, enjoy the rest of his vacation, and head home.

A few days ago, even the night before, Luke didn't think that letting it go would be possible, but with no evidence, few leads left to follow, and a police force who didn't seem to care about anything other than tourism, he was starting to wonder why he was fighting a battle no one was interested in.

He wanted to speak to the bar manager, but the young guy tending the bar had told him that the manager wouldn't be in for another hour, so he nursed his beer and ordered lunch. He had nowhere else to be right then. Luke made it three-quarters of the way through his beer when the bar started to fill up. Grady walked in with three other people Luke recognized as media. He excused himself from his colleagues and took a seat next to Luke.

"I'm heading home tomorrow," Grady said with a shrug. "We've covered about all that we are going to cover. Some of the network television stations might stay longer, but I'm hearing that their producers are pulling the plug soon. Det. Hanley has been fairly loud that these cases are runaways and accidents and there is no one saying anything different."

Luke took a sip of his beer. He couldn't blame Grady. The decision was higher than his pay grade. "The medical examiner said differently about Daphne Powers."

"We covered that. Even the medical examiner is refusing to say anything else in an official capacity. There's some speculation that the mayor's office has been shutting her down. I don't know if that's true or maybe she's tired of making statements. Either way, there's not much news for us to cover."

Luke took a sip of his beer. "I've accepted this is one case I might not solve. I hate feeling like this, but there's not much I can do without my full team here."

Grady looked over at him. "You're not the first detective to throw in the towel on a case. I don't know how you do your job day in and day out. It's difficult and heartbreaking at times. The Presleys gave me a statement a little while ago that they are heading home soon. Knowing that their daughter is deceased and that she was most likely dumped in the ocean, they don't feel like they can do anything else here."

Luke had assumed they'd be heading back soon. "I feel bad that we didn't get them more answers, but sometimes that's how it goes. Hopefully, they can make their peace with it. I know that's an impossible thing to do for some people..." Luke's voice trailed off. He felt the weight of his grief over his sister, Lily, settle over him. He took another sip of his beer and shifted his thoughts.

"Are you okay?" Grady asked, seeing the emotion on Luke's face.

"I'm fine," Luke assured him with a tone that said he wouldn't entertain any further discussion on it. He angled his head to look at Grady. "What's next for you?"

"Back to the grind. I don't know that I have what it takes for the crime beat. I might turn to softer news after this."

"You're inquisitive, a good researcher, and have good instincts. You have what it takes."

"I appreciate you saying that. My editor thinks I do. I don't know."

The normal hum of the bar suddenly erupted with cellphones ringing and the chatter growing much louder. Luke spun on the bar stool to look out over the bar area that was filled with journalists. Grady's phone had chimed as well. He looked down at his phone and then held the screen so Luke could see it.

The message read: *There's been a break in the Daphne Powers case. Det. Hanley is giving a news briefing at four.*

Luke checked his watch and he had forty minutes to finish his lunch, maybe interview the bar manager, and then follow Grady over to the police station. Grady excused himself as the bartender dropped off Luke's burger and fries. He wanted to grab some lunch and confer with his colleagues.

Luke wondered what the break in the case might be. He had no idea and hadn't been updated by anyone. It occurred to Luke that his visit to the state attorney's office might have prompted a phone call to the chief of police. Luke had no idea if it had, but if it did and Det. Hanley made some progress, then good for him. Luke wasn't worried who would get credit for solving the murder – he had more than enough solved cases under his belt.

Luke was finishing the last bite of his burger when the bartender introduced Adam, the manager of the Sunshine Bar. Luke wiped his hands on a napkin and shook the man's hand. When the bartender reached for Luke's plate, he nodded that it was fine to take it away.

Luke explained to Adam his role in the cases and that he had a few questions. "We believed that each of the victims went missing from your bar, but we've come to learn that isn't the case. I heard that you don't have any cameras in here. Is that true?"

"It is. We've never felt the need to install cameras. We are a beach bar and not much happens around here." Adam ran a hand through his blond hair. "That is until now. Our attorney has advised us not to get involved in these investigations. Given you're not in an official capacity, I can answer a few questions, but I don't know anything that can help you."

"Is there a reason you sought an attorney?"

"Liability. If the women were last seen here, then who knows what the families believe. No one here had anything to do with it. People are crazy with lawsuits though."

Luke took out his phone and scrolled through photos of each of the victims. "Do any of these young women look familiar to you?"

Adam glanced at each photo with seeming disinterest. He shook his head with each one and then raised his eyes to Luke. "These girls look like all the girls that come in here. I see so many every night that I can't tell one from the other."

Luke didn't have any reason to dislike Adam, but there was something dismissive about the guy that rubbed him the wrong way. He ran down the names of men on their suspect list without saying they were suspects. "Are any of those men familiar to you?"

"Well, sure," Adam said slowly. "Dylan and Ollie are in here most nights of the week. Andy Barber runs the scuba shop right across the way. He's in here sometimes."

"We know that Dylan has had contact with almost all of these young women. Ollie has claimed he wasn't here many of the nights the young women went missing. Do you know if Andy was in here any of those nights?"

Adam let out an incredulous laugh. "I couldn't tell you who was in here last night. I don't keep their schedules. You could tell me that a famous person was here and I wouldn't know the difference. This place gets so packed and I'm in charge of making sure it all runs smoothly. It's all a blur to me – all night, every night."

That was what Luke had assumed. He had interviewed bar staff on other cases and they had far too much going on busy nights to notice anything. "Is there anything you can tell me about Dylan and Ollie or Andy Barber that you might think is relevant?"

Adam shrugged. "I'm not sure what to say. Can I see any of them kidnapping girls? Is that what you're asking?"

"If you can answer that, yes. I'm mostly looking to see if you have any concerns about them."

Adam searched Luke's face as if wondering if he could trust him. Then he admitted, "We know that Dylan sells drugs. We don't allow him to do that here, but we know he's in here and that people know he sells. The transactions take place someplace else. We've stopped him a few times from doing that here. Ollie is kind of a quiet guy. I don't know much about him. Andy is the same. I've seen him with different women though. I don't know that he's ever gotten serious with anyone. He's a bit of a player." Adam stepped back from the bar. "I can't offer you anything else."

Luke thanked him and told him where he was staying if he thought of anything else. He asked the bartender for his check and was settling the bill when Grady stopped back over.

"I heard they arrested Andy Barber for Daphne Powers' murder."

Luke wasn't sure he had heard him correctly. "Did you say Andy Barber?"

"Yeah. I guess the cops got word that Daphne had stayed here in St. Thomas with Andy and then he killed her when she wanted to leave. I don't have confirmation on this yet, but it's what everyone is saying. We'll know more at the press conference. You coming?"

"I'll be there." Luke wasn't surprised that Andy had been arrested. He was surprised by the timing given Det. Hanley's refusal to believe anything they had told him. Then again, Luke reminded himself, between his talk with the assistant state attorney and Riley's call with Daphne's father, it might have been the push that was needed.

Luke followed Grady out of the bar and after a short walk, they were standing outside the police department in an area marked off for press. Det. Hanley and a few other people in official uniforms stood at the front near the podium waiting for the crowd to assemble.

It was weird for Luke being on the other side of a news conference. They were top of his shortlist of things he didn't like about his job. He hated the media's interference and having to give formal statements. It felt to him like the most unnatural way of speaking – even though everyone in his department praised him for the formal statements he gave.

Around him, reporters jockeyed for position, so Luke stepped off to the side. He had thought about texting Cooper and Riley but decided against it as Det. Hanley stepped to the podium. There would be no time for them to get there anyway.

Det. Hanley cleared his throat. "Thank you for being here today. As you were notified, through some great detective work from our office, we were able to determine that Daphne Powers intentionally separated from her friends while she was on vacation here. Before visiting St. Thomas, she had developed a relationship over the internet with Andy Barber. While she was here, they made a plan for Daphne to stay unbeknownst to her family and friends. As far as we can tell, she remained with Andy Barber for a few months before her untimely death. While initially ruled as an accidental drowning, more evidence has come to light to indicate that Daphne was strangled before she went into the water. Through additional evidence, we believe that Andy Barber is responsible for her murder. He has been arrested without incident and will be arraigned in the morning."

Det. Hanley stepped back from the podium as reporters shouted questions at him. He took one at a time but didn't offer up more information. He simply repeated what he had already said. He gave no indication what this additional evidence might be and would not confirm how they figured out Daphne had remained on the island with Andy. Det. Hanley wasn't going to give Riley credit for that.

As the press conference wrapped up, Grady yelled one final question, his voice booming louder than the others. "Do you believe that Andy Barber is responsible for any of the other missing women?"

Det. Hanley started to say no, but a man to his right stepped in front of him. He leaned over the podium and said, "We cannot confirm that at this time. It's certainly something we are looking into. If we have more information, we will let you know."

The man wasn't someone Luke recognized from the police department website. It wasn't the chief of police. Luke knew that much. As the crowd started to disperse, Grady walked over to Luke. "What do you think?"

"I know he's lying about a few things. Like it was Riley who figured out that Daphne had been living with Andy, but I'll let it slide if it means he's doing his job." Grady offered to write the real story, but Luke declined. "There's no point stirring up anything if he's finally taking this seriously. Write the story as they told it."

Grady looked toward the front of the police station. "Are you going to try to speak to him?"

Luke stared off in the same direction. "I've been thinking about it. Not sure that I'll get very far though."

"Might be worth a shot."

Luke agreed and shook Grady's hand. "If I don't see you before you go, keep me updated on your progress with the newspaper." He waited until Grady walked off and the rest of the reporters left and then made his way to the front door of the police station. Luke didn't know why, but he had the sinking feeling they were missing something.

CHAPTER 36

After Cooper and I finished speaking to Chef Andrew, we went into the kitchen and confirmed what he had told us with two of his staff members. The information was corroborated, and we knew now that Samuel Fletcher had lied on at least one thing that we could prove. *Prove* being the most important. Otherwise, we were still working with speculation as far as I was concerned.

"What's the plan now?" Cooper asked as we stood in the staff hallway.

I pointed toward an office door. "Vic said that he was going to get some surveillance video that I could go through. I want to see if we can catch who left Luke the note that pointed us to Fletcher in the first place."

"Do you want help with that?"

"All I want you to do is find Adele and enjoy the rest of the day. I've got this."

Cooper laughed and red rose in his cheeks. "She did text me and tell me that she bought something sexy that I'll enjoy."

"It's your honeymoon. Go, enjoy it." As we separated and Cooper headed down the hall and I went to Vic's office door, we were both stopped by a text. His phone sent a notification just as mine did. We both stopped and shared a look as we reached for our phones. "It's from Luke."

"Same," Cooper said and lowered his eyes to read it. "They have arrested Andy Barber for the murder of Daphne Powers and they might be looking at him for the other disappearances."

As much as I thought it might be him the day before, something didn't feel right. I walked down the hall to where Cooper stood. "What do you think about that?"

"I don't know," he said, shaking his head as his eyes hinted at the confusion I felt. "I don't doubt that he killed Daphne. He has the motive, means and opportunity to have done that. He's a creepy guy for sure. I don't know if I see him for the other murders."

"I feel the same way." While I should have felt happy and relieved that they had caught the guy, I was left with a sense of dread that they had made a mistake. "There are too many unanswered questions for me. First and foremost, how would he get in here? If we assume that what he did to Daphne he did to the other women, how logistically did he do that?"

"That's been tripping me up too." Cooper pointed down the hall. "It's reasonable that he could know that this door is left unlocked. It could also be reasonable that he might know his way around this hotel. He's a local and has had his business here long enough that I'm sure he's been inside this hotel. It's all reasonable he could be guilty, but..."

"There are parts of it that don't make sense," I said finishing his thought.

Cooper leaned against the wall in the hallway. "Let's say Andy does go to a local bar and picks up a young woman and he does bring her to the hotel and through that door and to a room – how is he getting her out? Does it seem reasonable that he'd carry her dead body to his boat? It's close but it's not that close. It also doesn't make sense that he'd get his boat out of the water at the dock and tow it over here for him to put her body in only to bring it back to the water."

"He could drive over here in his car, transfer her body, and then drive to his boat," I offered even though that didn't make much more sense to me. "I think the fact that he has a boat on the water and he could simply walk a girl to his boat, do whatever he was going to do on his boat, and then drive out a distance and dump her body is what's tripping me up. Andy would not need a hotel. It's an added step that could cause him to get caught."

Cooper snapped his fingers. "That's exactly it. He's already here within walking distance. Even the Sunshine Bar is down the beach. He'd have no reason to pass his boat and come up to the hotel. Let's take the Gia Tibbitts case for instance. She disappeared going to the bathroom, which is right near the back door to the deck and goes directly to the beach. Anyone could have stopped her, called her out to the deck, and led her down to the beach. If it was Andy, it makes no sense that he'd bring her up to the hotel when he could escape in the cover of darkness to his boat."

I recalled the night Cooper and I were down there at his boat in the dark. "It's much darker at night than I would have anticipated. I figured all the lights from the surrounding businesses would have made it much brighter, but where it sits in the cove blocks all the surrounding light." I pursed my lips in thought. "I don't think we can rule out that Andy didn't kill Daphne, but I don't think he's responsible for the other disappearances."

Cooper lowered his head to his phone. "I'm going to text Luke and give him the rundown about what we discussed, but I don't know that it will matter much to the cops."

"Worth trying, at least." We parted ways and I went to Vic's office and knocked on the door. He got up from his desk and I followed him down the hall to another office where he had set up a laptop and the surveillance video.

Vic logged me in, jotted down the login credentials on a pad of paper next to the laptop in case I wanted a break, and then left me to do my work. I slipped on the headphones attached to the laptop, clicked the start button for the first surveillance video, and relaxed back in the chair, settling in for a few hours before dinner. I had no other leads to run down so this was it for now.

I watched the videos on the slowest fast forward setting. People came and went from the front desk of the hotel but no one seemed to drop a note or leave anything behind on the desk. The front desk was staffed nearly all the time. There were only a few occasions where it was left unattended and even then, someone would be in the office right behind the front desk. The hotel was a busy place and the front desk had a steady stream of people both night and day.

Going into this, I had assumed there'd be a good deal of downtime outside of the check-in and check-out times. That wasn't the case so there was more video footage than I had anticipated.

After two hours of staring at the screen, my eyes needed a break. I hit stop, took off the headphones, and stretched my arms overhead. I got up from the desk and wound my way back through the maze of hallways to the front lobby and then out to the back deck to the bar. It was nearing five and I was meeting everyone for dinner around seven. I'd get a quick snack and something to drink to get me through.

I grabbed a Coke at the bar, ordered a small grilled shrimp appetizer, and then found a table. As I waited for my food, I pulled out my phone and scrolled through social media. My sister, Liv, had posted photos of three houses she was considering making an offer on. She had been living with my mother since a recent breakup and saving money. Liv said she wanted a place of her own even though this would be the third time that she had moved back into our childhood home only to move back out again. The truth was Liv didn't like living alone and my mother's house was big enough for her to stay. My mother, Karen, and her fiancé, Jack, wanted her there. There was no need for Liv to force herself to move out on her own. I knew though that Liv felt weird being in her thirties and still living at home.

I fought the urge to comment on the photos or tell her what she should do. We had played that game most of our twenties and it left both of us arguing with the other. Our relationship was finally amicable because I had learned to simply accept the decisions Liv made even if she came running back to me later regretting them.

I kept scrolling through her photos until I landed on a recent one of her, my mother, and a local politician. They had been involved in a community beautification project and the photo had been taken at a community ceremony that kicked off the initiative. I stared at the photo for a moment. There was something about the photo that was tickling a memory that I couldn't quite bring into focus. It connected to the case, but it was sitting there in the back of my mind.

The server came and dropped off my shrimp and I set my phone down to eat. While I enjoyed the scenery, ocean breeze, people watching, the photo remained present. I couldn't let it go. Before we left for St. Thomas, in a video chat with Liv, she had told me about some meditation techniques for memory recall she had read about. Even though I had teased her at the time, I tried one now.

I sat back in my chair and closed my eyes. I didn't try to force anything. I let thoughts come in and out like rolling waves. I don't know how long I sat there like that. I was about to open my eyes and give up when two words popped into my brain. *International relations.* The words hit me like a lightning bolt and my eyes sprang open. Daphne Powers had been studying international relations. I had read it in the notes that Adele had provided me from when she first spoke to someone connected to Daphne. I hadn't thought anything about it at the time.

I punched in the numbers for Kendra, Daphne's best friend. The phone rang a few times and I figured it was headed for voicemail when she answered. "I'm so sorry to bother you," I said as a greeting. "Did

Daphne ever meet Samuel Fletcher?" I started to explain who he was but Kendra cut me off.

"He spoke at our university our freshman year. Daphne was enamored with him, and he was quite taken with her, too. That was before all the scandal occurred and he went into exile. Why?"

"Did they keep in touch?" I asked, my voice raspy on the phone. My heart had started racing. It thumped in my ears over the sound of my voice. "It's important for me to know if they kept in touch."

"Yes, they did. I don't know how much they spoke or how often. What's going on?"

"Did you know that Samuel Fletcher is here in St. Thomas? He's staying at the same hotel that Daphne stayed in. Did she mention anything about him recently?"

There was silence on the other end of the phone. Then Kendra let out a short gasp. "Not specifically. Before she left, I had tried talking her out of going to meet Andy. She insisted she knew someone else in St. Thomas if she needed help. When I pressed her, she wouldn't say who it was, so I didn't think Daphne was serious. I figured she was saying that to make me feel better."

I didn't understand Kendra's dribble of information. That Daphne knew someone else in St. Thomas would have been helpful to know. I couldn't chastise her now. "You're sure she didn't say anything about Fletcher? When was the last time she spoke to you about him?"

"Probably a month or so before her trip. We had been talking about what he was accused of doing and how he had been stripped of his diplomatic title. Daphne was still upset by it and said she didn't believe he had done anything wrong. I thought she was a bit daft for that. All in all, we decided it was best not to talk about him, which is why she probably didn't tell me he was there in St. Thomas."

I asked her a few more questions and then thanked her for the information. I had the sinking feeling that the person Daphne called the night she left Andy was Samuel Fletcher.

CHAPTER 37

Luke had been sitting in the lobby of the police station for close to three hours. He had asked to speak with the chief of police and Det. Hanley, but so far, no one came to speak to him. The only person he had heard from was Cooper.

As far as Luke was concerned, he had no evidence to suggest that Andy Barber had anything to do with the disappearances of the young women. If there was evidence, he wanted to see it, even if to appease his doubt. Luke had called Assistant State Attorney Dale Bishop and left a message. So far, he hadn't returned Luke's call. He was starting to wonder if there was any point in waiting longer.

He was about to leave when he received a text from Riley with information that connected Daphne Powers with Samuel Fletcher. Luke would wait no matter how long it took. He leaned back in the chair, kicked his legs out in front of himself, and waited for a half-hour more. Luke heard Dale Bishop's booming voice before he saw him step through the doorway that led to the interior of the police station. He told Luke to follow him.

Luke met him at the doorway. "I had no idea that you were here."

"My phone was off while I was watching the interrogation. I had no idea you were out here until a few minutes ago." Dale walked down a stark hallway with his shoulders squared back and commanded those around him.

Dale pulled open a door and introduced Luke to two other detectives and the man in the suit who had said that Andy Barber might be connected to the disappearances. The man, Det. Mike Brown, was the head of the violent crimes division. He held the same title and position that Luke had back home. Luke had been under the impression that was Det. Hanley's job.

"I'm sorry we had you waiting out there. I couldn't bring you back yet, but I also didn't want you to leave," Det. Brown said, shaking Luke's hand. "We've suspended Det. Hanley for now. I don't know what will come of it, given his father is the chief. I'm his supervisor and haven't been happy with his work in a long time. Your meeting with Dale prompted some much-needed change in the department."

All Luke could do was nod once in understanding. He wasn't there to trash Det. Hanley's reputation. All he wanted was real police work on the case. "I have some concerns about Andy Barber. I'm not sure he's involved in this."

Det. Brown turned to the window that overlooked the interrogation room. Andy sat with his hands folded on the table. Gone was the hubris and arrogance. His complexion had paled and he darted his eyes around like a caged animal in total fear. "He hasn't confessed. I spent the hour in there with him and no matter what I said or how I said it, he's not giving anything up."

"That's what I'm saying," Luke reiterated, watching Andy through the window. Even seeing him now and the look of fear on his face, Luke had serious doubts that they had arrested the right man. He turned to Det. Brown. "I know Andy checks all the boxes. Trust me, we considered him, too. He has the means, motive, and opportunity to do this. Daphne was hiding out at his house. There are even things we uncovered that you don't know. That's why I'm here, but I still don't think it adds up to him being guilty of murder. I have nothing that connects him to the other victims other than that they used his business while on the island. That's hardly a smoking gun."

"What is it you know?"

Luke told him all the information that Riley had uncovered through speaking with Daphne's friend, Kendra. Det. Brown's face pinched as the circumstantial evidence against Andy grew. When Luke was done, he said, "I know it seems compelling. Andy was missing on the night of Laurie Presley's disappearance, but we have no evidence that he was anywhere near that hotel. The fact is we haven't been able to confirm an alibi for him but that doesn't mean he did it."

Det. Brown leaned over the table and stared hard at Andy. "I don't know that we even have enough evidence to hold him."

"What made you bring him in?"

He turned and looked over his shoulder at Luke. "Daphne's father is a powerful man. Once he found out that his daughter had been murdered and that she had been living with Andy during the time she had disappeared, he called us and demanded that we do more than we were doing."

"I'm surprised that Det. Hanley would take direction from him."

"No, he wouldn't," Det. Brown said sharply. "Daphne's father didn't call the police station. He didn't waste his time talking to Det. Hanley again. He called the state prosecutor's office. After speaking with you, Dale already knew that Det. Hanley had dropped the ball, so he called me, but it was too late. Det. Hanley had heard that he was in trouble so he jumped the gun and made an arrest to make it look like he was doing something."

Luke folded his arms and didn't quite know what to say. Det. Hanley had made another poor decision. The only thing worse than doing nothing is arresting the wrong person or the right person with no evidence to back it up. "What are you going to do now?"

Dale stepped toward Luke. "I thought you might interview him and see if you get anything. You and your team have some rapport built with him. He looks scared enough he might talk to someone who has no power to arrest him. At this point, he might welcome a friendly face."

That was what Luke had been hoping he'd say. "I can do that. You're going to have to roll with my direction and give me the latitude to work. I don't interrogate like most detectives. I have a different approach in instances like this."

Dale gestured with his hand. "Whatever you need to do. All we want is the truth because if it's not Andy then we still have a killer out there."

"How are you going to address this with the media if you have to let him go?" Luke was glad that he wouldn't be on the receiving end of the storm they had created for themselves.

"I don't know," Dale said evenly. "We can worry about that later. Let's get to the truth first."

Luke played out in his head how he'd approach Andy and then went to the room. As he opened the door to the interrogation room, Andy jerked back and his eyes grew wide. He watched Luke as he entered and sat across from him at the table.

"You look familiar to me," Andy said softly, searching Luke's face. "You're the detective who is looking for Laurie Presley. I met a woman and that other guy who is working with you."

"You've spoken to Cooper and Riley. They are the ones who figured out that Daphne was staying at your house. Cooper also met you on your boat. He said that you were less cooperative then."

Andy blinked rapidly. "Is that why I'm here? Did you tell the police I wouldn't speak to you?"

Luke leaned back in the chair. "We have nothing to do with you being here, but hopefully now that I am, I can help you get out."

Andy leaned to the right and pointed to what looked like a mirror. "They are watching me. That other detective that was in here said that he was going to throw me in prison no matter what I did."

Luke couldn't address what Det. Brown had told him. Cops could lie but it didn't always help in an interrogation. "Let's sort this out," he said, drawing Andy's attention back to him. "Would you like something to drink before we get started?"

"My throat is dry. Water would be great."

Luke got up and stuck his head out of the door and told Dale who had stepped out of the observation room. Luke told him he wanted water for Andy and then added, "Bring it in so Andy can meet you." Luke needed Andy to know it wasn't Det. Brown deciding his fate.

Luke sat back down at the table and rested his hands on the tabletop. "Assistant State Attorney Dale Bishop is here. I want you to meet him, Andy. He's going to take my recommendation after we talk and he'll make the final decision about what happens to you. All we need from you is the truth."

Andy lowered his eyes to the table and folded his hands. "I'll tell you whatever you want to know," he mumbled.

Andy started with what Luke already knew – the entire background of how Daphne came to live with him. Luke knew the story but what he was watching for was Andy's body language when he recounted the details to Luke. Andy had remained closed – sitting there with his shoulders hunched, chest caved in, and arms crisscrossed on the table. He rarely made eye contact with Luke.

When he led Luke right up to the night Daphne disappeared, he raised his eyes. "I feel terrible that this happened. I do, but I didn't have anything to do with Daphne's murder."

Luke didn't acknowledge his feelings. He pressed on. "We know that Daphne had concerns that you were out all the time in the evening and came home drunk and disheveled. She suspected that you were seeing other women."

Andy shifted his eyes to the side. "I cheated once or twice. Most of the times I was out with friends avoiding being home with her." He turned his head sharply to look at Luke. "Have you ever lived with someone who makes every single moment together miserable?"

"I can't say that I have."

"It's unbearable. Staying was Daphne's decision and she didn't even talk it over with me before the decision was made. We didn't know each other well enough to live together. I had strong feelings for her, but it was too soon. Add to that the issues with her father and the fact that she had run away and people were looking for her – it was too much for both of us. I got to a point where I couldn't stand being around her, so yes, I cheated and I stayed away from my house to avoid her. That's the worst thing I've done."

There was a knock at the door and then Dale walked into the room with a bottle of water. He handed it to Andy, introduced himself, and echoed the words that Luke had told him. Andy didn't make eye contact with him but thanked him for the water. Dale left and gave Luke a thumbs-up as the door closed. That was all Luke had hoped would be accomplished. It wasn't much but Luke hoped Andy would see there were people willing to help if he helped himself.

Luke rattled off a date. "That was the night Laurie Presley disappeared. We know that you weren't home that night after work. We know that you didn't come home until the early hours of the morning. Where were you that night?"

"My boat," Andy said. "I didn't cheat on Daphne often and the handful of times I did it was with a woman I had been seeing on and off long before I met Daphne. Most nights, I either went to a bar or grabbed a few beers and sat on my boat until I assumed Daphne was already asleep and then I'd head home."

Andy had put himself close to the hotel. Luke leaned forward. "Did you see anything that night out on the water?"

Andy leaned back and took another sip of the water. He set the bottle down on the table. "You know, there was a boat that night that sped across the cove in front of me. It was a small speed boat and didn't have a lot of light on it. I remember thinking that the idiot was going to kill someone. I had even wondered if he was drunk. It was quick though and I forgot about it shortly after. I didn't think much of it. People come here on vacation and do stupid things all the time."

Luke asked him a few more questions about the boat, timing, and details, but Andy didn't know much more. "Was the boat big enough to fit more than one person?"

Andy nodded. "It was a standard speed boat. I don't know how many people were on the boat. It was too dark to see."

Luke let that subject rest for now. He turned his attention to the night Daphne left his house and was never seen again. "Andy, this is a problem for you. Her body was found washed up in the cove where you work and have your boat. As far as I know, you were the last person to see her alive."

"What about the cab driver or whoever picked her up that night?" Andy rubbed his forehead and pleaded to Luke with his eyes. "I couldn't have been the last person to see her. I didn't kill her."

"No cab picked her up. I've confirmed that with the cab company."

"Then it was someone she knew. Daphne had called someone before she left and asked for a ride. I know she did."

"Isn't it possible that you were angry that she was leaving and you snapped and killed her?"

Andy shook his head. "I already told you I was sick of her being there. I had such conflicted emotions. I had started to fall in love with her but hated her at the same time."

"Hate is a powerful emotion. It can make a person do things they wouldn't normally do."

"No," Andy said with force. "You have to believe me."

"I want to, Andy. I do, but I need more than your word."

"Then I'm in trouble because I can't prove something didn't happen." Andy sat back in the chair, took another sip of water, and stared across the table at Luke locked in a stalemate.

CHAPTER 38

Cooper woke from an uneven sleep and stared at the blades of the ceiling fan. Adele had her hand thrown over his middle. They had made love well into the night and the lethargy that consumed him now had been worth every second.

He yawned and kicked a leg out from under the covers and traced his fingertips over Adele's back. "We should get up. Luke and I have that appointment scheduled to go scuba diving."

Adele stirred next to him and then disengaged her limbs from his and rolled onto her back, pulling the sheet over her breasts. "Have you heard from him yet?"

"Not this morning. He texted late last night that he was on his way back from the police station. He didn't tell me what happened with Andy though."

"I need coffee," Adele mumbled as she began to snore softly again.

Cooper swung his feet to the floor and reached for the phone to call room service. He'd order breakfast and then get himself ready before meeting with Luke. He placed their breakfast order and then after hanging up slid his hand under the covers to pinch Adele's hip. "It will be here in twenty minutes and I'm going to shower, so you better make yourself presentable."

Before he could stand, Adele reached for his hand. "I'm coming with you," she said with her eyes closed and a lazy smile on her face.

An hour later with a smile plastered on his face, Cooper met Luke in the lobby of the hotel. "Where's Riley?" he asked, looking around for her.

"She's up in the room. She said she's sleeping in and then will look through more of the surveillance video. She still hasn't found who left that note for me. She thinks it's going to be important." Luke checked his watch. "Where are we meeting the scuba guy?"

"Dave is meeting us at the docks. He has a boat on the other side of the island and another boat on the same docks as Andy Barber. He said Andy's got the majority of the business around here so he normally works on the other side of the island. I filled him in on the areas we were hoping to search. What happened last night? Andy still in jail?"

"He's still in jail. There is a hearing this morning, but I'm fairly certain Dale Bishop is going to drop the case for lack of evidence. It's going to make the police department look foolish for the arrest, but there's no case."

Cooper pointed toward the back deck of the hotel. "We should head down and meet him."

As they walked, Luke told him about what had happened the night before. "The most important thing that came out of the interview was Andy seeing a speed boat the night Laurie Presley disappeared. He saw it close to one in the morning. I believe him about not being involved in Laurie's disappearance."

"What about Daphne's murder?"

"There are two schools of thought. Either Daphne's case is connected to the others and if we rule out Andy for the others, then we have to rule him out of Daphne's. The flip side is that Daphne's case isn't connected to the others and there are two killers – one of whom could be Andy."

Cooper looked over at his best friend. "Which one seems more likely to you?"

Luke threw his hands up and said he wasn't sure. Then he grew quiet and considered it. "If I'm being honest, Daphne's murder is connected to the other victims, and Andy wasn't involved. I hate ruling him out that quickly because there is almost no other explanation for Daphne's murder."

Cooper raised his eyebrows. "Did you talk to Riley last night?"

"Not about any of this. She had texted me at the police station about Daphne and Samuel Fletcher but she didn't tell me how she figured it out. Do you know?"

"She remembered that Daphne had been an international relations student and went to a prestigious school in London. She assumed maybe a diplomat had given a lecture series or in some way interacted with the students. Riley told me she was shooting in the dark, but she spoke to Kendra and confirmed that after a lecture Fletcher and Daphne had met and then remained in contact."

"It didn't bother her that he had been accused of harassing women?"

Cooper shook his head. "Kendra told Riley that Daphne didn't believe that he had done that and that he'd been unfairly punished." He reached for Luke's arm to slow him down. "We know that Fletcher has access to the staff area of the hotel, even possibly unlocking the door from the inside. We know that he basically lives in St. Thomas and has resources here. He's been able to find drugs and prostitutes, so who knows what else he has been able to get or what other help he's been able to secure. He's a rich powerful guy even without the diplomat status. Plus, he has a history of assaulting women. There is the stressor of him losing his job and being exiled. It's the perfect storm."

Luke stopped and turned to him. "I'm not saying I don't believe you. Fletcher might very well be the guy, but there are too many unanswered questions and no solid proof. We need something –

some physical evidence or a witness who ties him directly to the disappearances. Powerful men like Fletcher do not confess even when you lay out all the evidence in front of them. He will either lawyer up, go back to London, or dare us to find evidence. He's not confessing."

Cooper knew that to be the case. "Let's pray for a miracle then."

Luke laughed. "You're not the praying type. Don't you usually leave that to me?"

"I might have to get spiritual under this circumstance."

Luke slapped him on the back and assured him it would all get figured out. They walked the rest of the way to the dock and then found the boat that Dave said would be there. It was a similar dive boat to Andy's.

A man in a pair of tan cargo shorts and a blue tee-shirt waved them aboard. "I'm Dave. I'll be taking you out today on a forty-two-foot dive boat. There is the large deck here in the back and ladder on its stern allowing easy off and on access for divers."

Cooper shook Dave's hand. By his tone and upbeat expression, Dave was proud of his boat and he had every reason to be. "We appreciate you taking us out."

"Either of you need a refresher on the equipment or anything?" Dave asked and then took them to the masks, regulators, fins, and other gear. "If you have trouble with anything let me know." He grabbed the first ladder wrung and climbed up to the cockpit that was shielded from the sun with a white hard-top canopy. He turned the boat over and hit the throttle, bringing them into the open ocean.

While they geared up for the dive, Luke asked Cooper if he were sure he was ready. He assured Luke he was set. "Slightly nervous but I'm good. Not a fan of sharks, so let's keep our fingers crossed we don't see any."

"Remember, don't panic, and look up if you get nervous."

Cooper tapped his head. "It's advice I never forget." Scuba diving always took a certain level of courage that Cooper didn't know he had until he was doing it. There was a point in the dive where you hit a point of no return if something went wrong. If he panicked, he'd suck up the oxygen at a faster rate than allowable and he wouldn't have any to get back to the top. Don't panic and look up was a technique he employed even on land when he needed to calm himself down whether he was dealing with fear, stress, or anger. It had never failed him yet.

Dave stopped the boat, climbed down from his perch, and checked their readiness. When all was good, he told them they were free to dive. They each made it to the end of the boat and then Luke leaped off the back followed by Cooper. They hit the water with a splash.

As soon as Cooper started his descent his heart rate slowed and he remembered how much he enjoyed scuba diving. The waters of the Caribbean were a clear blue and perfect for a dive. He looked over at Luke who seemed to be enjoying himself as much. They gave each other a thumbs up and Luke pointed in the direction he wanted to go and Cooper followed.

Cooper wanted to enjoy the time even if that wasn't the only reason they were doing it. He needed to be on the lookout for anything unusual, but that didn't mean he couldn't have fun while they were there. About an hour ticked by as they explored a nearby coral reef that had been on the list of one of the best dive sites in St. Thomas. The beautiful marine life kept his attention and he had to keep reminding himself that he was on the lookout for anomalies.

Cooper was so focused on a school of yellowtail snappers that he didn't see Luke pointing to an area just below them on a reef they hadn't explored yet. When Luke finally got his attention, Cooper swam over to the area and stared down at the same spot. Twisted up in the reef was a shoe. Cooper could make out the back part of the heel. He had no idea how Luke had even spotted it.

Luke used hand signals to communicate the plan. He would swim down and extricate the shoe and then they'd bring it back up to the surface when they were ready to finish their dive. Luke had secured a small mesh bag onto the side of his shorts in case they found anything.

Cooper waited while Luke swam down five feet and tugged on the shoe until it came free. He held it in his hand in front of him as he swam back to Cooper. It was a woman's sandal with one of the straps torn and the buckle missing. The toe of the shoe appeared to have divots and marks like something had been nibbling on it. Even in its state, it looked familiar to Cooper.

They continued their search for another two hours without finding anything else. When it was time, they slowly made their ascent back to the surface. Cooper reached fifteen feet below the water's surface when he remembered the shoe in Fletcher's closet. He had no idea if they were similar, but he'd had the foresight to snap a picture. He'd have to get back to the boat before he knew for sure if they were a match.

CHAPTER 39

I leaned into the laptop, hit the pause button on the video, and adjusted my headphones. After more hours than I cared to count, I finally found the person who had slipped the note onto the front desk of the hotel. I hit rewind to watch it a third time.

I had been playing the video on fast forward when I came upon a woman walking up to the counter, speaking to someone at the desk, and then moving into the lobby area. At first, it looked like she was waiting for someone. She even sat down for a while, but she didn't meet with anyone.

Instead, when the lobby quieted and the woman at the front desk went into the office behind the desk, the unknown woman got up from the lobby chair and walked to the front desk. She reached her hand over the side and dropped an envelope.

I took a few screenshots of the woman and fast forwarded to the point where Vic stood at the desk early the following morning. He picked up the envelope and examined it. Then he headed toward the elevators and out of frame with the envelope in hand. That had to have been when he delivered it to our door.

I stopped the video and leaned back in the chair pouring over the screenshot photos. I didn't recognize the woman at all. She seemed about my height with a slender frame, olive skin, and long dark hair. She was dressed in a simple summer skirt that flowed around her ankles as she walked and a green tank top that showed off her toned arms and hugged her breasts. She hadn't done anything to try to shield her identity, but unless someone was doing what I was doing now, no one would have even noticed her dropping off the envelope.

I got up from the desk and went to find Vic. I stopped at his office door, but the door had been left open and the lights were off. I headed back to the lobby and found him at the front desk speaking to a woman and man who had a map in their hands. He smiled as he pointed to destinations on the map and then laughed with them over something I couldn't hear.

When they walked away, I rushed to the front desk. "I found the woman who left the note. Does she look familiar to you?" I handed him my phone. "I took screenshots from the video. You can watch the video if you think that will help."

Vic stared down at the first photo and then scrolled to the second and third. He raised his eyes to me. "I don't need to see the video. This is Connie Francis. She works at the front desk of the hotel next door. I know her well. I don't understand why she'd leave this note or how she'd know Samuel Fletcher."

"Maybe she was working that night and saw him with Laurie."

He handed me back my phone. "You'll have to ask her. She usually works during the day, so you can probably find her at the front desk."

I thanked him and left the hotel practically in a sprint. I slowed down when I nearly bumped into an older woman as she was approaching the hotel. I offered my apologies, she cursed young people in a hurry, and I power-walked my way to the hotel next to mine.

I walked through the automatic double doors and right away spotted Connie behind the front desk. I stood off to the side in the lobby observing her for a few moments. Nothing seemed out of the ordinary though. I waited until a hotel guest left and then I approached.

"Connie Francis?" I said, leaning into the front desk.

"Yes, can I help you?"

Connie had an easy smile and her dark hair wrapped up into a loose bun. She had the relaxed professional demeanor of someone who had done the job for a long time. She reminded me of someone ready for anything, as if she had seen and heard it all. She probably had.

I explained who I was and why I was there. Her smile stiffened when I mentioned the envelope with the note. Her eyes shifted to the woman at the desk standing next to her helping other guests and then back to me. "Meet me outside and I'll speak to you in a moment."

I backed up from the desk, wondering if she were serious or trying to get rid of me. But when she waved me back again and then turned to her co-worker, I took my cue and left. I stood outside the front door of the hotel for a few minutes before she came out.

"Let's walk down to the beach," she said, not stopping long enough for me to answer. She marched past me and kept on going, leaving me no choice but to follow her.

When we got down to the beach and out of sight from the hotel, she stopped walking and turned to me. "How do you know about the note?"

"Luke is my husband. We've been searching for whoever left the note. I finally found you on the hotel surveillance."

She winced. "I didn't realize that anyone would be going through the footage to find me."

"Did you not want to be found?"

She shook her head. "I left the note for your husband who I saw on the news. I knew he was next door because I saw him going in and out of the hotel. I figured someone at the front desk would get it to him."

"Did you see Samuel Fletcher with Laurie Presley that night?"

"No."

"How do you know him?"

"I don't."

I took a breath. She wasn't going to make this easy. "You were right that it was Fletcher in the video. I don't understand how you knew that though."

Connie looked away from me and out toward the water. "I just knew."

"That's not true and we both know it."

"If I tell you, I'm putting someone's life in danger. It's why she didn't call the police or the tip line herself. She's in a precarious position." Connie turned and locked eyes with me. "She's not safe and there's no one who can protect her."

"Connie, I'm not going to pretend that everything is going to be okay. I can't offer her protection. All I can tell you is that if this person knows who is responsible for Laurie Presley's disappearance, then she's in danger by not telling."

"It's not just Laurie Presley. She has information on all the missing women."

My stomach somersaulted. "How does this person know?"

"She was told."

"I'm assuming we are talking about Fletcher. If he told someone about his crimes, then she is in danger with him free. Her only hope is to come forward and see that he faces justice. It's the only way she will ever be safe."

Connie crossed her arms and turned her body to face the ocean. "She's done enough by telling me and having me leave the note. We delivered him to you. Why can't you figure it out on your own?"

"Connie, the note led us to Fletcher, but he said he walked her to the front of the hotel and left. He gave us an alibi for that night and the other nights when women disappeared. We have no direct evidence to the contrary. There is no physical evidence. There is no witness statement evidence. There is nothing. We need more than helping a drunk woman on the night she disappeared. We are dealing with a total lack of physical evidence. Trust me, if I had more and the police had more, he'd be arrested by now."

She scoffed. "You think anyone is going to arrest Samuel Fletcher? He's been getting away with his crimes for years. He's untouchable. Look at those women who came forward and said he was sexually harassing them. He lost his job and now lives here in St. Thomas. That's hardly a punishment."

I couldn't argue with her. She was right – rich, powerful people got away with criminal activity all the time. Even when they were caught and tried and convicted, their sentences were often much lighter than someone else convicted of the same crimes. It wasn't a reason to deny families justice though.

"Then why come forward with the note if you didn't want someone to know?"

Connie turned away from me again. "It was a desperate attempt to help a friend. We thought if we pointed investigators in the right direction, they'd be able to do the rest. I never thought he'd be held accountable, but I thought he might leave St. Thomas if there was enough pressure."

With both of us turned toward the ocean, staring out at its vastness, I pled my case and hated myself for the argument I made. "If Fletcher is the one responsible, then the only thing that matters right now is stopping him from doing this again. If your friend won't come forward, she is putting other young women at risk. I know that's a terrible burden to put on her, and it's a horrible argument for me to make. It's not her responsibility, but someone somewhere has to stand up for these young women. These families need justice, and more than that, they need answers about what happened to their daughters."

Connie breathed in and out so loudly I heard every breath. The seconds ticked by while we stood side by side in silence. I was quickly giving up hope that she'd tell me more. Then when I was about to thank her and walk away, she said, "You've already answered your question."

I let the words sink in and it hit me all at once. I turned to her. "Are you talking about Charmaine? She'd know better than anyone what his ring looks like. She is also his alibi."

Connie didn't say anything but she nodded her head once. "I don't think she'll speak to you. I don't even know that she'll go on record that she lied about his alibi. It's more than that though."

I couldn't imagine any more of a win than that. I waited and allowed Connie to say it in her own time. I knew how difficult this must be for her.

She turned to face me. "Samuel Fletcher told her the night after he killed Laurie Presley. He said he thought he might have been seen by someone and that he needed an alibi. He threatened her that she had to be his alibi or he'd kill her, too. Charmaine isn't stupid. She had sex with him and then when he wasn't paying attention, she hit record on her phone and then asked him about the murders. He had been lulled into such safety and who'd believe a whore, right? She got a confession on video. She's been holding onto it this whole time. She doesn't believe that even with it he will be held accountable. She's terrified of him but figured if he tried to hurt her, she'd tell him she had recorded it and that it would be released if anything happened to her."

I couldn't believe what I was hearing. It was the evidence we needed. "I need to see Charmaine now."

"I don't know that she'll speak to you, but I'll give you her address." She gave me the address and then some quick directions to get there.

I knew Luke had been to see her once already. He hadn't told me where she lived or much about their interaction other than he hadn't fully believed her. He had called her difficult and non-compliant.

I wondered now if he was just dismissive of her because of the sex work. “I don't know if I should tell you to tell Charmaine we spoke so maybe you can convince her to speak to me or if I should show up unannounced. What do you think will work better?”

“Show up and convince her the way you convinced me.” Connie turned back to the hotel. “I need to get back. Good luck.” She walked off before I could say much more.

Since Luke and Cooper were on the scuba trip, I'd go alone and convince Charmaine to come forward. At the very least, she might let me listen to the recording of the confession. If nothing else, I'd be able to tell Ava and Bill what happened to Laurie.

I called James, the cab driver, to see if he had time to take me over there. He had been so kind to us already and Luke said that he knew Charmaine. He said he'd be there in ten, so I walked back to our hotel and waited in front. As soon I told him where I was going, he apologized that he hadn't been able to get Charmaine to change her story about the alibi.

“I'm hoping to do the same and have a little more ammunition with me this time,” I said from the passenger seat. James felt like a friend now so I was riding shotgun.

He glanced over at me. “Charmaine is a handful. Don't underestimate her.”

“I won't.” I wasn't feeling cocky about it. I was more apprehensive than I was letting on. I felt like this was our one shot to find out the truth and prove it. “Charmaine is our only hope to find closure for these families. I need to convince her of that.”

“Play to her ego.” James drove us directly to Charmaine's. There was a car in the driveway, but otherwise, the house didn't look like there was anyone home. The front door was closed and the blinds were drawn. James stopped in the road in front of her house and cut the engine. “I'm not leaving you here. I'll wait and she can see that I'm out here. She won't mess with you as long as I'm here."

I walked to the front door and knocked twice and waited. After a moment I knocked again. This time a pretty woman with round eyes and her hair swept on top of her head answered the door. I asked if she was Charmaine and she nodded.

"I need to speak to you about Samuel Fletcher."

Her eyes got wide and she shook her head frantically. "You need to go."

"I can't go. I need to speak to you."

"It's not safe for you. You need to leave now," she said again, her voice trembling.

I knew Connie had told me she was afraid, but this was over the top. "It won't take more than a few minutes."

"No..."

Before Charmaine could finish her sentence, the door opened wider and Ollie appeared, moving her out of the way. "Come inside. Charmaine will tell you what she knows."

I turned back to James but he wasn't looking toward the house. If I had been listening to my gut I wouldn't have gone inside. The truth was too important. As soon as I stepped into Charmaine's house, I understood her fear.

Samuel Fletcher sat in a chair in the corner of the living room. "I guess we are going to have to get rid of two of you now," he said, looking to Ollie.

CHAPTER 40

Luke stood on the boat and pulled his scuba gear off, leaving it on the deck. He grabbed a towel and dried himself enough that he wasn't dripping water all over the place. "Dave, that was an amazing dive. That water is crystal clear. It was probably one of the best dives I've been on in a long time."

Dave held his hands out. "It's why I've got a booming business. See anything of interest down there?"

"A shoe," Cooper said, getting himself out of his scuba gear.

Luke pulled it from the mesh dive bag. "I'm not sure that it means much. I assume there are many party boats in these waters. Doesn't surprise me someone lost a shoe."

"Pretty common," Dave echoed, sitting down on the side of the boat. They were still rocking out in open water. "You wouldn't believe some of the things tourists lose overboard, especially if they have been drinking."

Luke palmed the shoe, which was a woman's strappy sandal. It had been covered in sand and other ocean debris so it was hard to see what color it might have been. Turning to Cooper, he asked, "What do you think?"

Cooper reached out his hand and took the shoe. He examined it and brushed some of the debris from it. "I've seen this somewhere before." He handed the shoe back to Luke and went to the shorts he had worn over his swim trunks. He pulled his phone from the pocket and brought up his recent photos. His eyes got wide and then he handed the phone to Luke. "Doesn't that look like this shoe? This one is a mess and torn, but it's the same shoe."

Luke looked at the photo and studied the heel and the side strap, which was all that was visible in the photo. Then he looked over the shoe again and it did appear that they were a match. "Where did you see this shoe?" he asked, pointing to the photo.

"In Samuel Fletcher's closet. It was on the floor kind of poking out of the open door. I didn't have a chance to go into the closet and get a better look though."

"Let's head back to the hotel and clean up this shoe and figure out what to do next," Luke said evenly, but he felt anything but calm. He didn't want to jump to conclusions though. It could mean everything or it could mean nothing at all.

Dave took a look at the photo and the shoe and he agreed that it was similar. He climbed the ladder to the cockpit and drove them back to shore as Cooper and Luke dried off in the sun.

Once they were back on the dock, they thanked Dave and gave him a generous tip. He assured them if they needed to go back out, he'd rearrange his schedule to accommodate them. Luke thanked him and they went on their way.

"What are we going to do if it is the shoe?"

Luke gripped the shoe in his hand. "Let's go in and speak to Vic. Maybe we can speak to some of the housekeeping staff that clean Fletcher's room. They may have seen this shoe. It could be a common shoe. You might not have been able to see the pair in the closet. There could be several explanations and I don't want to jump to conclusions."

Cooper agreed with him. They walked past diners on the deck and entered the hotel. From that vantage point, Luke could see Vic helping a guest at the front desk. When Vic finished, Luke approached and gestured to the side of the desk. He slipped Vic the shoe. "We need to talk about this. We think Fletcher might have the same shoe in his closet."

Vic looked over his shoulder to the guests milling around the lobby. "Let's take this to my office." They followed him down the hall, and when they were seated with the door closed, Vic put the shoe on his desk. "What do you mean you saw it in Fletcher's closet?"

Cooper explained, "I went to speak to him to ask him about the disappearances and when I was in his room, I looked around a little while he thought I was in the bathroom. When I looked in his bedroom, I saw a shoe similar to this sticking out of the closet door." Cooper pulled his phone from his pocket and showed the photo to Vic.

He studied it and then looked at the shoe. "They are similar. I don't understand the significance though."

"We aren't sure," Luke admitted. "Could we speak to one of the housekeeping staff to see if they have seen women's items? Our concern is that this might be one of the victim's shoes, and if it is, then Fletcher may have the other."

"Like a trophy or something?" Vic asked, pulling back in horror.

"Exactly like that."

Vic grabbed the phone and punched in some numbers. He held the receiver to his ear, but never spoke to anyone. A moment later, he dropped it back in its holder. Then he pulled out a desk drawer and grabbed a red keycard. "I can do one better than speaking to hotel staff. I called Fletcher's room and there is no answer. We are going to check for ourselves."

Cooper raised his eyebrows and looked at Luke. "Can we do that?"

Vic waved him off. "I can go in any room in this hotel if I have cause. If we were the police, we'd need a warrant. We aren't the police. Let's go."

Luke wasn't sure it was the best idea, but there didn't seem to be any stopping Vic. If he thought he had the right to look in Fletcher's room, Luke wasn't going to argue. The three of them walked to the staff elevator and went straight to the top floor. Luke hoped that Fletcher wasn't in the shower or ignoring the phone. They'd look stupid showing up to his room like that and he'd probably refuse them entry.

A few moments later, that wasn't a concern. Vic knocked on the door, called Fletcher's name, and then opened the door with his keycard. The room had recently been cleaned by housekeeping. There was the faint smell of a disinfectant in the air.

"Let's be quick about this," Vic said, heading right for the bedroom. Luke followed behind while Cooper stayed in the living room area and started to look around.

Vic slid the closet door to the side and right there on the floor was the shoe Cooper had mentioned. "There it is," he said, bending down to pick it up but Luke stopped him.

"Don't touch it. We don't know if it's evidence yet." Luke stepped around Vic and slid open the closet door the rest of the way. He bent down and looked over the shoe and then compared it to the one in his hand. They were the same size, same straps, and there were small markings on the strap where the flower would have been. "It's a match. There's no other shoe in the closet like it, so this one might be its other half."

Crouched low, Luke examined the rest of the contents of the closet. In the far back behind a large suitcase was another smaller one with its zipper half-open. Using just his fingertips, Luke nudged the tops of it open so he could see the contents inside. There were several women's items in there including a blouse and a red lacy bra. Luke had no idea why Fletcher would have these items or who they might have belonged to.

He stood up and turned to speak to Vic who was across the room now looking in the bedside drawers. “I think we need to get out of here and call the police.”

Vic stayed motionless as he stared down into a drawer. “I’m not going anywhere.”

There was a sadness in Vic’s tone that Luke hadn’t heard before. “Are you okay? What did you find?”

Vic pointed down to the contents of the drawer. “Amani’s sapphire earrings. Her mom had bought them for her birthday. She was wearing them the night she disappeared. My aunt argued with her about not wearing them out because they had been expensive and she didn’t want Amani to lose one. Amani loved them and for three weeks she had refused to take them off.”

Luke put his hand on Vic’s shoulder and peered down into the drawer. Sitting there in a clear plastic bag were two sapphire earrings. They had sterling silver posts and backing. “Are you sure they are the same?”

Vic nodded. “Amani was so proud of them. I’d know them anywhere.”

A sinking feeling spread through Luke’s gut. “We need to get out of here and call the police. Can you change the key to this room so Fletcher can’t get back in?”

“I can do that downstairs.” Vic turned to leave the bedroom. “Are you going to wait here to make sure he doesn’t come back?”

“I’ll leave Cooper here. I want to find Riley.”

“Riley’s not here,” Vic said, looking up at him. “She figured out who left you the note and went to speak to her.”

Luke wasn’t surprised she had figured it out, but he didn’t like that she had gone alone. “Who was it?”

“Connie. She works at the desk at the hotel next door.”

“I’m going to find her and Cooper will stand guard. I’ll call the police while you change the keycard. Please don’t touch anything in here.

This is an active scene now."

Vic assured him he wouldn't do anything to jeopardize the case and then left.

Luke followed him out of the bedroom and found Cooper going through cabinets in the small kitchenette. "We need to get out of here. I found other women's clothing and Vic found his cousin's earrings in Fletcher's bedside table. I'm fairly certain Fletcher is our guy, Cooper. I need to convince the cops."

He explained to Cooper what Vic was doing and asked him to stand guard on the floor outside of the suite door. He also told him about what Riley found. "She should be next door talking to a woman named Connie. I want to update her and tell her to keep her guard up in case she sees Fletcher."

Several minutes later, Luke stood dumbfounded outside the hotel next door as Connie explained what she had told Riley. "Was she going to see Charmaine alone?"

"I think so. I gave her the address and she said she was going to speak to her. I assumed she was going right away." Connie looked over her shoulder at the hotel and then turned back to Luke. "I'm sure she will be fine. I need to get back to work."

Luke thanked her and she was on her way. He pulled his phone out of his pocket and tried to call Riley. Five rings and then it went to voicemail. He left her a detailed message about what they found in Samuel Fletcher's room. Next, he called Dale Bishop.

"Dale, we found something on Samuel Fletcher," Luke said rushing the sentence after the man answered. "You need to get the cops to get a search warrant and take a look at what we found."

"Can you tell me over the phone?"

Luke detailed the items found in Fletcher's hotel room and how they were found. "Vic said he had a right to search the room. I'm not in a law enforcement capacity so I'll let you sort out those details."

"Are you sure it was Amani Hanley's earrings?" Dale shouted to someone on the other end of the line to get him the chief of police on the phone. Then back to Luke. "We have to be certain. It's what will get us the search warrant. The other items could be his girlfriend's clothes."

"Vic assured me they were his cousin's earrings. It was compelling."

"It's enough. I'll get it and get a crime scene unit over right away. Is the room secured now?"

"I have Cooper standing guard. We have no idea where Fletcher is or when he will return."

"Keep me updated if Fletcher gets back."

"Vic changed the access keycard so Fletcher can't get in even if he wants to."

Dale clicked off and Luke was left standing in the hot sun wondering if Riley was okay. She hadn't called him back yet so he fired off a text and went to join Cooper.

He went back into the hotel and found Cooper slumped against the wall reading from his phone. He raised his head to Luke. "Police coming?"

"Dale said he'd be able to get a warrant. We need to wait for them to arrive."

"Hear from Riley?"

Luke shook his head and explained what Connie had told him. He wasn't sure why he was worried. Riley could handle Charmaine, but given she had probably lied about Fletcher's alibi, it wasn't sitting right with him that she was there alone. "Do you have this on your own? I want to find Riley. I don't like the idea of her being out there alone while we have no idea where Fletcher might be."

Cooper saluted him. "No one is getting in that room unless it's the cops."

Luke punched Cooper in the arm affectionately. "I'll let you know when I find her. Keep me updated." As Luke turned to head back to the elevator his cellphone rang. He reached for it excited that it might be Riley. He was surprised to see it was James.

"I was just going to call you for a ride. Riley is at Charmaine's."

"I drove her there," James said. "That's why I'm calling. She's been in there a long time, Luke. Too long and I'm concerned something is wrong. Just a bad feeling that doesn't sit right with me. I didn't know if it was my place to intrude on her meeting. I'm in the cab outside of Charmaine's house."

"Wait for me and we'll go in together. I'll be there in ten minutes. If anything goes wrong between now and then go in and get her."

"Roger that." James clicked off.

Luke locked eyes with Cooper down the hallway. "I knew something was wrong."

"You want me to go with you?"

"No. Stay here. Call Adele and make sure she's safe, and if she's in the hotel, tell her to go to your room and stay there."

CHAPTER 41

I had been sitting on the couch in Charmaine's living room trying to figure out an escape plan while Ollie and Samuel Fletcher argued about how they were going to get rid of us in daylight. Neither had admitted anything yet regarding the young women who were missing, but the look on Charmaine's face told me she knew what they were capable of.

My patience had grown thin. Even though I had no weapon and nothing in the room looked like it could be used as a weapon, I didn't want to sit there and wait to die. I whistled loudly, and when all eyes turned to me, I asked, "Why do you need to kill us?"

Fletcher smirked. "Why are you here to see Charmaine? Seeking some advice on how to keep your husband happy?"

"My husband is more than satisfied. Charmaine might have some information I want."

"About me," Fletcher said, a statement not a question. "I know who you are. You're the wife of that cop running around here trying to find those missing women. Why couldn't you people just enjoy your vacation instead of getting involved in all of this?"

I leaned back and crossed one leg over the other. "That's a great question. For once, I wanted to enjoy a vacation. Unfortunately, you chose to kidnap and kill young women around the age of my husband's sister who was murdered in college. I don't get why you did it. You're a decent-looking guy. You've got money. You could get any woman you wanted."

When Fletcher didn't respond to me, I looked to Ollie. "How are you wrapped up in this?"

"Shut up! You talk too much." Ollie turned back to Fletcher. "Let's kill her first and then we can take care of Charmaine."

"I know I talk too much," I said interrupting him. "I'm thoroughly annoying. It's like a superpower. If you're going to kill me, the least you could do is let me die knowing the truth. I wasted my whole vacation on this."

Charmaine kicked me in the leg with her sandaled foot. "Stop antagonizing him."

"I came here for the truth and I'm not leaving without it."

"You're not leaving at all," Fletcher said, his tone menacing.

I got up from the couch and Ollie shouted for me to sit back down. "I need to stretch. I'm not a threat. If I had a weapon, I would have shot you already." I pretended to stretch and he turned back to Fletcher. They had no weapons either, but I knew Daphne had been strangled so one of them got their rocks off strangling women. I assumed it was Fletcher. I sized him up from across the room and I didn't know if I could take him if I had to. I had some fighting skills but not many.

With both of them distracted, I started to make my way toward the front window. The blinds were closed and I wanted to alert James. As soon as I reached my hand out to separate the blinds, I was jerked backward by my hair. I stumbled back a few steps and then landed on my backside in the middle of the living room.

"I said sit down!" Ollie shouted in my face. "If you won't listen, then I'm going to make you listen."

Charmaine cursed at me. "Do as they say. They aren't playing around."

I pushed myself off the floor until I was standing again and brushed down my shorts and adjusted my shirt. I was going to blow this whole thing up. I didn't have any other moves. "I know exactly what I got myself into. Fletcher over there kidnapped several young women, took them to the hotel where he raped and killed them. My guess is Ollie is his lackey who helped him clean up afterward and dump the bodies in the ocean. I bet you didn't count on Daphne floating back to shore."

Fletcher sighed loudly. "I didn't count on a lot of things."

"Can I take that as a confession?"

"You can take that however you want to take it."

I sat back down next to Charmaine who continued to plead with me to shut up. "I can't figure out why you killed Daphne. I spoke to her friend, Kendra, and she said you two hit it off. Why would you kill her?"

Ollie turned to me, his eyes glaring. For a moment, I thought he might come back and strike me again. Fletcher told him to calm down. He shooed Ollie to the side of the room and then locked his gaze on me. "You really want to know?"

"I want to know."

"I'm sick. I get these headaches," he said, holding the side of his head. "It hurts so bad and then I have to hunt women and kill them. Then the headaches go away." As he finished, the sides of his mouth turned up in a sick grin. "Is that what you wanted to hear?"

"Not really. I already know that you're sick. I wanted to know why you chose Daphne as one of your victims. It's what led me to you. It's how I figured it out. If it had not been for that, I might have still been considering Andy Barber. It was only after I realized your connection to Daphne that I zeroed in on you."

Fletcher sighed and rolled his eyes at me. "She called me the night she left Andy and wanted to see me before she left for the airport. I had Ollie pick her up and bring her to me at his friend's boat. I wasn't going to risk bringing her back to the hotel when people were already looking for her. If I was going to the trouble of seeing her, I wanted sex. She didn't want to give it up and one thing led to another. She's dead. If she had given me what I wanted, who knows how it would have turned out for her."

I knew a few things right then – I had been right about Fletcher killing these women and Ollie had access to a boat. I assumed then that the rest of the women were in the water. "How did you choose your victims?"

"Don't you ever shut up?" Fletcher asked, shaking his head. There was a smile on his face though. He had told me about Daphne and he enjoyed reliving it. "I don't see why you want to know all this. You're not going to be able to do anything with the information. You'll be dead."

"I don't like unfinished puzzles."

Fletcher pointed to Ollie. "Pat her down and make sure she's not wearing a wire. It should have occurred to me sooner."

"If I were wearing a wire, the cops would already be in here." I stood from the couch and raised my shirt and spun around enough for them to see that I hadn't been wired.

"I can't take all the credit," Fletcher started, folding his hands on his stomach. He was dressed in khaki shorts, a Polo shirt, and sneakers. He was hardly dressed for murder and had an air of confidence as if no matter what he said, he was getting away with it. He waved his hand dismissively. "Ollie selected a few of the girls for me. He started with Amani. She was my favorite of all. But that was fraught with problems. We decided picking local girls probably wasn't going to be the best bet. Too many interested people on the island. Tourists would arouse less suspicion and it did for a while. Ollie screened them, selected them, brought them to my special spot, and then got rid of them for me. I got away with it until you people showed up here. Now,

I need to get rid of you and get out of St. Thomas – go somewhere they can't extradite me until all this blows over."

The cold unfeeling way he described the murders disgusted me. "Was Amani your first?"

"On St. Thomas," he said matter-of-factly. "There have been others they will never tie to me."

I turned to Ollie. "What was in it for you?"

He shook his head like I was an idiot. "Money. Best paying job I ever had."

My mouth hung open in shock. "Young women are dead because of you. Entire families have been destroyed. What about Dylan? Was he involved in this?"

Ollie tipped his head back and laughed. "He'd never be involved. He's too much of a baby. He's too chicken to ever do anything really bad. And those young women deserved what they got."

Anger bubbled up inside of me. "How so?"

"Getting drunk and taking off with a stranger. What did they expect was going to happen? It's their fault. They were chosen for their gullibility. Laurie got away from me that night. She's the only one that got away. We still got her."

"You were there that night?"

Ollie laughed again. "I'm always there, lurking in the shadows. I was on the back deck of the bar for most of the night. Dylan never saw me. No one notices me. That's *my* superpower."

I wanted to ask why. Investigators always want to know why as if it will somehow make sense of senseless murders. Ollie had already answered the why and I was sure that Fletcher didn't have one other than murdering these young women was what got him off.

I looked right at Fletcher. "Did you dump them all in the ocean?"

He pointed to Ollie. "Once he picked them up from me, I have no idea what happened."

"They are all in the ocean, probably fish food by now." Ollie pointed to Charmaine and me. "That's exactly where the both of you are going. Once you're gone and he leaves, no one will ever know my involvement."

"That's not true," Charmaine said, jutting her chin out. She had grown some confidence in the last few minutes. She raised her eyes to Fletcher. "I recorded you when you were talking about the murders. You thought you were safe talking to me because no one would believe me. If anything happens to me, I've got a contact who will take the recording right to the police. I've made several copies and a few people know."

"You're lying," Fletcher said but his voice betrayed him. "You're nothing but a whore."

Charmaine laughed. "A smart whore." She turned to Ollie and grinned. "That's my superpower."

Fletcher shook his head. "I don't believe you."

"Why do you think I'm here?" I asked. "I found someone who has the recording. They tried to alert us before which is how Luke knew it was you with Laurie the night she disappeared. We didn't know the full scope of your involvement until we tracked down the person who anonymously alerted us. Luke is bringing that recording to the police right now. It's only a matter of time and you're done, Fletcher."

He puffed out his chest. "I'm untouchable."

"You're not and if you kill us, it's going to tie right back to the two of you. My husband is a detective and has connections with the FBI and Interpol and whoever else will work with him to hunt you down like a dog. You can pretty much forget the justice system because he will kill you both if anything happens to me."

Ollie whipped around to Fletcher. "You confessed? Are you kidding me?" He cursed a long streak of words telling Fletcher exactly how stupid he was for telling anyone. He ran his hands through his hair and then pulled it from the roots, pacing back and forth. "What are we going to do?"

"Stick to the plan," Fletcher said calmly. "I don't know what game these two are playing, but Charmaine doesn't have the nerve or the smarts to record me. They're bluffing."

Ollie turned sharply and charged me, yanking me up by my hair. "Are you lying? Tell me now!" he shouted into my face. He dragged me across the living room by my hair. His eyes bulged out of his head. He had become unhinged with the thought of getting caught.

"I'm telling you the truth. Luke is with the police right now. That's why I'm here to see if Charmaine is willing to come to the police station and give a statement," I lied with ease.

Ollie cursed and raged on, jerking me around the room by my hair. With my eyes pinched tight I had no idea what Charmaine or Fletcher were doing. I tried to grab Ollie's hand for him to release me but he kept a tight hold. "Let me go!" I shouted as loudly as I could. I hoped that James could hear me.

In response, Ollie only gripped my hair tighter. He cursed at Fletcher more for putting him in the situation. "I don't know what to do," he said over and over and over again, the panic rising in his voice. He thought he'd never be caught.

I winced against the pain and took a swing for his gut. I missed the first time and then used the self-defense technique I had been taught and moved toward him, loosening his grip on my hair. I swung again, this time connecting. When he doubled over in pain, I kicked him square in the crotch, which made him howl in pain and crumple to the floor holding himself.

I jetted toward the front door, and as my hand grabbed hold of the doorknob, I pulled the door toward me but a hand above my head slammed it shut. Icy fingers wrapped around my neck from behind, trying to squeeze the life out of me. Today wasn't my day to die. I wasn't going out like this.

I slammed my whole body back into him with the full force of my weight, knocking him off his feet. We tumbled backward and I landed on top of him, both of us on our backs. His head hit the floor with a sickening whack. He grunted and moaned while I scrambled to my feet. I didn't make it far when the door flew open and James and Luke stood with guns aimed at us.

"Down on the floor," James said moving past Luke and aiming the gun right at Fletcher's head. The man barely moved a muscle. I assumed the full effect of my weight and the force with which I shoved us backward had given him a fairly good brain bump. "Please move so I can blow your head off," James shouted but Fletcher didn't budge.

I didn't care if he shot Fletcher or not. Luke wrapped his arms around me. "Are you okay?"

I wriggled loose and turned. "Where did Ollie go?"

Charmaine pointed over her shoulder. "He went out the back door."

I pushed Luke. "Go, stop him. He helped Fletcher. He found the girls and then dumped the bodies in the ocean. Don't let him get away."

Luke pulled me closer. "We'll let the cops handle that." He looked over at Charmaine. "Are you okay?"

She nodded and pointed to me. "That one's tougher than she looks. Who knew that big booty would be a lifesaver? She knocked Fletcher clear across the room." She laughed.

Luke pulled me into him and kissed me. He dropped a kiss on my lips. "I told you you're perfect just the way you are."

I cringed inside, but I couldn't help but smile. Luke gave James a thumbs up as the sirens from nearby police cars got closer. I was glad they'd handle it from here. We had two days left to our vacation and I needed a drink.

EPILOGUE

We extended our vacation by five days. Vic had been so grateful that we helped figure out what happened to his cousin, Amani, that the hotel comped us a few more days. James, Luke, and I had waited at Charmaine's house until the police arrived and arrested Fletcher, who kicked and screamed his whole way to the police car. He demanded that the cops release him given his status. They laughed in his face and threatened to taser him if he didn't comply.

With Charmaine's statement and her recording of his confession along with my statement about what he had confessed to me, there was no chance that Fletcher was ever going to be released. The court had denied him bail, took his passport, and locked him up. He sat in prison awaiting trial, but Dale Bishop had a feeling that with new evidence mounting it was a lock for a guilty verdict. There was no way Fletcher was going to publicly admit what he did and take a plea though. The case would be a full trial, in which I would be called to testify.

The biggest surprise was that not even an hour later the cops tracked Ollie down at his house. The reason they found him so quickly was that he had fled Charmaine's house and confessed everything he had done to Dylan, who wouldn't let him leave, and called the cops himself. He may sell drugs and sleep around, but he drew a line at murder, even if it meant turning in his family.

We heard right before our flight home that Ollie was willing to testify against Fletcher for a shorter sentence. It wouldn't be that much shorter, but it might shave off a couple of years.

I'd like to say that we used our last days to unwind and drink fruity drinks while lying in the sun and playing in the ocean. We did our fair share of that, but once the news media heard about the arrests and how they came to be, we had a line of media interviews set up.

There was hardly any escaping it. We were all staying at the same hotel and even when Vic tried to get them to leave us alone, they hounded us. We finally decided that the best approach was to give them the story and they could be on their way. Luke had kept his promise and gave Grady the exclusive. After that, we sat down with each of the networks and gave them the interviews they wanted.

We had inadvertently turned into celebrities – on a global stage. Luke had even fielded a few calls from agents who offered to represent him and make him something of a law enforcement expert on the media circuit. He declined, and as he told them, he wanted nothing more than to get back to regular detective work. Cooper and I knew his answer before he ever said it. If there was anything that Luke wasn't going to do, it was purposefully take a job where all he did was speak to the media.

After all that was said and done, Bill and Ava and Vic scheduled an impromptu memorial service out on the water. We joined them as they said goodbye to their loved ones. It was a somber moment, but Bill had assured us that he'd rather know the truth than leave St. Thomas never knowing what had happened.

A few nights after getting back, we were all seated around my kitchen table. Life was returning to normal. After clearing the plates after dinner, I asked Adele, "Do you have any regrets your wedding turned out how it did?"

Adele reached for Cooper's hand and smiled over at me. "None at all. It was marked by tragedy but in the end, we provided several families the closure they needed and we stopped a killer from continuing his reign of terror. It's hard to regret something that brings a little more peace to the world."

"Besides," Cooper said, squeezing her hand, "we made it through the wedding without incident. I worried Adele was going to leave me at the altar."

"Where would I have gone?" she laughed. "We were on an island. It's not like I could run far away." Adele looked around at all of us. "So, what's next for all of you? Got any cases pending?"

Luke hadn't been back to the office yet. "I'm sure they will have something for me. Crime never stops."

"I want to listen to the podcast that's all about us." I had found the website and started listening on the plane back. Even though I had worked the cases, it was riveting. Luke wanted me to call her and set up a meeting. I'd do it eventually.

As far as new cases, I knew that Cooper had been fielding a lot of calls since getting back, but I didn't know if he had made any decisions about what cases we were taking. I refilled my glass with sweet tea and sat down. "Cooper, your work phone hasn't stopped ringing. What's next for us?"

"Business has never been better since we did those media interviews. We are in demand around the country – around the globe if we wanted. I'm not licensed in any other states. You have your license in New York and we are both licensed here. I don't know that we want to branch out further with just the two of us."

Luke raised his eyebrows. "Looking to expand and grow your business?" There was a hint of disappointment in his voice. I knew he was worrying that I'd be away from home working cases in other states. It wasn't something I wanted to do anyway but didn't want to put a damper on Cooper's business.

"I don't want to work in other states necessarily," Cooper said much to our relief. He looked over at Adele. "I don't want to be far from home too often."

Luke asked, "Did you get any calls that interest you?"

"Most were routine cheating spouses and child custody cases, but there was one." Cooper paused and seemed to consider. "Actually, it's more than one. It's close to thirty cases across ten states."

"A serial killer?" I asked, my eyes growing wide. I had had enough of those.

"I don't know. Have you heard about the cases of young men drowning after a night of drinking?"

We had all heard about those cases. I had investigated one years ago in New York. They were all suspected of being tied back to a serial killer or, as some detectives who had taken the cases and made a public spectacle out of them noted, a gang of serial killers roaming around the country drowning young men. They had all these clues and signs that they were connected. Mostly what they had been doing was making huge leaps without any hard evidence to back it up.

The case I had in New York, these other detectives, retired cops, had worked the family into such a frenzy that it was a serial killer, the family didn't want to hear any evidence to the contrary. Eventually, I dropped the case because there was no point. No one wanted to hear real evidence.

"I'm not getting involved in that," I said to Cooper and then explained the details of the case I had been involved with. "It's a mess. Not only was it a local mess, but it's also a national mess with so many different rabbit holes you could get sucked into."

Cooper grinned. "So, it's a no."

"It's a hard no. Hard pass not going to happen." I sat back in the chair and held firm.

Luke and Adele watched us, shifting their eyes back and forth across the table as we sat in a stalemate. I knew Cooper had wanted to sink his teeth into it. He didn't shy away from messy cases.

He relented a moment later. "We'll table this for now." He reached his hand to Adele. "I want to get my bride home."

After they left, I dried the last of the dishes. As I put the last dish in the cabinet, Luke came up behind me and nuzzled my ear. "Cooper isn't going to let it go."

"I don't want to think about that tonight."

"What do you want to think about?"

I set the dishtowel down on the counter and turned in his arms. I kissed his lips. "Let's go upstairs and I'll tell you." I led my husband up the stairs, knowing that he was right. Cooper wasn't going to let the case go. I was going to be sucked back into the worst case of my private investigator career.

About the Author

Stacy M. Jones was born and raised in Troy, New York, and currently lives in Little Rock, Arkansas. She is a full-time writer and holds masters' degrees in journalism and in forensic psychology. She currently has three series available for readers: paranormal women's fiction/cozy mystery Harper & Hattie Magical Mystery Series, the hard-boiled PI Riley Sullivan Mystery Series and the FBI Agent Kate Walsh Thriller Series. To access Stacy's Mystery Readers Club with three free novellas, one for each series, visit StacyMJones.com.

You can connect with me on:

- http://www.stacymjones.com
- https://twitter.com/SMJonesWriter
- https://www.facebook.com/StacyMJonesWriter
- https://www.bookbub.com/profile/stacy-m-jones
- https://www.goodreads.com/StacyMJonesWriter

Subscribe to my newsletter:

✉ http://www.stacymjones.com

Also by Stacy M. Jones

Watch for the next PI Riley Sullivan Mystery Book #8
THE DROWNING BOYS - Fall 2022

Access the Free Mystery Readers' Club Starter Library
PI Riley Sullivan Mystery Series novella "The 1922 Club Murder"
FBI Agent Kate Walsh Thriller Series novella "The Curators"
Harper & Hattie Mystery Series novella "Harper's Folly"

Sign up for the starter library along with launch-day pricing, special behind-the-scenes access, and extra content not available anywhere else. Hit subscribe at
http://www.stacymjones.com/

Please leave a review for Harbor Cove Murders. Reviews help more readers find my books. Thank you!

Other books by Stacy M. Jones by series and order to date

FBI Agent Kate Walsh Thriller Series
The Curators
The Founders
Miami Ripper
Mad Jack

PI Riley Sullivan Mystery Series
The 1922 Club Murder
Deadly Sins
The Bone Harvest

Missing Time Murders
We Last Saw Jane
Boston Underground
The Night Game

Harper & Hattie Magical Mystery Series

Harper's Folly
Saints & Sinners Ball
Secrets to Tell
Rule of Three
The Forever Curse
The Witches Code
The Sinister Sisters

Made in United States
Orlando, FL
01 August 2023

35641917R00193